32 Horror Tales Best Read Over Water

Compiled & Edited by
Bret McCormick

A HellBound Books Publishing LLC Book
Houston TX

A HellBound Books LLC
Publication

Cover and art design by Kevin Enhart for
HellBound Books Publishing LLC

www.hellboundbookspublishing.com

Printed in the United States of America

CONTENTS

Foreword

I imagine everyone who speaks English as their primary language has heard the phrase 'scared shitless.' Though, in most cases, the speaker is not using the words in the literal sense, this cliché has a meaning well-rooted in reality. You see, mammals – all mammals, humans included – have a shit triggering mechanism built into their nervous systems. In cases of extreme duress, when the 'fight-or-flight' instinct kicks into overdrive, mammals evacuate their bowels. Evolutionary biologists have speculated that this action may decrease the body weight, enabling the frightened creature to run just a little bit faster, providing that tiny edge that could mean the difference between life and death. It's also been suggested that the odor of the sudden fecal download may distract the predator, allowing the intended prey to escape. In any case, history is full of tales of folks, often soldiers, so distraught by life-threatening situations they lost control of both bladder and bowels. This sort of experience is commonly considered so humiliating, that many of us would rather take a bullet than be remembered as the guy who crapped his pants under pressure.

Such is life. Just another of the oddities that make being human so damn interesting.

And while we're on the subject of excretory trivia, I'd like to point out that the typical American diet often results in constipation. Constipation means prolonged periods spent sitting on the toilet, waiting for things to happen. Several of the older men in my extended family were known to refer to the bathroom as the 'reading room.' When one announced he was going to the reading room, we knew he meant he was going to monopolize the facilities for a good long while. These extended stays were made more enjoyable by a stack of magazines and the odd novel by the likes of Edgar Rice Burroughs, Louis Lamour or Ian Fleming. Nothing too intellectual, mind you, just something to entertain. Something you wouldn't have to think much about once you'd done your business.

Along the way, some enterprising people, realizing how common this phenomenon truly was, began publishing books specifically for the bathroom. Ever heard of Uncle John's Bathroom Readers? When I was in retail book sales, I sold a ton of books in the Uncle John series. The numbers were right up there with cookbooks (which I learned everybody buys, but precious few actually use) and children's books (even folks who never buy a book for themselves, will jump at the chance to buy one for their kids).

Somewhere in the midst of all this, I seized on the idea of a bathroom reader of terrifying tales. A book full of stories designed to 'scare the reader shitless!' Undignified? Perhaps. Pandering to baser interests? Of course. A brilliant idea, nonetheless? I thought so.

Fortunately for me, the folks at HellBound Books agreed. Well, I could be overstating their enthusiasm, but they let me run with it anyway.

The submission process for Toilet Zone was unparalleled in my experience. Sure, there were the usual clunkers and well-intended near-misses, but I found an inordinate number of truly inspired horror stories in my inbox. I've chosen what I thought were the best out of the two enormous batches of story files the HellBound crew sent me. I've got my favorites and I'm sure you'll find some gold nuggets of grim delight.

Now you've got more reason than ever to continue the low-fiber, high fat diet that generates those mega-colon-cloggers. Take your time. Don't strain. Now you've got an excellent incentive to linger in the smallest room of the house. If, perchance, one of these tales goes beyond scaring you shitless and causes cardiac arrest, don't worry. It's not the most conventional way to go, but it was good enough for Elvis. Right?

Bret McCormick, Bedford, Texas, July 2019

THE
TOILET
ZONE

An Appalachian Tale

EV Knight

Some people are just born wrong. Most times, they look no different than you or me; no one's the wiser to what sorts of madness is incubatin' inside. Festerin' sometimes for generations before some aberration of nature is born and it's too late for the wretched little thing. Ayuh, eventually, lunacy tells. It starts to leak out, you see, it's in the genes. The Clantons were just that sort of folk. They kept to themselves mostly, but living up there in that half cave-half shack, the whole lot of them were often the subject of many a front porch speculation. Now, you might think I'm waxin' philosophical with all this talk of madness and monsters—I ain't though. I got a tale to tell and I suppose it's high time I got to it.

The story of Brucie Clanton begins about three

months before yours truly was due to make his own entrance into this wild and crazy world. But I can tell it true enough. My mama was a midwife in these parts at the time. You know, I hear talk about the ghettos and vagrants sleepin' in subway cars but you ain't seen poverty til you seen Appalachian mountain poverty. Weren't no doctors or hospitals within fifty miles. None would have even been willin' to subject themselves to our kind of livin'. My mama; well, she was taught by her mama and her gran before her. Three generations of women bringin' babies into life in dirt-floored drafty cabins.

The night one of Ruth Clanton's brood came runnin' down the mountain shoutin' for the midwife to come, my mama was just puttin' her feet up to rest, bein' heavy with me in her belly. She wasn't expectin' any deliveries 'round then. You see, The Clantons birthed their own. No one'd ever been in that strange domicile. Fact was, no one even knew how many offspring Ruth and Roy had at this point or how old any of the kids might be. But my mama said that didn't matter none to her. She was called to deliver babies, not to judge how they were made.

Well, Mama made her way up the side of the mountain and they let her in. Turns out it wasn't Ruth Clanton in need of assistance at all but one of her daughters, who couldn't have been more than fifteen. Mama said the smell in that place about knocked her over but she had a job to do. So, Ruth tells Mama that this girl, Delilah was her name, been laborin' goin' on three days now and they figure the baby's dead. Ruth tells her she felt the head yesterday but it got hung up on somethin' and the girl was just about beat to hell. Ruth wanted Mama to cut that baby out before it killed Delilah.

My mama, bein' the kind of woman she was, puts

her head down to the girl's belly and listens. "This baby's still alive" she tells them. Then she rolls up her sleeve and takes a feel. Now, I ain't professin' to know anything about birthin' babies but Mama reaches up and fiddles around. She figures the baby is just in the wrong position for comin' out and she pushes and maneuvers it, until finally and with a few more hard pushes, Brucie Clanton came out.

Only he came out all crippled up like a crab, arms and legs bent up at unnatural angles. His head was all misshapen and his left ear curled up like a rose on the side of his neck. His right ear was impossibly small and he had a clubfoot. He had a cleft lip and his nose was flattened out like a gorilla. Brucie was covered in a fine pelt of dark hair. This was all terrible enough, but the worst part was the third arm that grew out of the center of his chest. The fingers on this hand were webbed together and so were the fingernails. They had grown into a thick, yellowed claw-like growth at the end of a crippled hand, so that it looked like he carried a small garden trowel with him all the damned time. The shock of lookin' at him put Mama into labor. Said she got queasy then and the stink of the place only added to the queer situation. She excused herself outside and vomited. That's when her water broke. The thought of givin' birth in that filthy dump with all the wild eyed, unkempt bodies staring at her was more than she could bear and so she ran all the way home. She said I was delivered on my own front lawn because her fleein' shook me right out.

And so, Brucie and I came to share a birthday, but it was Brucie alone that became a local legend. The crab boy. Turned out he was also a dwarf. No matter how straight up I grew, Brucie stayed low to the ground. Brucie was the only Clanton people bragged about havin' seen with their own two eyes. The stories were as morbid as the boy's look. Men would tell of comin' upon the boy using his claw hand to gut animals and rip out chunks of meat while feedin' himself with the other two. Kids would tell each other ghastly tales of Brucie catching fish with his extra hand and eating them whole and the older ones would go out late at night tryin' to see him. The stories of the monster were as vast and varied as the imagination of us mountain folk. But that's all they were -- stories. Tales about a deformed boy from a feral family of inbreedin' loonies.

Until Martha McCoy vanished. Martha was two years older than me; she would have been eighteen at the time and she'd gone missin' while mushroom pickin'. A bunch of us went out lookin' for her. We found a pile of torn up guts, coulda been Martha's innards but that seemed such an improbability when it coulda easily been a deer or a dog. What did we know? We never told no one. Probably shoulda, might have had more people out there lookin' or at least more people watchin' a little more closely. Might not have lost Billy Dalton. Billy was only ten and was noodlin' for catfish when he went missin'.

This was the second missin' kid in a month. At that point, all the men got together and had a meetin' about it. At sixteen, I was part of that meetin'. All them tales of Brucie Clanton and his wild animal behavior came up over and over until we were all whipped up into a frenzy. The whole lot of us headed off to the Clanton cave. Well, good sense kicked in 'bout halfway there and it was decided only two of us should go. One to do the distractin' and one to look around. The rest of the men would scatter about the place. in case back up was needed.

'Twas me and Ol' Roger Brundel picked to go have a talk with the Clanton bunch. Roger's always been a talker, so naturally he took the job of knockin' at the door (which I might add wasn't a door at all but just a wood frame with a heavy blanket tied to chicken wire). I went around to the side, tryin' to peek through the cracks and tripped over a pile of bones. Looked like the whole lot'd just been chucked out the window. Now, I ain't no rocket professor but they sure did look like human bones to me. And some still had meat attached. There was a mix of smaller ones and bigger ones. I didn't see no skulls though; in fact, I don't know that anyone ever did find the skulls for those two poor kids.

Now, while I was fallin' over femurs, Roger was chattin' it up with Roy Clanton. Roger, he said the stink comin' out of that place was somethin' fierce and his throat kept closing up on him tryin' to bring up his lunch right there on the Clanton's doorway. So, Roger's tellin' Roy 'bout the missin' kids and askin' if either of 'em came up this way. Well, Roy is protestin' in a most suspicious way when little Brucie came galumphin' out from the cave squallin' like a wild boar. He held his arms up for Roger to pick him up and Roger, being the kinda soul he is, did it instinctively. He's since told us all the boy looked so pitiful and mistreated no one could have denied the poor creature the least bit of tenderness. Well, Roger's humanity led to his own downfall. The little beast reached out with that crippled up third claw hand and sliced Roger's belly open.

Roger's surprised grunt hit my ears just prior to the wet splash and plop of his bowels hittin' the ground. That mass of incestuous cannibals heard Roger's disembowelin' too and headed to the doorway for dinner. Yep, you heard me right, my friend. The whole lot of 'em turned out to be cannibals. Right away I whistled to the others and headed around the side of the house where Brucie was usin' his good hands to pull out Roger's intestines while his third hand scooped them up to his mouth. He tore at them in a frenzy the likes of which I've never seen nor hope to again.

Ol' Roger, he was amoanin' and cryin'; beggin' him to stop. When shots were fired, the Clantons retreated back into the house. Well, all of 'em 'cept for Brucie and Roy. Roy had a cleaver in his hand and when he heard the shots, he brought it down on Roger's outstretched arm. I watched him rip it free from the old man's torso just as a gunshot exploded in Roy's face. He was there one second and a shredded mass of bone and brains the next. His head rained down on Brucie who stopped to see what was goin' on above him.

That's when I made my move. I dove across Roger and landed on the boy, who should have, by all rights, been the same size as me. But he hadn't grown much since he was four. We wrestled around; Brucie slashin' out with that damn third arm of his. I couldn't handle all three appendages. The next thing I knew, he was on top of me. His stinkin' breath sickened me. I choked. He used that abomination of a limb to try and slit my throat. He would have done it too, 'cept somehow Roger had gotten up, his bowels draggin' at his feet like a saggin' jump rope. He had the cleaver Roy had used to chop his arm off. I thought for a moment he was a ghost, so white and frail lookin'. But that old buzzard was tough, like all us mountain folk. He brought that cleaver down into the middle of Brucie's forehead just before he passed out.

There was a humorous moment where Brucie crossed his eyes to look up to see the cleaver buried in his head before he fell off me dead, and I suppose it was my nerves that made it so funny but I started laughin' and didn't stop til they shot me full of Thorazine in the city hospital.

Now, I'm not so big on doctorin' and hospitals; I'd take my mama's herbal teas over their IVs and catheters. But they managed to save Roger sans a few feet of intestines and a left arm. But Ol' Roger gets around just fine without 'em. I got some nerve pills I carry 'round with me but otherwise, there's nothin' to show for that ordeal with my dichotomous twin. That's alright anyhow. When I heard about all them body parts they found in that cave shack and the great number of Clanton kids that had to be placed in a juvenile care facility while their parents stood trial for murder and cannibalism, well, I decided that sometimes its best for the damage to be on the inside, with no one on the outside the wiser. Some people are just born wrong and some go wrong because of circumstances beyond their control and sometimes it's hard to tell the difference.

Company Man

Carson Demmans

I watch my victim as she approaches. Young and beautiful, but aren't the young always beautiful? She is unaware of me as she approaches, nonchalantly chewing her gum. I am on her before she realizes, clamping a hand over her mouth as I twist and bring her body to the ground, using my weight against her. She is helpless, confused, and seconds later dead. I stop to relish my victory.

But there is no time for that. As soon as the life escapes her body I am pushed aside by men in uniform.

"Thanks, Henderson," one of them mumbles, without actually looking at me. "We'll take it from here."

"Damn janitors," I think to myself. "If they don't want to clean up the mess, why point the girl out to me?"

Of course, I already know the answer to that. She was chewing gum, of course, and it's easier for them to clean up a corpse than it is to scrape that dumb stuff off something.

Anyway, my shift is almost over, so I begin walking back to my locker. I don't have a uniform like the snotty janitors do, but I do get a locker with my name on it where I can stow my coat and lunch while I work. I used to keep trophies from my victims there too, until management found them in a routine search. They were looking for drugs and found jewellery and knick knacks from a dozen dead people. They weren't amused. Apparently, I couldn't take trophies, at least not the way any other serial killer could. The item in question had to be turned into lost and found and, if nobody claimed it in 7 days, I could have it -- but only if I took it home right away. Does that make any sense to you? I take the stuff off dead bodies, for crying in a pee bucket! Who do they think is going to claim it besides me?

Certainly not the family of the dead. Usually nobody ever knows they are dead. The janitors do their job well. No bodies are ever found. I've never asked why. I don't care. I mean, that is the good part. I don't have to worry about getting rid of the evidence or finding victims. They are pointed out for me and then disposed of. Troublemakers who have no place here.

Mind you, the management have a different definition of troublemaker than most. It includes gum chewers, graffiti taggers, skateboarders, and anybody else who disrupts their fascist version of heaven, otherwise known as the largest theme park in the world. I first came here a couple of years ago. Lots of people meant lots of victims, I thought. It also meant lots of witnesses. I wandered around for days, until one night a janitor pointed out a kid doing graffiti for me. He must have known what I was up to, because the body disappeared shortly thereafter. I assume there are others here like me, working other shifts. Otherwise, how could I have been promoted from nights to day shifts last week? Somebody like me retired, I guess. I lose the shift differential but at least I can see what I'm getting paid to do.

Yes, I get paid. I belong to a union, get paid vacation every year, and punch a clock. I know what you are going to say.

"When my grandfather was a serial killer, he had to walk 3 miles in snow up hill each way to kill someone and never made a nickel doing it."

I admit, on paper it looks like I have a good deal. But, working for a living has its drawbacks. There is paperwork to fill out, quotas to meet, and I have to work if I'm sick or I lose my job. Other employees can get doctor's notes if they are too sick to work, but not me. Can you imagine it?

"Mr. Henderson is too sick to kill anyone today. He should be back next week if he gets plenty of rest and fluids."

Not likely. My doctor won't even see me without an appointment.

So, I toe the line, killing who they want me to kill, when they want me to kill them. The other employees pretend they don't know what's going on, but don't believe that. They know there are more than enough customers to deal with even after I've done a shift, and they just want their lives to be easier, the same as me. Why else would they silently point out my next victim with a quick glance, rather than politely serving the troublemaker with a fake grin?

I get to my locker and grab my stuff. I give Sullivan a quick 'good bye' as I pass him. I feel sorry for Sullivan. He sells cotton candy and has been doing it so long his hands are permanently stained every color in the rainbow.

No matter what you do for a living, somebody else has it worse, right?

In the Darkness of his Lair

By Richard Raven

It was once a staging area and service entrance, one of many located along the length of the city's massive and sprawling underground sewage and drainage system. The concrete tunnel entrance was situated at the base of a sloping mound of earth, the wide passageway beyond gradually descending until it reached the rank and vile depths of the system itself. The grounds surrounding the entrance were enclosed by three tall, interlocking chain-link fences, all topped with multiple curls of razor wire. They could be entered through only one gate just off the highway that led to the city a few miles away. The tunnel entrance itself was secured by a pair of tall, wide steel doors, which were also locked tight when not in use.

In its time, it was often a busy place, the entrance and the entire length of the tunnel brightly lit by floodlights. But its time had come and gone.

It was over thirty years ago that municipal vehicles and equipment last jammed the grounds and crews moved in and out of the entrance like droves of ants. That was when the system, after much financial wrangling, got a much-needed overhaul. Entire sections of the underground labyrinth were rerouted, in some cases reducing the overall length by miles. This one entrance, secure within its fenced perimeter, was cut off from that which it had served. Reduced to a man-made cave extending some three hundred yards into the hard-packed clay before ending abruptly at a new concrete wall. The original plan called for the entrance and tunnel to be demolished, but the project ran out of money before that could be accomplished.

So, instead, new locks were installed on the double steel doors at the entrance and the one access gate in the fence. The place then abandoned, the grounds left to nature to reclaim at its leisure. Over time forgotten by most…

…but not by everyone.

The crowd was gathered in the forecourt in front of the county courthouse at the north end of the old city square. All eyes were focused on the gazebo and the woman who stood at the open end of it, facing them. Flanked on either side by the Chief of Police and the Mayor and various members of their staffs and families, the woman was addressing the crowd through a PA system in a soft, trembling voice.

"What was once…a peaceful city…has now become anything but that." This was turning out to be more of an emotional ordeal than Jennifer Metcalf had first thought. The glare of floodlights and TV lights wasn't helping, though it did make it all but impossible for her to see many in the crowd beyond the first few rows. The faces she could see through squinted and red-rimmed eyes that were leaking fresh tears all wore sympathetic, even pitying expressions. In the hand of each person visible to her was a guttering candle. As she paused to compose herself, her thoughts turned acerbic, resentful.

Before this began, moments before she mounted the gazebo, a woman—one of the Mayor's aids—had whispered in her ear, *"We put the crowd at close to two hundred, and the number will probably go even higher. A good chance this will go viral on social media, as well as picked up by the national media.*

A couple of hundred...out of a city of thousands." Jennifer let her eyes roam over the faces staring back at her. *How many of you are secretly glad—even thrilled—that this isn't happening to you? How high would that number go? Any chance that would go national or viral?*

Jennifer had never wanted to do this. Reluctant from the start to even be part of it when one of the local TV stations had approached her with this idea. Her reluctance wasn't because she didn't care about the six women who had gone missing in the past six weeks. What she objected to was that she believed this staged event really had nothing to do with the missing women. Merely a chance to generate great PR for the Mayor and the local cops who, alongside the FBI, were investigating the disappearances. Not to mention a chance to boost the TV station's ratings.

This was, after all, big news.

In the end, under great pressure from the TV station (*"This is a chance to reach out to the kidnapper and appeal to that person as a human being."*), from the Mayor (*"Ms. Metcalf, you're a nature! You do the TV spots for your company, and the camera loves you!*), and from the Chief of Police (*"How can you refuse this when one of the victims is your own sister?"*).

Jennifer visibly winced at the thought of her younger

sister, Melinda Sanchez. She hadn't slept more than a few hours a night since Melinda disappeared a week ago to the day. Melinda, who was just breaking into the world of media as a weekend TV news anchor, was among the last living family she had left, and they had always been close. Melinda, in the most ironic of twists, worked for the TV station that had approached Jennifer about doing this live remote, though she wasn't their first choice. They had first gone to Melinda's husband, Hector Sanchez, who was one of the VPs at the investment banking company where Jennifer worked.

"I feel the same way you do about it," Hector had confided to Jennifer. "I want her back, of course, I do, but I want no part of some…some dog and pony show just to make the assholes look good who can't find them or the nut that took them. But, Jennifer, if you can't bring yourself to do it…then I'll suck it up and do the best I can with it."

Hector was hurting and terribly torn; Jennifer could see that and hear it in his voice. He was also quite correct in that the various law enforcement agencies had found nothing so far to go on. No DNA, no trace evidence or fingerprints, and no eyewitnesses to any of the disappearances. Nothing at all to even point them in a direction from which they could begin searching for the women or their abductor. It was as if the women had simply vanished from the face of the earth.

Worst of all, it had been a week since Melinda, the last, had disappeared…and the kidnapper had struck once a week for six weeks.

That was the greatest pressure brought to bear on her.

Someone had to do something, for God's sake!

Jennifer raised her eyes to the glare of lights, swallowed, and continued speaking, now addressing herself not to the crowd or TV cameras, but to the kidnapper.

"Now this entire city lives in fear…people afraid to leave their homes day or night. I'm sure this, at least in part, is what you hoped to achieve and, I'm sorry to say, you've done that." This wasn't strictly according to the script given to her to follow so as not to antagonize the kidnapper, but Jennifer couldn't help herself. She was on the ragged edge with worry and dread that her sister, to say nothing of the other women, were already dead and would never be coming home. After all, except for a couple of cranks who had been tracked down and revealed as the headcases they were, there had been no credible ransom demands. There seemed little hope to cling to.

"If you can hear my voice right now, I have to ask what, exactly, did Melinda or any of the others ever do to you? Did you ever know any of them? Work with any of them or at least had some contact with them? If not, then why inflict your…your rage on them and to cause their families so much pain and grief? I ask you to put yourself in my place and in the place of the other families. How would you feel to be deprived of someone you cherish?" She paused to gather her thoughts, and then, more or less, returned to the script. "My sister is Melinda Sanchez, but she is more than a sister. She is my best friend, and I love her and miss her very much. As for the others," she began and went on to name each of the other women, touching on some virtue they shared and their positions in the community.

When she went silent again, she was finished. She had nothing more to say and wanted only to flee this place and this spectacle that was growing more obscene to her by the second. Without another to the crowd or to any of those standing with her, she turned and left the gazebo by the stairs at the rear. There were a few shouts of encouragement from the crowd, some subdued applause, all of which she ignored as she pushed her way through a growing throng of cops and city leaders and TV people gathering behind the gazebo. Many hands reached for her, gripping her hands and touching her back and arms; words of thanks and sympathy spoken to her in reverent whispers. Jennifer hurried along as best she could, emotion welling in her throat and feeling as though her head was going to explode.

Finally, thankfully, she was free of the mob and striding toward her car parked on the street cattycorner from the gazebo. There were still many people milling about, but none of them seemed to notice or have any interest in her.

Except for the tall and shadowy figure of a man who was suddenly standing in front of her, blocking her way. Jennifer was digging in her purse for her car keys when the man appeared as if from out of nowhere. She stopped dead, her hand slipping out of her purse, and she stared at the man. Without the glare of the bright lights and her eyes still adjusting, she could distinguish nothing about the man beyond his height and slender build. A perfect silhouette backlit by nearby streetlights.

"I hope I didn't startle you," the man said in a soft, yet deep voice.

"No, not at all," Jennifer lied, her eyes cutting surreptitiously at others who were moving past them. *I was surrounded by them only minutes ago, and now there isn't a cop in sight!* "Is there something I can do for you?"

"No, not really. I just wanted to tell you how much I admire what you did and the courage it must've taken to do it. I was genuinely moved by your words."

"Thank you," Jennifer murmured, now looking past the man at her car. She was about to step around him when, to her surprise, he extended his hand. Irritated, but not wishing to be rude, Jennifer felt obliged to extend her own hand.

When his fingers closed around her hand, it was all she could do not to gasp.

His hand was soft and moist, and it felt like she was gripping a piece of raw liver. A chill rippled up her arm.

He quickly released her hand, then he turned and walked away, quickly melting into the crowd moving along the sidewalk. Jennifer stood rooted in place, staring at the last spot that his back had been visible to her. Finally, releasing the breath she had been holding, she looked down at her hand. It still felt dirty and defiled.

Who was that guy? There had been nothing about him that she could see or hear in his voice that seemed remotely familiar to her. Nor had there been anything overtly creepy about him or even threatening in his words or actions.

Then why the hell was she standing there feeling like she had been assaulted?

Jennifer closed her eyes and breathed a heavy sigh. This had been like some horrible nightmare ever since Melinda failed to show up where she was supposed to be; now the ordeal was really beginning to exact a terrible toll.

Now she was jumping at shadows—and at shadowy men!

Forget it. Just someone who showed up for this tonight. No big deal. Just let me get away from this madness and make it home and get the door locked. Maybe, then, I can relax a little and try and pull myself together…while I stare at the phone, hoping it'll finally ring and I'll hear Melinda's voice.

"I hear you did well," Hector Sanchez said in

Jennifer's ear. "Better than well, in fact. The word is that you made it look easy."

"It wasn't easy, I assure you," Jennifer said into her phone. She was on her street and drawing close to the house where she had been living alone for almost two years.

"Jennifer…it should've been me, and I'm ashamed I couldn't do it."

"There's no reason for you to feel that way. This has been forced on us—shoved down our throats, to put it bluntly. Tell me, how are you holding up?"

A sigh at the other end, then, "Not good, what can I say? I feel like if I don't stay busy, that if I stop for even a second, I'll go to pieces."

"Call me if you need to talk," Jennifer said as she steered off the street and into the driveway that ran along one side of her house. The security lights all came on as she pulled in, the entire front of the house lit up with halogen brightness. "Better still, if you need some company, I probably won't get any sleep tonight, so come over if you feel like it."

"I might do that and thank you—and the same offer is open to you."

Jennifer was already getting out of her car when she hit disconnect with her thumb and dropped her phone in her purse. That side of the house was mostly in darkness and shadows, but it was only a few steps to the brightly lit front.

She never made it.

She had bumped the car door closed with her hip and had taken only a single step toward the light when strong hands grabbed her from behind. Before the scream of surprise and fear that had reached her throat could burst from her mouth, an arm snaked around her neck and a hand holding a wad of cloth was pressed to her nose and mouth. She never had a chance to make a sound. She tried to struggle but was no match for her assailant. The cloth reeked of a harsh and raw chemical that filled her throat and lungs.

She was still clinging to consciousness when she felt herself being dragged further into the darkness on that side of the house. The shoe on her right foot slipped off and there it remained on the ground for a time until a furtively moving shadow returned for it. Then the shadow vanished again as quickly as it had appeared.

Less than a minute later there was the sound of a car driving sedately away by way of the alley that ran behind the house.

She came awake slowly, groggily, her throat and mouth as dry as sand. Her eyes began to clear; she became aware of dim points of dirty yellow light. As awareness crawled and crept back to her, two things hit her one after the other: the first was that she was naked; the second was that she was sitting upright, her back pressed against something hard and uncomfortable. A dank and chilly draft of air rippled her exposed skin with gooseflesh. She realized that what she sat upon had the cool and smooth feel of concrete. When she tried to move, first her arms, then her legs, she found that nothing was working right.

Oh, God, I'm tied up…

It was then that the full weight of her predicament began to hit home with her. She began trembling violently.

…and this is week seven—and I'm number seven!

Her mouth was uncovered, but even as she drew in a breath to scream, the smell assailed her. A heavy, cloying, putrid stench that left her gagging and coughing.

"So good of you to join me," said a soft and deep voice from somewhere to her left.

When the coughing fit eased, and she could control her gagging spasms, she looked that way. She saw the shadowy figure of a tall and slender man, a silhouette backlit by the dim wash of dirty yellow light. Something about the figure struck a familiar chord…

"The TV thing," she murmured in a voice raw with fear. "You're the one who came up and surprised me. The one who spoke to me and shook my hand."

"Very good. I see you're recovering from the chloroform nicely."

"You're the ***one***—and you were ***there***?" It was all Jennifer could do to get her mind wrapped around it. Jesus, the sheer nerve of it to…

"Why not? The cops have no idea who they're looking for. Besides, even if the assholes had my name and knew what I looked like, it would've been worth the risk to see your incredible performance."

Jennifer was preparing again to scream; again the pervading stench stopped it in her throat. "What is that smell?" she rasped.

"Come now, I'm sure you can figure that out if you think about it."

The women… Melinda. Lord, no, not that.

"I see by the look on your face you have figured it out. Like I said, I was moved by your words and your obvious love for your sister. So, why deny you the chance to spend your final hours—more like minutes, really—with her? She's close, by the way. On the other side of that piece of old equipment that you're tied to. Or, I should say…what's left of her. She's not a pretty sight right now, I must admit."

"What have you done to her?" Jennifer wailed.

"Me? Why nothing at all. Well…nothing beyond bringing her here, that is."

"Did you rape her, you sick fuck? Is that what you're going to do to me before you kill me and leave me here to rot?"

For a long moment, there was no reply, only a heavy and ominous silence. Finally, "Spare me, please" the man hissed in a voice dripping with contempt. "Seven of you I've brought here—and every single one of you has asked that same damn question. I swear, you bitches are sure pussy proud—you believe the whole world revolves around what's between your fucking legs, don't you? Well, let me put that bullshit idea to rest right now. That is ***not*** why I brought you here, and it won't be me who kills you, either. That will happen in its own time when they discover there's fresh food."

"They who?" Jennifer demanded. She was staring at the man, trying to distinguish anything about him, but there was nothing but his silhouette and his scathing words. "Who the fuck are you and what is this place?"

"It will do you no good to know my name. Sorry. This place? It's an abandoned part of the sewer system. Since no one's had any interest in the place for so long…well, let's say I acquired it for my own use. To answer your first question, it's not who, but what…and it's the rats. Somehow, they get in here—and they're big fuckers, too. Believe me, I've seen them many times. Even watched them feasting on bitch number three. Hard thing to watch, though, and I didn't watch for very long. Just left them to their meal."

"You can't be serious." Jennifer was well out of her mind with fear by this time.

"Oh, I'm very serious. You want to know why? You asked me a question at the doings there in the city square. You asked me to put myself in your place and that of the other families and how I would feel to be deprived of someone I cherished, remember? Well, let me tell you, I ***know*** what that's like. My father worked for the city water works and was part of the crew that reworked this place. Near the end of the project, he died in a cave in…not far from this very spot. And you know what the city did? They left him buried here. Never even made it public. There's no record left that he even worked for the city or was within miles of this place when he died. Just paid my worthless ass mother a big pile of money, which she blew on drugs and alcohol. I was only nine years old when it happened…and my father was my whole world. I've thought about it all these years and finally decided that each of you would know the fear he experienced and that your damn families would know the pain I've endured. But it doesn't stop with you seven. Oh, no…It goes on and on until someone finally figures it out and stops me."

"But…but…" Jennifer stammered.

"Shut up," the figured barked, his raised voice reverberating. "Enough talk. It's time for the rats to feed. I can hear them scratching, anxious to get in here, but they won't as long as the light stays on. Once they dig in, though, the light doesn't bother them. Besides, I need to start scouting number eight and learning her habits. I've already picked her out, by the way. That pretty blonde wife of the Chief of Police? Ah, yes, the rats will just love the taste of her."

Without another word, the silhouette figure moved out of Jennifer's limited line of vision. A few moments later the dirty yellow lights began winking out, one after the other. Soon after the last went out, plunging her into total darkness, the low thrumming sound she had been hearing and thinking was all in her head abruptly stopped.

A generator…

"Wait!" she wailed. "Don't do this, please!"

No reply, the only sound to be heard that of heavy and receding footsteps on the concrete. Then there was the loud and echoing slam of steel against steel, followed by what sounded like a padlock snapped closed.

How long had passed since she was left entombed there in the darkness with the dead and their stench she had no idea. She was still thrashing against her bonds, beyond the point of hyperventilating, when she heard the click of scurrying claws on the concrete.

She stopped thrashing, her chest heaving.

Oh, God... no... no...

She heard a soft squeak and a curious chitter to the right of her, the sounds then repeated to the left as a second joined the first. Then, in what seemed like only seconds, there had to be hundreds of them, the noise they made rising to an unholy chorus. She could tell by the odious stench of them—worse even than that of the corpses sharing the darkness with her—that they were surrounding her, edging closer.

Please, God...help me...

But there would be no Devine intervention. She both heard and smelled them as they rushed at her from out of the darkness as a single hellish entity. She was already screaming, a shriek of insane fear that reverberated off the concrete walls, when the first needle-like teeth tore into the flesh of her naked thigh.

The din of the horde rose as they crawled over her, climbing up and over her head and heaving shoulders, nosing between her thrashing legs, covering her like a foul and fury blanket. Several of the frenzied vermin went for her throat at the same time, finally silencing her hysterical screams of pain and terror.

Then they began feeding in earnest. No part of her escaped their ravenous fury, and it continued long after she had stopped breathing.

THE END

Keepsakes

Alyssa N. Vaughn

"Just toss it!" Rhiannon rolled her eyes at me and carried on unpacking the kitchen.

"Are you kidding me? I'm keeping it forever!" I clutched the brass figurine to my chest in mock horror. My wife glared at me, but didn't object.

"Is it haunted, Dad?" my oldest son, Wes, asked excitedly.

"No!" his brother Michael answered for me, vehement. "There's no such things as ghosts, are there Dad?"

I thought about teasing him, just a little, but I felt Rhiannon's gaze burning holes in the back of my head, heard her clear her throat in a "you're getting up with him if he has nightmares" warning. I judiciously decided to take the honest-but-technical route.

"Well, Mikey, there certainly hasn't been a lot of widely-accepted scientific proof of—"

Rhiannon cleared her throat louder.

"No, Mikey, there's no such things as ghosts." I saw his little shoulders relax, and figured my wife had made the right call. No sharing the bed with the five-year-old tonight, at least.

"But Dad!" Wes protested, "You said that the movie with the creepy doll was based on real people!"

"What movie?" Rhiannon demanded. It was regrettable that she had decided to unpack all the steak knives at that moment.

"The one we watched while you were at book club with Auntie Sharon."

I turned very, very slowly, and met her icy gaze with a tentative smile. She kept sliding knives into the slots on their little wooden block with undue force. I gulped.

"So, this could be haunted, like the doll in the movie, right Dad?" Wes shoved the little brass figure toward my face. The boys had found it in an upstairs cupboard, wedged into a back corner, behind a box filled with power strips and extension cords. It was probably from the sixties or seventies, and I vaguely recalled seeing a collection of similar brass animals in one of the pictures posted with the house's online listing. Those had looked a little more detailed though. This one was … kind of a blob? Sort of bowling-pin shaped, with ovular, rabbit-like ears sprouting from the sides of its head, a cylindrical snout like a pig, and two slanted indentations that must have been meant for eyes or eyebrows. There was also a kind of tail, curling around the base. It was weird-looking, for sure.

"The lady that used to live here had a lot of those things." Rhiannon finally put down the kitchenware and came for a closer look. "They probably just left it behind by accident. I'll email the realtor, see if they can get in touch for us."

Wes looked crestfallen.

"Hey, cheer up," I put my hand on his shoulder, "Maybe there's something haunted in your bedroom!"

"Yeah!" His face lit up and he raced back up the

stairs whooping with delight. Michael was hot on his heels, wailing that there better not be anything haunted in *his* room.

"Great job, Paul," Rhiannon deadpanned, "there's no way *this* won't turn out well."

I shrugged. It was just a little harmless fun, but when it came to the boys, she was always a little overcautious. A little *too* serious.

Everything would be fine.

Around 3 a.m., I got up to pee. The renovations to the master bathroom weren't quite done, so I stumbled down the dark, not-yet-familiar hallway to the bathroom the boys would be using.

Our new neighborhood was much quieter than the midtown apartment we had come from. There were no sounds of cars or nightlife, no bright lights seeping in around the edges of our blackout curtains. There weren't any country sounds either. No frogs or crickets or anything like that. It was pervasively and quite impenetrably quiet. It unnerved me.

I finished my business and hurried back down the hallway. There's something about moving fast in the dark. As much as it makes you feel like you're getting away safely, it reinforces that feeling that there's definitely something waiting in the shadows that you need to get away *from*. I found myself stuck in a rapid cycle of increasing nervousness, which increased my speed, which increased my nervousness, all accompanied by the completely delusional notion that everything would be fine if I just got back to the master bedroom. Of course, everything would be fine, I told myself scornfully, even as I quickened my pace. There was nothing coming for me.

Then, just as I was passing the staircase, I heard a thump from down in the living room. I froze, running through the list of possibilities. One of the stacks of boxes overbalanced and fell? The house was settling? A bird or a cat or a raccoon in the bushes outside? Someone trying to get in the window?

I was about to head down and check, when there was another noise close behind me – a whisper. Whirling quickly, my foot landed strangely, slipping out from under me. I was suddenly falling backwards. The free fall really did feel like it happened in slow motion, strangely weightless, suspended in mid-air for ages. Then I hit the first stair.

A few days, between six and ten million x-rays, and innumerable cups of coffee later, I was settled back at home on the living room couch. The consensus was that in the dark, I'd slipped on one of the boys' toy cars -- they had been sending them rocketing down the stairs after dinner -- after I'd been startled by what was probably an overzealous raccoon checking the trash cans. I had a broken ankle and a minor concussion, which was getting off lightly, all things considered.

I'd been prohibited from all work-related activities, and most leisurely ones as well. No television, no computer, no reading for more than a half-hour at a time. Just rest. And the busted ankle meant that rest would be happening in the living room.

During my hospital stay, Rhiannon had the boys working like mad getting as much unpacked and organized as possible, and by the time I came home, the place looked less like a hoarder's paradise and more like a comfortable, lived-in home. It's amazing what getting rid of a few cardboard boxes will do.

The warm summer weather had the kids outside, with Rhiannon keeping a watchful eye from the window of her office at the back of the house. She left some audiobook playing for me, a British murder mystery, all Dukes and Colonels and manor houses. It would do …

as background noise for a nap. I closed my eyes, got really comfortable on our plush, deep seated sofa, and drifted off.

I was sitting on the couch, facing the built-in shelves. I knew, somewhere in my brain, that our couch faced the fireplace. And wasn't covered in plastic. And didn't have blue irises embroidered all over it. But here I was. The shelves were covered in brass figurines. Peacocks, horses, swans, cats, mice, a huge eagle on the bottom shelf, a series of very small unicorns on the top.

"Do you like them?" A warm, pleasant voice. I looked to my left and met the cheerful

gaze of a tall, gray-haired woman. She sat in a high-backed armchair upholstered to match the sofa. A willow-pattern cup and saucer lay on the coffee table in front of her, and I realized a matching set were in my own hands. I set them down gently.

"Yes, my grandmother had a collection like that," I found myself saying, "much smaller though. She inherited it from her sister."

"Parts of mine were also inherited," the woman's smile was warm, prideful. She wasn't my mother, or a relative …

"From your family, Miss Wright?" I asked.

"Please, call me Glory! You're not in my History class anymore, dear." She leaned over, picked up a teapot and refilled her cup. "Yes, I inherited several pieces from my mother when she passed away. I continued collecting because it helped me to feel close to her."

"Were you very young when she died?" I immediately winced at my own question. How tactless of me!

"Oh, about twelve years old," Glory Wright didn't seem to mind my bluntness. "My father traveled a lot for work, and he started bringing me new pieces, a compensation for the fact that I was left with relatives or friends. And then other people started gifting them to me for birthdays and graduation and things like that. I keep the ones from my mother on the top shelf, and the ones from my father on that special shelf in the middle."

I looked at the shelves again, and saw that there in the middle was a perfectly square cubicle. It was rather sparse, only eight or nine figurines in it, but arranged with care. Evenly spaced. Unlike the rest of the shelves, it was completely free of any dust.

I nodded.

"My dad wanted to start giving my grandmother figurines to help build up her collection, but she wouldn't let him. She said it was too painful."

Glory cocked her head, offering me a platter of elegant flower-shaped cookies.

"Why keep the collection at all, if she felt it was too painful?"

I took a bite of cookie and shifted uncomfortably in my seat, the plastic squeaking underneath me.

"Her sister, my Great-Aunt Lydia, died when they were younger. Still in high school. She was, uh … I mean, someone killed her."

"Oh, how dreadful." Glory touched my shoulder, her eyes full of sympathy.

"Yeah. It happened while she was home alone one night, and … and the killer took something from her collection. She had three little … well, they were supposed to be cats, I think? And after they found her, um, her body … well, there were only two. My grandmother always left a blank space for the one that was missing."

"I'm so sorry," Glory squeezed my knee, "That must have been so difficult for her. They never discovered who … did it?"

"No," I sighed, fidgeting with the cookie, turning it round and round in my hands, "It's just a family legend now. We'll probably never know."

"Families are difficult things," Glory said, contemplating that middle shelf, "My father was always a very forbidding man, a stern presence, you know. I suppose I hang on to these little trinkets because they were one of the few ways he was ever … soft. I came back here to take care of him, you know, when he was older."

"I didn't know that. You grew up here?"

She nodded, her smile beginning to return.

"Right here in this house." And then her expression faded back to something else, something akin to regret, or fear. "I thought about leaving, after he died, but … I never could bring myself to do it. I kept thinking of how angry he'd be."

Both of us seemed to shiver, then we sat in an uncomfortable silence, both feeling we'd revealed too much of ourselves.

"I'd better go." I stood up, "Since I've been home from school, Mom's been making extra effort for family dinners."

Miss Wright made as though to stand, too. She opened her mouth to say something, but was interrupted by a THUNK. We both looked at the shelves. A figurine had fallen from the middle cubicle onto the plush shag carpet.

"I'll get it," I gestured for her to keep her seat.

"That's all right dear, I can get it later …" But I was already across the room.

I picked it up, surprised as I always was by the heft of the little things. I turned it over in my hands. The shape of the ears and snout, the slanting eyes, the tail wrapping around the base … I knew this.

"That's so strange," I laughed in disbelief, "this

looks exactly like the one from Lydia's …"

I looked at Glory. Her stare was no longer warm and friendly. Her eyes looked black as she stared at the figure in my hands. She was hunched low in the chair, her hands clutching its arms. I couldn't tell whether she was ready to scream at me for touching it, or preparing to run like it was going to come after her.

I heard something just overhead, drifting down the stairs ... or was it behind me?

A whisper.

"I think you should leave."

I woke with a start.

The backdoor slammed and Wes and Michael raced through the house hollering at the top of their lungs. They stampeded through the kitchen and up the stairs. Rhiannon walked into the living room with her arms crossed.

"What's wrong with them now?" I asked, bleary and fairly irritated at being awoken.

"They're arguing about that damn rabbit. Or rat. Or whatever it is. I told you we should just get rid of it!"

"I thought you were going to email the realtor and get it back to the lady that lived here."

Rhiannon looked surprised.

"Oh gosh, I guess I never told you. He emailed me back while you were still at the hospital. He couldn't get in touch with the executor of her estate. He said it probably wasn't that important if they just left it here, so do whatever we wanted with it."

The boys came stomping back down the stairs, sounding like an angry pack of elephants. Wes held the little figure high above his head where Michael couldn't reach.

"It's *mine*. You didn't even *like it* until Dad said it wasn't haunted."

"I like it *now*, and I'm the one who *found it*!"

"I am going to take it away if you don't stop this fighting!" Rhiannon had her hands on her hips, in the ultimate Mom-means-business posture. Both boys turned their wailing on her like twin fire hoses.

She held up one hand and they fell silent. She pointed to Michael.

"I want her to stay with me in my room. I named her!"

"Your name is *dumb*!" interrupted Wes, unable to control himself, "She's staying with me in *my* room, and her name isn't *Glory*."

"*Glory* is not any dumber than *Lydia*!" Michael fired back, sticking his tongue out for good measure.

I felt a chill run up my spine.

"Glory? And Lydia?" I asked, trying to remember where I had heard those names before.

All three of us jumped and turned to stare at the built-in shelves as the books lined up in the center cubicle started to fall, one after another, off onto the hardwood floor with a loud THUMP. THUMP. THUMP.

I turned toward Rhiannon, who was reaching for the boys, pulling them close. Behind her, the pots and pans in their cabinets began to clang and thunk against each other. Something upstairs began to swish smoothly through the halls, coming closer and closer to the stairs.

"Honey, I think we should leave."

Last Ride

Madison Estes

The concept of *stranger danger* had never totally clicked in Katie's head, she realized. Now, at the age of twenty, she heard her mother's concerned voice when she stuck her thumb out to flag down the grey Ford Taurus. As the rain pelted her, she didn't care about *stranger danger.* She wanted heat and a place to dry off. Most importantly, she wanted to put more miles between her and her cheating ex. Besides, she had a cell phone and a hidden pocketknife for protection.

The headlights blinded her as the car came to a stop. She jogged to the passenger's side door. A large man with a scraggly beard introduced himself as "Buck" and offered her a thin, wool coverlet from his backseat. He looked to be in his mid-to-late fifties. She slid into the seat and shut the door.

"Thank you," she said.

"What?" he said, his hand cupping his ear.

"Thank you," she repeated, a little louder.

He nodded. "You headed north?"

"I'm headed anywhere that has a heater and a roof."

Buck chuckled. His laugh was warm and comforting, like a blanket just pulled out of the dryer. She noticed a Bible in the console, a golden cross plastered across the face of it. She took that as a good sign.

"Are you a believer in Christ?" he asked.

"I don't go to church much, but I am."

"That's good. It's good to have faith," he said. "This world needs it more than ever now."

"Thanks again for picking me up," she said, trying to change the subject. She wrapped a part of the coverlet around her hair and squeezed some of the water out.

"Honestly, I almost didn't. This has been shaping up to be a really bad night, but I have a daughter about your age. I'd hate for something bad to happen to you. This is a dangerous world."

"Yeah," she said. She checked her phone and found no signal. "I didn't plan on hitchhiking tonight. Especially not in the middle of nowhere."

"I didn't plan on being out here either," he said. "This is not how I wanted to spend my Saturday."

"Why did you come out here?"

"Work," Buck said briskly.

"What do you do?"

"Freelance."

She wanted to press further. Writing? Photography? But somehow she didn't think he was out in the woods taking pictures or writing stories.

As the road made a winding turn, a loud rumble from behind jolted her. With a backwards glance, Katie deduced that it must have come from the trunk. She almost asked about the noise, but hesitated. By the time the courage to speak returned, she felt the moment to ask about the sound had passed.

Something must have fallen over in the trunk, she

thought. *That's all.*

"What kind of freelance work did you say you do again?" she asked, fidgeting with the chain of her gold necklace.

"I didn't say."

There was a long, uncomfortable pause during which Katie kept a lookout for a public place to distract herself from her hammering heart. She imagined opening the passenger door, covering her head with her arms, and rolling out of the car. If she saw a gas station on the road, she thought she might try it.

Something tumbled around in the trunk again. There was nothing but empty, straight road ahead. The rumbling intensified.

"Tell me about yourself. Where did you get that necklace?" he asked with a smile, as though he hadn't heard anything.

"My mom," she managed to get out. She ran her fingers over the engravings. "It was a high school graduation present. Most kids get class rings, but I wanted a locket so I could put pictures of my parents—"

Her eyes widened and her mouth snapped shut as muffled screaming filled the car. A rhythm emerged:

Thump-thump-"Hellllllpppp!"

Thump-thump-"Hellllllpppp!"

"I bet your folks thought that was sweet."

"I don't feel very good," Katie said, her hand going to her stomach. As she hunched over, she remembered the pocket knife in her boot. Using the two-inch blade to stop a man of his size felt as practical as trying to catch minnows with the plastic ring of a six pack, but it was better than nothing. She used her long dark hair to hide what she was retrieving. With the blade tucked into her sleeve, she felt a sense of control. She repeated the plan in her mind.

Plan A: Get out and run

Plan B: Get out and stab

"Please pull over, I think I'm going to throw up," she said, a gagging noise erupting from her throat as the thumping in the trunk turned into pounding. His hearing couldn't have been that bad, and surely he could feel the vibration in their seats.

"Okay, I'm pulling over."

Katie's hand leapt to the handle. She threw herself from the car as it parked. The rain blasted the ground steadily; she had no sense of direction, and couldn't tell where to run. She fell to her knees and pulled the blade out, waiting. He waddled his way toward her. She said a prayer of thanks that he left the car running. As he put a hand on her back, she sunk the blade into his side and ran back to the car, the headlights guiding her way.

Buck howled.

As she drove off, he called out, "Hey, wait! Don't. DON'T!"

As his voice faded away, the beating and screaming escalated. It continued while Katie drove.

"It's okay. We got away from him. You're safe now," she yelled. Her hands gripped the steering wheel until her knuckles whitened. The trunk went silent. Katie decided whoever was in there must have either heard her or passed out. A few moments later, Katie decided there was enough space between her and Buck to pull over and let the prisoner out.

She got out and inserted the key into the trunk. It popped open. She lifted the top, and as she had expected, found an unconscious woman inside. One second there was nothing but a huddled body lying on its side. Before Katie could blink, massive claws emerged from the woman's torso and slammed the sides of the trunk, causing the entire car to sway side-to-side. Black liquid splattered from its talons like ink from a leaky pen. The woman's form wilted, transforming into something tall and reptilian. The creature opened its ravenous mouth and splashed more of the dark substance onto Katie. Dozens of spiked teeth jutted from its grey gums. It smiled, exposing hundreds more.

"No," Katie said. She shook her head, backing away from it. "This isn't real, this isn't—"

Buck shut his eyes and made a sign of the cross when he found her. A half-consumed limb here, long-haired skull fragments there. He sighed when he stumbled upon the blood-coated necklace. He opened it and looked at the happy family inside. He shook his head.

"This really is shaping up to be a bad night."

He lit up a cigarette and reached into the backseat, pulling the covers aside, and retrieved the holy crossbow and Bible he had stashed there.

"This is not how I wanted to spend my weekend."

Panic Attack

D.W. Jones

His sneakered feet pounded the ground like a furious war drum demanding his strength and speed. Looking ahead, Brian felt a wave of confusion slowing him as he searched for whatever it was, he was running towards, but found nothing. His feet ignored the absurdity of the notion and pounded that much harder. There must be something amongst the empty blackness ahead that beckoned him. He looked down to find the same darkness beneath his feet, offering no clue as to what was going on or where he was. Glancing to his side, he found his surroundings in the same desolate manner. Empty. Dark.

Considering the word *empty*, he wondered why he was running so hard in the first place. He turned his head slowly to get a peek at whatever horror he was fleeing from. His eyelids widened when he saw nothing there. Just the same empty pitch-blackness he was running towards. There was nothing there except Brian, running like a mad man. He blinked twice thinking that this didn't seem right. It was like a strange dream, and with that realization, he awoke.

"Hey Freddy," announced a man's voice off in the

far distance. "I think he's coming around." The last of his words grew in volume, like an echo, gaining a life of its own with each reverberation.

The darkness from his dream seemed to bleed out into reality, keeping everything around him veiled in an eerie secrecy. Brian closed his eyes tightly and slowly reopened them to find that the colors of the real world were beginning to emerge from the pitch. Looking to his right, he found a blurry image, slowly sharpening into the wobbly visage of a man. He tried to reach out to the shape but found himself immobilized.

"It's ok Mr. Haney, just relax," the stranger said softly, "You've been in a car accident." His voice lagged a second behind the motion of his lips. Brian thought the man was possibly the best damn ventriloquist he'd ever seen. He brought a small pen light toward Brian's face and said, "My name's Charlie. I'm an EMT and we're bringing you to Jackson Memorial." He flashed the light into each eye and clipped it back to his shirt pocket with an assuring smile.

"I can't move," Brian complained as he pushed his eyes around his surroundings looking for something familiar to latch onto when a sharp pinch on his arm caused him to gasp.

"Just an IV-line sir," Charlie stated calmly.

Brian looked up to the bag of saline hanging overhead and followed the clear tubing down to his right arm. With his senses regained he relaxed, recognizing he was in the back of an ambulance strapped to a gurney. He took a deep breath and exhaled as normal consciousness swallowed the confusion.

"We have to keep you strapped in for own safety," Charlie explained, "Especially with the way Fred drives."

"Blow it out your brown eye old man," Freddie shouted from up front as the ambulance lurched to the left.

"Always the comedian," Charlie snickered. He checked the straps around Brian's head. "Mr. Haney, do you remember anything from the accident?"

Brian closed his eyes for a moment, moving the question around the darkness like a worm on a hook. The only thing to bite was fear. He was running from something...but he couldn't recall what. "I don't...remember."

"That's typical when you've been through a traumatic experience," Charlie explained, retrieving a pair of scissors from the stow away cabinet overhead. "By the time we showed up, the fire department was using the jaws of life to cut you out of the car."

Brian blinked hard as he latched onto Charlie's words. "Jaws of life". He felt something was coming back to him. A memory trying to wake from a coma. As he dissected the words, he kept circling back to the first; Jaws. It kept pulling him back to some vague image of him running like Hell away from something. The hair of his arms stood on end, raising their alarm to him, if only he was willing to listen. Something about that word. A tug on his lower half pulled his eyes back to Charlie who was now at the other end of the gurney.

"You have some blood on your pants," Charlie explained, "I'm going to have to cut these jeans off and make sure there isn't another injury."

As the EMT cut the pant legs lengthwise, he asked, "What's our E.T.A. Freddy?"

"Just one more minute," Freddy replied, "Doesn't look like they've made it to this part of town yet."

With the pant legs sliced open to Brian's groin, Charlie reached up, placed the scissors back into the cabinet and pulled out a small metal box. "You look a little nervous Mr. Haney."

Brian looked back to Charlie who was staring at his

crotch with a smile. He felt a familiar wave of heat blossom atop his head, seeping quickly down his spine. A tinge of nausea bubbled in his gut and his hands began to tremble and sweat. He always felt this way when his anxiety got out of control. Fight or flight was what his doctor called it. Since he could not simply get up and run away, he would have to fight it. He was supposed to find some object to focus on and the panic attack would eventually subside. Brian chose the metal box that Charlie was opening and stared intently as he counted backwards from thirty.

"We're here," announced Freddy.

"See Mr. Haney, when you get nervous, the muscles around your scrotal sack reflexively contract to pull your testicles out of harms' way. Kind of deflates your bag so to speak." Charlie continued to smile as he opened the small box, retrieving a large syringe.

Brian's focus moved from the box to the needle that Charlie held. The heat running down his spine spread quickly across his chest. His eyelids fluttered, and the darkness once again invaded the corners of his vision. On the verge of fainting at that point, he almost welcomed it.

"Now Mr. Hadley, we can't have you losing consciousness again," Charlie admonished as he pushed the contents into the IV line.

"Can I turn the siren on now," Freddy asked like a kid getting to ride in a cop car for the first time, eagerly awaiting a reply.

"Yes Freddy, you can turn on the siren," Charlie answered impatiently, " And you may as well hit the lights."

Brian's eyes shot open, threatening to blast out of his skull. The darkness was gone, and his heart pounded hard against his rib cage. The siren blared against the flashing red lights washing through the front window.

Everything became so bright and vibrant. His teeth chattered uncontrollably, his muscles tensed and he pulled painfully against the straps.

"O.K., so the adrenaline is really for me," Charlie admitted as he tossed the needle aside and pulled a stained scalpel from the box. "It makes the fishing more fun. I like to see 'em move if you know what I mean."

"Ding ding goes the dinner bell bitches," Freddy shouted pumping out a beat with the horn on the steering wheel, trying to match the rhythm of the siren.

Brian growled through his teeth, straps bit into flesh. "What the fuck is going on?" he shouted as he struggled frantically to no avail. He wasn't going anywhere, but he no longer had a choice. The adrenaline said it was fight or fight.

"Just a little slice will do," Charlie whispered as he brought the scalpel to Brian's scrotum.

Searing white heat burned away what little rational thought Brian had, leaving him with nothing but a primal scream of pain.

"Now, to separate the vas deferens," Charlie said, tugging hard.

Brian released a scream, he had never heard himself make before, as his testicles were torn from him. Without the adrenaline, he would have passed out.

Charlie held the two testicles up for inspection. He chose one and said, "Here you go man," as he tossed the smaller of the two to Freddy. The bloody ball bounced off the dash board and wobbled across the floor. Freddy snatched it up, blew some dirt from it and announced, "Five second rule," then, popped it into his mouth.

Charlie slid his tongue along his prize and said, "You see, Freddy and I have a bet going. He says *they* pass over people who are sleeping because *they* enjoy the screams of *their* victims."

"Yeah man. *They* like all the yelling and

screeching," Freddie concurred as he chewed his snack.

"I think it's a bit more than that though," Charlie corrected as he took a delicate bite of his own treat. "I think they detect and track consciousness. They're literally blind to the sleepers."

"That is some mystery box bullshit there, man," Freddy said with a sneer, wiping his mouth on his sleeve. "Oooh, *they're* here." He cackled as a shadow scuttled across the windshield.

"It doesn't really matter anyway," Charlie admitted. "*They* multiplied like rabbits, so you can imagine the difficulty in keeping them fed. Now that *they've* surfaced, *they* only keep the two of us around to gather up the sleepers. We get a piece of the action of course, but *they* get the rest."

Brian's memories slammed against the pain, pushing and shoving for room. There was no car accident. He was being chased by one of those *things* when he fainted from a panic attack. The jaws framing a black hole of crowded teeth spread wide open and greedy for his flesh.

Charlie stood up and unlocked the back door. Freddy moved to the foot of the gurney and smiled. "Now that we've had ours, it's time to give *them* theirs." Charlie threw the doors open and winked. The darkness beyond the door was not empty nor desolate. Teeth, gnashing hungrily waited just outside. "He's all *yours*," Charlie announced as Freddy pushed the gurney into the waiting jaws of a painful oblivion.

Reclaimed

By DJ Tyrer

"James." Hillary King's voice was sharp. "My office, now, if you please."

He dropped the phone back into its cradle as if his hand had been stung. The 'please' had not mitigated her tone.

Slowly, he scraped his chair back and rose. He knew she would be watching him from her office. Like a condemned man in chains, he shuffled his way to her office.

Hillary nodded for him to enter when he paused at her glass door. He went in and she gestured for him to sit.

"Gemma," she said and he felt a chill run across his back. Office romances were strictly forbidden and she hadn't been in for a couple of days. He'd assumed the flu, but had there been a complaint?

"You live near her," Hillary continued.

Not understanding where she was going with the statement, he nodded. "About a mile, or so."

"She hasn't been in to work."

"I noticed. I assumed she was ill."

"Gemma hasn't called in sick and isn't answering my calls. I hoped you might check in on her, see if she's okay."

James tried not to stare. Hillary had never led him to believe she had a heart.

"Her project is late. I need her here."

Maybe she didn't have one, after all. Still, he nodded, concern nagging at him.

"I can check tomorrow morning, on my way into work."

Hillary sniffed, but nodded. "Very good." She waved him away. "Go."

Delaying the visit till the next morning, James had hoped his car would be ready for him. Something electronic had gone wrong with it and the garage was in no hurry to fix it. They still hadn't.

Which meant his wife, Polly, was giving him a lift.

James drummed his fingers against the side of the passenger seat as they drove to Gemma's house. Polly despised office parties and worked longer hours than James, so there wasn't normally a risk of her and Gemma meeting. This was asking for trouble.

"I hate this place," Polly complained as they turned into the housing estate where Gemma lived. She turned off her phone's satnav, which was protesting the road didn't exist.

"You lost the fight, babe, your newts were evicted, and it's time for you to get over it."

Water sprayed as the car splashed through a puddle around an overflowing drain.

"I didn't mean that," she said, slowing the car to check for the road they wanted. "Well, I do hate it for that, but that wasn't what I meant."

"Er, next left, I think," he interjected.

"Right."

"No, left." He laughed, trying to inject some humour into the sound.

"Very funny. No, I meant, this place feels dead… soulless. I haven't seen a single person."

James took out his phone and checked the time. "Probably all on their way to work." He tossed the phone onto the dashboard.

Polly shook her head as she turned the wheel left. "Half these houses have cars out front."

"Two-car families," he said. "I think – yeah, twenty-four – this is it. Pull over here."

The car slowed to a halt by the curb and Polly put it in neutral.

Glancing out at the house, she said, "Looks like she's home."

Gemma's car was parked on the drive.

"I shouldn't be long." James popped his belt, then opened the door and climbed out.

Grunting an acknowledgement, Polly slipped her phone from the holder, where it had been serving as a satnav, and opened up an ebook.

Moments later, engrossed in the romance, she started violently at the sound of a tap on the passenger-side window. It was James.

She pressed the button to lower the window. "Yes?"

"No answer. I'm going to go round back," he gestured to a side gate, "see if I can find her, if she's skiving rather than off sick."

"Sure." She sent the window back up and returned to the story.

With a start, she realised she'd been reading for

some time and James hadn't returned. She checked the time on her phone: ten-to-ten! James had been gone the best part of an hour.

Automatically, she went to call him, then saw his phone sitting on the dashboard.

What was keeping him? She pressed the horn and waited. He didn't emerge. Looking about, she still saw no one. Nor had she registered any cars drive past while reading, not that that was conclusive. The estate was like a ghost town. She wondered how many of the houses remained to be sold.

"Where are you?" she muttered, tapping her nails against the steering wheel. Annoyance mixed with concern and another couple of minutes passed.

Slipping her phone into her pocket, Polly got out, pressing her key-fob to lock and alarm the car behind her as she walked around it to the curb.

She stepped onto Gemma's path. The slab shifted a little beneath her foot with a soft, moist sound.

Polly shook her head. It was just as they'd warned the developers: the groundwater was close to the surface; one good rainfall and there would be a flood. Idiot developers couldn't seem to grasp what the 'flood' in floodplain meant. Served the purchasers right; not that it helped the animals displaced by their houses.

The rest of the slabs were the same as she approached the front door.

Halting before it; Polly pressed the doorbell and thought she heard it ring within. She waited a few seconds before pressing it, again. Then, she tried rapping with the knocker.

There was no response. A drop of rain splashed her cheek. She looked up: The sky was darkening.

Where was he? If he was inside, surely one of them would open the door. What if his co-worker was sick? No, he would've called for help. All she could think was he'd gone around the back; had an accident and she'd been too engrossed in her book to notice.

Heart beginning to quicken, she hurried across mushy lawn to the side-gate and pushed it open. The rear garden was devoid of anything but turf, not yet tended to. Despite her concern, her lip twitched in disapproval at the bland scene. Then, she spotted that the patio door had been slid open; James had to be inside. Splashing across sodden grass, she went over to it.

Polly called out his name as she stepped into the open-plan lounge-dining room. An inch or so of water sploshed about her feet, having, apparently, risen through the floorboards.

She paused, bemused, and wrinkled her nose at the unpleasant smell of damp and mold and something like wet fur. Looking about, she could see patches of black and bluish mold on the lower parts of the walls and speckling the white leather of a matching settee and chairs. It was disgusting! No wonder James' co-worker wasn't home: Polly couldn't imagine anyone wanting to stay in a dump like this; unless the woman was ill from the state of it.

But that didn't answer the question of where James was. Unless… A sudden thought struck her: Might he have fallen ill from the mold spores in the air?

Just in case, Polly pulled her scarf from around her neck to cover her face. It helped a little with the smell, at least.

She called his name, again, voice muffled, but still there was no reply.

Her footsteps splashing as she went, Polly headed into the hallway, glancing into the kitchen as she passed. No sign of James, but both hall and kitchen were in an even worse state. Water bubbled up out from the kitchen sink and ran down the stairs in a series of dirty cataracts. Both were rife with mold.

To Polly, it seemed nature sought to reclaim the land stolen from it, to return the home to a previous state before it was built. She thought she spotted something splashing in the corner of the kitchen, a frog, perhaps, come to reclaim its stolen home.

Despite the perverse twinge of satisfaction such thoughts gave her, there was still James to concern her and he still wasn't answering when she called his name. She put one foot on the bottom step. The sound it made and the slight shudder didn't reassure Polly as to its ability to support her weight. Water continued to pour down the stairs as she climbed.

Then, she heard a movement from above.

Polly paused and listened. She caught a splash and a possible creak upstairs.

"James, is that you?" she called.

There was still no reply and no further sound. She shivered, wondering if she had disturbed a burglar. Had they harmed James? She resumed her climb with more caution. There was still no sound, save the splash and creak of her progress up the stairs.

Polly stopped on the landing; the short passage was dark. There were two doors to the front of the house, both shut, two to the rear, one open and one almost closed, and an airing cupboard door at the end. Water ran from under the door that was ajar. Vomit rose in the back of her throat at an unpleasant smell. Polly was certain she felt a tremor run through the floor beneath her feet.

Without a conscious thought, her body twisted halfway back towards the stairs, ready to run; but she fought the urge.

"James? James, where are you?"

She splashed a couple of steps forward, not waiting for a reply and pushed the almost-closed door open. Murky water ran over the rim of the toilet and the edge of the bath. The walls were black with mold.

With a sudden loud splash, something large and black exploded from the toilet bowl and surged toward her in a spray of foul water.

It ran straight at her and she lurched back, kicking at it, limbs flailing, into the opposite door. She felt a wild scrabbling at her trouser leg, cloth tearing, then her flesh. Screaming, Polly managed to kick it off and stumbled away from the thing along the corridor until she hit the airing cupboard door.

The rat squatted on the floor of the corridor, staring at her, its body heaving with each breath. About the size of a large cat, it glared at her with rabid eyes and there was something wrong with its fur.

Polly's body trembled. She felt blood dribbling down her shin.

Not taking her eyes off it, she reached blindly to her right and groped for the open door, easing herself sideways into the bedroom that lay beyond.

She slammed the door shut, turned – and screamed with even greater terror than before.

The wall near the bathroom was black with mold, water pooled against it. But it was the thing on the bed – half-slumped on it, half onto the floor – she stared at. It, too, was black with mold and, although the bloom of the mold blurred its form, was clearly the body of a woman in baggy pyjamas.

Polly vomited, tugging the scarf away from her face to do so, then fell to her knees as shock and the terrible smell overcame her. Her body shook as she sobbed out choked shrieks of horror and disgust; unable to tear her eyes from it.

Shaking her head in disbelief, she pushed backwards up against the wall, continuing to stare, and put out a hand to steady herself. She immediately snatched it back, desperately wiped it on her trouser leg, the black mold cloying upon it.

A sudden movement from the corpse made her scream: The torso juddered horribly and a rat pushed its way out of the belly, blinking at her with eyes set in a mold-stained face.

Stumbling to her feet, Polly threw herself at the door, desperate to escape. She managed to yank it open and lunged through, tripping over the rat outside as it snapped at her ankles. She fell against the door opposite. It swung open and she crashed through to the floor.

For a moment, she was stunned, then managed to kick the door shut. The door shuddered as a rat threw itself against it. She heard it scrabbling at the wood.

Polly turned to a sound. She was in a second bedroom, this one fairly dry, and, slumped upon the bed, was James.

She managed to stand and stepped over to him.

Polly gagged. His right leg was a bloody mess, his lower arms gashed and bloodied, his throat was torn and his nose and lips chewed away. There were already patches of black upon his skin. Yet, despite it all, he twitched slightly and a rattling wheeze echoed from the tear in his throat.

Then, as she leaned toward him, a rat darted forward to take another bite from his flesh.

Polly clamped her hand over her mouth, stifling her cry, but the rat turned its head to look up at her, a little piece of bloody flesh dangling from a tooth.

Then, the rat opened its mouth wider and liquid began to dribble out, not blood, but dirty water.

She grabbed a lamp from beside the bed and threw it at the rat. It retreated a short distance.

Looking down at James, she shook her head, unable even to think how to begin dealing with his wounds.

She pulled her phone out of her pocket, but the screen was smashed. She tapped it, but it was dead.

“Wait here,” she said. “I won’t be long. Sorry.”

Opening the door, she kicked out at the rats, driving them back. Then, they surged toward her, biting and clawing. More were pouring out of the bathroom, charging at her with wet hissing sounds, swarming onto her.

Polly swatted them off as best she could and ran, tumbling down the stairs, bones snapping in her ankle and wrist. Sobbing, she ran for the front door, the rats swarming after her, growing in number, snapping hungrily.

Managing to unlock the door, she stumbled outside, ran along the unsteady path to the car. The key slipped from her hand. She grabbed for it, a rat snapping at her finger, tearing flesh free. She managed to grasp the key. With a bleep, the door unlocked.

Somehow, she got inside and fell back, breathing heavily and bleeding in the passenger seat. Rain speckled the windscreen like tears. She was soaked.

She slammed her hand down on the horn, the blaring sound horribly loud and raucous in the silence. There was no response. There was no sign of anybody around. Even the rats were gone.

James’ phone was on the dashboard: With some difficulty, she tapped 999.

“Police. I need help.” Her voice was barely a whisper. “It’s my boyfriend he’s hurt. I’m hurt.”

A police car arrived within minutes.

“A paramedic’s on the way,” one of the policemen said as he looked in at her through the open window.

“My boyfriend’s inside. Hurt bad. Upstairs.”

“What did this?”

“Rats.”

“Rats?” He looked sceptical, but shrugged. “Okay,

we'll take a look." He turned to his colleague. "Come on."

His partner looked at the house. "What a mess."

Polly watched them head inside and, somehow, knew they wouldn't make it out.

She heard sirens in the distance. But, as she waited for help, a rat clambered up onto the bonnet of the car and looked in through the windscreen at her. She had to get out of there, but she felt so weak, could hardly move.

Her wounds were black gashes in her flesh; her skin was darkly blotched. Water dribbled down her chin.

Outside, the house trembled, again, as its foundation sank a little more.

It was too late: None of them would make it out.

Her last thoughts were of James and a desperate sadness at losing him. Then, the watery darkness of death claimed her.

Ends

Rest Stop

Brian James Lewis

Despite his inner miseries, Bill smiled when he saw the green and white sign informing him that a rest stop would be coming up in 3.7 miles. Finally, he would be delivered from the purgatory of straining to hold his body's waste products in! Super-sizing his meal seemed like such a great idea thirty miles ago, but now Bill was experiencing the real reason they called it "fast food."

But just as he clicked his blinker on, a frown crossed Bill's face. "What the hell?" Someone had slapped a large "CLOSED" across the beautiful rest stop sign. Below it was the cheery announcement that the next rest stop was 47 miles away. What? There was no way that he'd make it that far without exploding. To confirm this, Bill's body went into a fresh bout of peristalsis that brought tears to his eyes. Whoever heard of a rest stop being closed? They were one of the few things you could depend on in life, ranking right up there with death and taxes. Usually they weren't too lovely, but at least you could do your business and hit the trail feeling a bit lighter and somewhat refreshed.

Sure, he'd heard all kinds of horror stories about these places in the middle of nowhere. But most of them were rumors that had ballooned into National Enquirer territory. Strange sexual practices, kidnapping, and meth making were the crimes often hung on rest stops. Yet in his 20-something years of popping into these places Bill had never had a bad experience or witnessed any crimes. The worst things to happen to him were no soap and a couple stalls sans paper after doing a number two. While these things were bummers, they weren't totally unexpected, and it would be ridiculous to call them crimes. Nobody died because they couldn't wipe their ass or wash their hands. But being closed? Now THAT was a crime! Not to mention inconsiderate, and rude as hell.

Bill sighed and wiped his hands across his sweaty face. "Now what?" Maybe there *was* another rest stop in 47 miles, but there was no way he would last that long. Whatever he did, it would have to be here, so he continued to drive slowly up the access road looking for a way in. If he could at least pull into the parking area, then he might find a hiding spot to unload his burdens. It would be messy, but certainly better than nothing at this point...

However, the entrance road to the rest stop was completely blocked by huge hunks of concrete traffic barrier wall that extended fully across both the asphalt and the grass. Not only that, but there was a second closed sign, and this one meant business. Instead of a neatly added on metal sign, huge letters were slashed across the green and white sign in red paint...

"CLOSED!!!" The paint had splattered and run dramatically, making the letters look like dried blood. Bill thought it could be the work of someone who was very angry or, perhaps, deranged. Great! How very reassuring. Something caught the corner of his right eye. Bill looked and almost ignored it. But then his unbelieving eyes picked out a nice set of tire ruts worn through the grass creating a handy bypass around the blocked road.

"Well, well!" Bill grinned. "Looks like somebody uses this place after all!" Hell, there was nothing else for miles and he couldn't be the only person who'd been in this predicament! Between the highway crews and State Police, there must be a few regulars. Well good deal! He too, would make use of these fine facilities! After all, he was a taxpayer, just like anybody else, and right now he needed to use this rest stop that his money had built.

His Lincoln wasn't exactly a pick-up truck or even a heavy-duty police cruiser, but Bill figured that if he went really slow, he'd make it to the parking lot without much damage. "Easy does it." He crooned as the big car wobbled along. Finally, with a lurch and a scrape, the Lincoln emerged from the weeds and came to rest. With a sigh of relief, Bill popped the seat belt and opened the Lincoln's door.

But his happiness waned as he stepped out of the car and into the totally empty parking lot. His feet kept moving him toward the rest stop entrance; his eyes scanned his surroundings. Suddenly Bill got a major case of the creeps that grew until his feet stopped. He hadn't expected a crowd, but it was 2 in the afternoon on a weekday for gosh sakes! It was also dead silent. Usually these places always had at least one giant motor home and a couple of semis idling while their owners slept. Often there were kids running around, playing Frisbee, or people walking their dogs. Sometimes there were busloads of people milling about, smoking cigarettes, eating and drinking vending machine crap, and taking pictures. It always amused Bill how especially the foreign tourists had to take pictures of

EVERYTHING, even a dingy old rest stop. Then there were the picnic tables and barbecue grills for your convenience. Bill couldn't think of anything more depressing than driving out to a rest stop to have a picnic, but he had seen people doing it. They seemed to be having a hell of a good time, too, so who was he to pass judgment? Not his cup of tea, but hey, whatever works.

None of that was happening here. There was just the sound of the wind and the constant roar of the busy highway behind him. It was so quiet that Bill could hear the sound of his footsteps echoing hollowly as he approached the big glass doors. "Tick-tack...tick-tack..." went his dress shoes on the stained concrete. Man! He just felt like he was an actor in an Alfred Hitchcock movie, or maybe an episode of, "The Twilight Zone"...All of which was making him want to just turn around and climb back into the Lincoln and drive as far away from here as fast as possible. His tires would burn some rubber as he roared away from the rest stop, never to return...

So what if he shit his pants? At least he wouldn't get hacked into a million bloody pieces by the axe murderer who was lurking inside the dark building. Bill could almost see the guy. He'd be skinny with greasy long hair tied back with a red bandanna, sleeveless Iron Maiden t-shirt, torn jeans and filthy high top sneakers. In his right hand, a rusty axe. The blade of which would be encrusted with dried blood from all his earlier victims. He would be crouching behind one of those huge wooden racks chock full of unhelpful maps and brochures for places like, Abe and Kathy's Alpaca Farm – *Good clean fun for the whole family!*

When Bill bumbled through the door in search of the men's room, the axe would come down with a sickening splat. As his head and body parted company, the axe dude would hold Bill's head aloft by the hair, yelling, "Hot damn! I got me another one! Yeee-hawww!" Bill's body would land with a squishy thud, blood still pumping in jets from his carotid artery and soaking into the carpet.

Whoa. Wait. Hang on a second. Bill shook his head to clear it of the horrible scene it was spinning out. What the hell was he doing, thinking like that? The damn place was probably locked anyway. Well, he'd give the door handles a shot, but most likely he'd end up out back, pissing in the grass and shitting in the woods. He'd probably wipe his ass with poison ivy, too.

"Here goes nothing" Bill grumbled as he wrapped the fingers of his right hand around the grungy metal handle. The door opened easily when he pulled it. But instead of striding on in, Bill let go of the handle and jumped back a step. What if there really *was* an axe murder hiding in there? Or anybody else for that matter? Maybe an escaped convict, or a loony from the local bin? Whoever they were, they were just waiting for him to step inside that dark, creepy rest stop, and then...

"CLANG!!!" Went the big metal trash can as Bill backed up and knocked it over. This startled him so badly that Bill screamed like a schoolgirl and ran, face first directly into the tempered glass doors of the rest stop. "Aaaaaaggggghhh!"

Blood spattered the dirty grey concrete as he backed up woozily from the impact. Feeling ashamed, he was actually glad that no one had been there to see a solid, six foot two, former high school football player nearly scare himself into a concussion. Bill yanked a handkerchief out of his pants pocket and pressed it to his nose to stop the bleeding. But instead of helping, it made him gag as the acrid smell of urine invaded his nasal passages. "Oh great" Bill sighed as he looked down at his tan slacks and saw that they were soaked.

"Great...just great" Bill sighed. "Nothing like pissing your pants to make you look like a tough guy!" He laughed and groaned at the same time. He just wished that he knew whether it was safe to go inside the rest stop or not. But if he spent much more time doing this stupid stuff out front, it really wouldn't be necessary. Bill took a deep breath, grabbed the door handle, lunged inside and…

Nothing happened.

Well, that wasn't entirely true. As the door rattled shut behind him, Bill heard a low growling sound, followed by a hiss. What the hell was that? He backed up fast, whacking himself briskly on the tailbone with the door's metal push bar. Even though he bit his lips to keep the groans of pain from blaring out, Bill couldn't keep his whimpered, "damn it!" from slipping out.

He looked around wildly for the source of the sound. Unfortunately the only light source was coming through the dirt streaked glass doors behind him and it wasn't much help. There were dark shapes looming from the walls on either side of him and farther back, Bill could see some shadows. Maybe there was a possum or raccoon crouching in there just waiting to bite him when he got close enough! With his luck, it was probably rabid too, or at least sick. According to those bullshit nature shows that his wife liked to watch, they were the only ones that attacked people. After a few moments standing motionless in the gloom, Bill didn't see anything moving. So he began to inch his way toward the large arrow-shaped sign that said, "Men's" and pointed to the right.

The result was another series of growls and hisses, only this time they seemed closer. Bill tried to freeze, but his spasming colon forced him to make a dash for the men's room. There was no sense getting bit by a rabid raccoon AND shitting his pants! Neither was the best option, but at least he had a chance to solve one of his problems. Maybe whatever the other thing was would go away while he was relieving himself. He pushed open the door and did some growling of his own as he stepped inside.

"GA-Awwwkkk!" Retched Bill as the smell of the place assaulted him. It was a solid wall of stink, the essence of every ounce of waste that had ever been deposited there, with maybe a couple of dead bodies thrown into the mix. Good lord! He could barely stand to breathe in there. It felt like he was sucking in actual molecules of the stuff right into his mouth. The thought made Bill gag, but he managed not to toss his cookies and that was a good thing. In the dim, urinal lined area of the men's room, the floor was already squishy and slippery with stuff that Bill couldn't see. Whatever it was, it made walking into a slip-and-slide type operation. Think trying to cross a Crisco covered floor on Jell-O roller skates in a hurry.

"Owwwww! Shit! Damn! Fuck-all!" Bill cried out as he took a big slide sideways that ended with him mashing his balls forcefully against the corner of a wall mounted sink.

"Ohhh mannn! Mmmm!" he nearly wept as he held onto the sink for support, doing his best to stand upright. Then he noticed that there was something very waxy feeling on the sink. Grunting, he took his hands off of it as soon as possible. His palms were covered with some sort of brownish-green substance that maybe was backed up sewer sludge, or a big colony of mold. Disgusted, he wiped his hands on his already wet pants and moved on in search of a stall.

As he came around a little corner of sorts, there was at least a little light from a small bunch of glass block windows, enough to show Bill his destination, the stalls. There were four of them and Bill kind of had to do the

Goldilocks thing until he found the right one. The first stall door was locked, the second toilet was smashed to pieces, and the third stall was making an odd gurgling sound that Bill didn't like very much. It sounded too much like something might be living in there. The murky water bubbled and splashed as if maybe a good sized snake had gotten into the plumbing system. Not good. So stall number four was kind of a relief. It was cleaner than the others and, "Hey! Special bonus for you Mr. Bill Stinson...There's even still paper on the roll!" Bill just stood there for a moment, afraid that this was all a set up and that some giant horrible mutant would come crashing through the glass block windows and eat him alive as he sat. Nothing like that happened.

So he finally sat and took his well-deserved dump, but he didn't waste a lot of time. This rest stop wasn't the kind of place where one lingered half asleep and read all the graffiti left behind by other travelers. It was there, of course. "Call Mary for a 777-4949" or, "Chico likes it up the ass!", "Me too!" wrote Big Tex on 12/12/2012. No more time for that. Bill kept thinking that any moment, the giant black widow spider that had been hiding under the toilet seat just waiting for this moment would sting his balls, or that a giant dripping hand would come up through the smelly filth and get him. There would be a sudden grasping, and poor Bill Stinson would be pulled down into the depths; possibly by the thing that was causing the gurgling in the toilet next door. But nothing happened, and Bill was able to finish his business with no incident. He could even wipe. Ahhh...happiness!

The sinks were those new electric models and didn't work when Bill tried to follow his usual routine and wash his hands. Well that was okay; he had some hand sanitizer back in the car. The trick now was going to be getting back to the Lincoln. For just a second, something darkened the glass block window. Bill glanced over and felt a chilly tingle slide down his back. There was a face pressed against the glass and staring directly at him! Then it was gone just as quick and Bill questioned if he'd seen anything at all. He hoped it was just a lonely dog or cat but he wouldn't know for sure until he got out of the stinky place. It would be great if whatever had threatened him on the way in had decided to take a stroll, but Bill was pretty sure it hadn't. It always seemed like those kinds of things stuck around until they did whatever it was they were going to do. He sighed and abandoned the sinks.

It was time to get the hell out of the foul crapper, so Bill shuffled over to the exit door, his ears listening for any sound that might give the creature outside away. He heard nothing but the squeak of his 200 hundred dollar shoes on the squidgy floor. With the light at his back, Bill could see the reason for the floor's rubbery slipperiness. The grimy floor was littered with a large quantity of used condoms.

What a totally romantic spot to take your lady love for a little bumpin'! Some people just had no class. It was amazing just how little some of us had evolved. Or maybe the human race was already started back on the return trip to being prehistoric knuckle draggers who fucked anything with a pulse. Yeesh!

Anyway...what he was really here for had been accomplished and he needed to get out of this disgusting, smelly place before he lost his damn mind. Something he didn't feel was too far off. Slowly he opened the door and peered cautiously into the gloom.

The big wall shadows he'd feared on the way in, turned out to be candy machines. However, all these candy machines had been reduced to open front cabinets with no wares for sale. The work appeared to have been done by smashing the glass fronts, perhaps with an axe

... Bill's examination of the machines ceased when he heard a low growl, followed by a hiss close to his left. With a gasp, Bill stepped back and let the big wooden door close.

Well that was just peachy! What the hell was he supposed to do now? Obviously the rabid wild cat, raccoon, possum, coyote, or squirrel was just waiting for its chance. As soon as he left the sketchy safety of the men's room, whatever it was would lunge from the shadows and tear his calves into ribbons. Bill's flesh would be ripped and torn painfully while his blood flew and he was infested with rabies or whatever health issues this thing had. What a way to go! He could just picture the newspaper headlines, "Man killed by wild animals while using a closed rest stop on route 88" While that was bad enough, the real hell of it all was what if they didn't find him right away? After just a couple of weeks, he would be a decomposing blob, lying there on the filthy carpet, his face as white as a sheet of paper because all of his blood had drained to the back of his body. Maybe there would just be a bunch of bones that had been gnawed clean by the attacking beast, and they would have to identify him from his dental records.

Bill shivered involuntarily as he thought everything over while walking back and forth in the warm and smelly bathroom. What to do? How could he get out of the rest stop building without getting bit? Maybe the true answer was that he couldn't, but he had already been stuck in this rest stop way longer than he wanted to be. Especially this horrible, toxic bathroom he was attempting to use as a shelter. Some shelter! He was just as likely to get hurt, or go stark raving bonkers in here. At least if he got to the lobby there was a chance he could get outside. Whatever happened, he had to get out of this freaky, disgusting place before he started throwing up all over himself... He had to fucking roll, man! Get the hell out of Dodge City.

He took the most primal approach and ran for it like the Devil was on his tail. Bill shot out of the men's room screaming. He thought he could hear something scampering along behind him, hot on his heels, but he didn't dare look. If he did, he just knew he would feel hot breath and then sharp teeth on his legs. He raced to the front door, slamming the metal push bar so hard that the door glass cracked. Still screaming, Bill literally flew out of the rest stop. His momentum carried him on staggering legs halfway down the concrete path to the parking lot. Only then did he stop to look behind himself.

Nothing was there except an ancient and very dirty rest stop that probably really did deserve to be closed. Bill wiped a shaking hand across his sweaty face and took in a deep breath. The air outside, even with the interstate so close by, seemed wonderfully fresh and cool. Delicious even. After just standing there and taking deep, slow breaths, Bill felt himself relax a little. He had survived!

Well maybe that was overstating things a bit. He might have been a bit foolish, back there. Correction, he had acted like an idiot, a big crybaby for gosh sakes! Nothing really bad had happened, except for a chubby, middle aged man letting his mind run away with itself and taking him along for the ride. Without a doubt, he had completely and totally lost it back there! He'd

peed his pants and had just narrowly missed taking a dump in them also. There hadn't been any heavy metal head chopper hiding inside, and that growling thing, well ... Bill debated that point with himself. That had seemed pretty real, and he had felt something ... Maybe?

With a sigh, Bill dug the Lincoln's remote out of his still damp pants pocket and headed towards the parking lot. One thing he knew for damn sure was that he had no intention of stopping at this rest stop ever again. He clicked the unlock button, still staring at his shoes moving across the concrete. Then he clicked it again, but no clicks, boops, or beeps greeted his ears.

He tried his eyes instead, but they didn't offer any improvement on the situation. "Oh no…Oh no..." Bill said. "No! It can't be!" Oh, but it was, and his backbone felt as if it was full of cold jelly as he looked right, looked left and saw nothing but asphalt.

The Lincoln was gone.

Retired

James Pyles

She could feel the hot grease from Allen's left haunch dripping off swollen lips and down her pointed chin as she savored the zesty essence. He tasted more like roast pork, but the muscle and fat smelled like liver. The first bite slid down her throat leaving a delightful aftertaste.

"Pretty good, but not as good as Gwenny. She was more like…" Leslie sputtered and coughed. "What happened to my voice? I sound like a…" In spite of Allen's deliciousness, she gagged and almost vomited him back up. "Where am I?" Panicked, she swiveled her head around looking for some clue as to what happened to her. "Oh my God! My hands. They're a man's."

Reality fragmented like a shattered mirror, shards falling into her eyes and then her brain. Campfire. Remote site. Sierra Nevada. Hitchhiker. Allen. Surgical tools. Sunset. Tall pines. Plate of beef and fat. No, not beef, Allen. Allen's head on a pike on the other side of the fire. Organs packed in an ice chest. "I ate that runaway girl, Gwenny, three months ago."

87-year-old Leslie McLean woke up screaming!

"Mom, it's okay." Dan McLean gripped his mother's dry, wrinkled hand, large, violet veins crisscrossing in freeway exchange design, and watched her green eyes flutter open, then go wide with shock.

"I'm right here, Mom. You're going to be okay." Her face was the one he always remembered, but time had drained it of vitality. Leslie's hair was the color of snow but as arid as straw. The standard white hospital blankets covered the humiliating gown she was given to wear after surgery. Her 63-year-old son could feel his mother's pulse start to slow, but her gaze was vacant.

"Danny? Where am I?"

"You're in the hospital, Mom. You came out of surgery four hours ago. You're going to be fine."

"Surgery?

"How's everything in here?" Her voice came from the doorway and her nametag said "Pam Peters, R.N."

"I think Mom had a nightmare." Dan held onto Leslie's now trembling hand as he sat helplessly, watching the 30-something nurse glide over the vinyl flooring in her silent, cushioned shoes. Shoulder-length auburn hair bounced jauntily as she checked the disturbingly arcane monitors wired to Leslie's fingers, upper chest, and the shaved area on the back of her skull.

"Looks like you had a bit of a shock, Leslie." Pam's pastel-patterned top reflected light from the windows behind Dan like worn polyester as she swiveled toward the bed. "How are you feeling now?"

"I…guess okay. Who are you?"

"I'm Pam, your nurse."

"But why am I here?" She was a frightened child, lower jaw quivering, eyes watering with tears waiting to drop.

"Mom, your doctor said your memory wouldn't improve right away, isn't that right?" Dan had inherited Dad's brown eyes but, fortunately, still had a full head of iron-gray hair. He looked from Mom to Pam seeking reassurance.

"That's right." Pam raised her voice as if Leslie had hearing problems. "You should start remembering things better pretty soon, maybe within a few days or a week. Dr. Maier's already made a referral to the memory rehab clinic." The nurse touched the old woman's shoulder. "Why in a month, you'll have the memory of a twenty-year-old."

"Memory?" Leslie looked from Pam back to Dan, then past him to the window, watching endless bits of dust pirouette in the filtered streams of sunlight, or tiny, burning bodies writhing in agony in their last moments of life.

"I remember, Danny. You said surgery. Surgery to fix my broken memory."

"Well, not exactly broken." He moved his hand to the bed railing. "You were having a hard time remembering things. It happens to some people when they get older."

"Short-term memory loss. I have short-term memory loss." The code phrase for her dementia had long been her litany.

"You qualified for a new treatment, Mom. Experimental, actually. You received injections of a donor's RNA."

"RNA?"

"It's like getting a transplant from an organ donor, only instead of a heart or lungs, it's a better memory."

"Remember. I remember." Leslie closed her eyes and saw firelight casting ghastly shadows amid fluttering gold and crimson on Allen's face, glazed charcoal eyes staring lifelessly at her.

"You look confused, Mom. Are you alright?"

"I'm thirsty. Something tastes bad." Leslie ran her tongue around the inside of her mouth. "Pork fat."

"What?"

"Here you go." Dan hadn't noticed Pam take the large, plastic container off Mom's tray and fill it. "Have a sip." She held the handle and maneuvered the straw close to Leslie's mouth. The elderly woman sucked greedily, then opened her wizened pale pink lips, drops of lukewarm water dribbling down her chin like hot grease. She shuddered at the thought, but it also made her hungry.

"Thanks."

"No problem, Leslie." Dan thought Pam's practiced smile could have been painted on, like lipstick or makeup. She sat the super-sized water bottle on the tray attached to the bed, then deftly jockeyed around the medical machines and back toward the door. "I'll peek in a little later. Dr. Maier said he'd check with you in about an hour."

"Thanks, Pam." Dan's voice sounded tired. He was exhausted emotionally. Looking down at his Mom again, he saw his wife's face, but Mom was alive, and cancer took Wendy and his Dad both within a month of each other two years ago. He wondered if Mom would remember them now.

"Surgery. I had surgery, right?"

"That's right, Mom." He'd have to ask for a cot to be brought in again tonight. There was no way he could leave her alone, and he couldn't stand the thought of wandering around his empty three-bedroom house. If only Jeff could have come out from the coast, but his wife April and the three grandkids decided to all get the flu at the same time.

He felt his Mom brush against his hand, still resting on the side of the bed. She used to touch him like that after he had a nightmare when he was a little boy.

"Danny?"

"Yes, Mom." He tried to smile, but his lips only flattened.

"Who's Allen?"

"You're sure you'll be alright alone, Mom?"

"Really, Danny. It's been over a month since I was discharged from the hospital and I'm in an independent living home. It's not like you're abandoning me in the middle of nowhere with nothing but a campfire and a cooler of raw meat to survive on."

He stood by the kitchen counter looking back into the living room of Mom's one-bedroom apartment. Leslie had started dyeing her hair again, just a light frosting with a kiss of violet, a color she'd never chosen before. Dark t-shirt, jeans, barefoot, which wasn't so strange, except before, she'd always insisted on wearing slippers at home. The real shock had been her asking for a laptop. After Dad died, she'd lost all interest in computers. Now she was consuming the internet like a millennial.

"Yeah, Mom. I know, but…"

"No buts, Danny." She finally looked up from the screen, put the computer on the coffee table in front of her, then reclined casually against the sofa back, her face and voice carrying annoyance. "I haven't thought this clearly in years, at least as far as I can remember." Leslie chuckled humorlessly. "I'm fine and you have a home of your own."

"You kicking me out?" He was only half-kidding.

"Yes."

His jaw nearly dropped because it wasn't a joke.

"For years I've been flailing about, my life completely out of my control. Now I can think again. I had scrambled eggs and toast with coffee and orange juice for breakfast this morning, and a very disappointing eggplant parmesan with peas and carrots for lunch. I'm considering the shrimp scampi for dinner, but wish they were serving a really tasty pork roast swimming in fat. How's that for memory?"

"Not bad." He crossed his arms. "I guess you've got most of your memory back. "You seem different, though. I'm not quite sure how to describe it."

"You got used to me being a scared little rabbit with no will of my own, always uncertain of everything. I'm myself again. I thought you'd be happy. Now you won't have to hover over me like a helicopter."

He looked at her splitting her attention between him and whatever was on her computer. "I don't know."

Her face softened as she got to her feet and walked over to him. "Come on. Give your mother a hug." She held out her arms.

"Sure, Mom." Embracing, he put his palms gently on her back. "Wow, that's some hug, Mom. Taken up weight lifting?" He snickered as he let go and stepped back.

"Olympic power lifting. It's the latest rage among women in their eighties."

"Well, try not to make Arnold Schwarzenegger look like a wimp."

"He'd be lucky to keep up with me. Now shoo. Mommy's got work to do."

"If you say so, Mom. I'll give you a call in a day or two."

"Fine. Look forward to it." She took his arm and guided him to her door, then opened it and stood expectantly.

"I love you, Mom."

"I love you too, Danny. Have a good evening."

"You, too. Enjoy the shrimp."

Leslie watched him walk into the corridor and turn left toward the elevator. She briefly admired his rear end, not as an erotic object but rather a culinary consideration. Nah. Too old.

"Sandy, don't!" Before she could close her door, Leslie was accosted by her neighbor Mary Poole's irritating toy poodle. She had to resist the overpowering urge to step on its head as the pampered canine continuously yipped while nipping at her toes.

"I'm so sorry, Leslie."

"If you don't keep that thing on a leash…" She gritted her teeth while staring down at Sandy, watching Mary finally clip the strap to the dog's pink leather collar.

"I said I was sorry." Indignation shadowed Mary's heavily lined face and flashed in her blue eyes. She was one of the few like Leslie who were completely ambulatory, which only meant that she could be knocked on her privileged ass. "We're just going for a walk across the road."

"It's an undeveloped vacant stretch of sand and scrub brush. Maybe you could arrange for your mutt to get lost there."

"Come, Sandy." The four-legged ball of fluff yelped as Mary tugged the leash whilst still glaring at Leslie.

Tracking their every step down the carpeted hall toward the elevator, Leslie's gaze possessed a tightly controlled hate and then another emotion.

The pair rounded a corner and vanished. "Finally." She closed the door and locked it.

Strolling back to the couch, her gait became masculine. Leslie sat down heavily and then put the laptop across her thighs again, grateful that the screensaver had concealed her web browser tabs. "35 Unsolved Missing-Persons Cases," she muttered, her fingertip tracing a line across the touch pad, scrolling through the names on the list.

"Allen Raymond Pratt, age 47, frequently transient, told friends he was hitchhiking to his brother's home in Reno. Last seen September 12, 2013." Leslie ran her tongue around the inside of her mouth again and across her teeth, vividly recalling his taste, the odor of his cooked meat, how she'd buried the brain and liver as inedible, but she'd left the skin on his forearm after shaving it. "Tastes like pork rinds. Wonder which list little Gwenny is on?"

She turned her thoughts to that cute 19-year-old waitress who had served her a crappy lunch a few hours earlier, then shook her head. "Sweet like Gwen, but too skinny."

With reluctance, Dan started keeping his smartphone on the nightstand next to his bed just in case Mom needed anything, and when it rang and his bleary eyes managed to lock onto the dull red characters 3:26 a.m. on his alarm clock, his arm shot out from under the covers at the offending object. Fumbling, he slid his finger across the screen to answer, saw the dreaded and familiar number, and pressed the electronic rectangle next to his face. "Hello. Mom?"

"Danny?" She was crying.

"Mom, what's wrong?" What's going on?" He felt his pulse throbbing in this throat.

"It happened again."

"What happened?" He used his free hand to push himself up, leaning against the wall while taking mental inventory of the location of his wallet and keys, anticipating a late-night excursion.

"The dreams. Danny, the nightmares are horrible."

"It's just a dream. Dreams can't hurt you." He moved the phone away from his mouth long enough to stifle a yawn.

"I was … it's too disgusting. Danny, I dreamed … that I'd eaten someone." She dissolved into tears and misery.

"Do you want me to come over?"

"No. It's too early. I just need to talk."

"I can try to get an earlier appointment with your psychologist." Power of attorney let him read Leslie's medical records, and he wasn't surprised that there had been some differences in Mom's personality profile compared to her pre-surgery state, but Dr. Ballinger thought they were pretty minor. For her, the only unanticipated manifestation was the macabre nightmares about murder, dismemberment, and cannibalism, although half the time, Mom denied all of that just days or weeks after her revelations.

"I want them to stop, Danny. I wouldn't hurt a fly, you know that."

"I know, Mom. Maybe Dr. Maier could prescribe something to help you sleep."

"I can get to sleep, but these horrible dreams … I can't stand them. They're so vivid, like I'm remembering …"

"Mom, I know you don't want to hear this, but maybe you need to go back into the rehab clinic."

"Oh, Danny, I don't know."

"Mom, I'm really concerned. This is the third time this week you've called me in the middle of the night."

"Really?"

"Don't you remember?" An icy hand gripped his chest.

"Oh yes, of course I remember. I'm just rattled. The dream."

"I'll call Dr. Ballinger's office in the morning. I'm sure she'll be able to find an earlier appointment."

"I can … taste her, like veal, the smell of her

cooking. I can feel her blood going down my throat. See it covering my hands, except they're a man's hands. Danny, I think I'm going crazy."

"I'm coming over, Mom."

"Mom, we've got to do something about this."

"About what, dear?" The afternoon sun warmed Leslie as she took Dan's extended arm, so he could help her across the parking lot, back to the facility's awning covered main doors. She noticed the police car first, sitting just forward of the shaded entryway.

"Wonder what's happened?"

"Danny, I've been meaning to confess to you."

"Confess what, Mom?"

"My shadow career as a bank robber. I'm sure they're here to take me away."

The sides of his mouth upturned. "Now that's the Mom I remember, quirky sense of humor and all." He palmed the automatic door switch mounted on a nearby wall sending the first set of front doors slowly opening, then after a few steps, did the same for the second set.

"Wait here and I'll sign you back in." Dan left Leslie by the lobby's reception counter. She normally said "hi" to whoever was on duty, right now it was Cyndy, but the concierge was paying rapt attention to the two uniformed officers speaking to a distraught Mary Poole.

"What do you think the cops want with Mrs. Poole?"

Leslie had been so enjoying Mary's distress; she hadn't paid attention to Dan coming up behind her. "Beats me. Take me to my room."

"Sure. Now, about what I was saying. I got you an emergency appointment with your psychologist and you soft soap the whole nightmare thing."

"I was just being a silly old Mommy when I called you. Like you said, it was only a dream."

"Dr. Ballinger said that the nightmares could be an effect of the RNA injections. Remember, it was experimental, and you were only one of thirty people in the country accepted for the trial."

"You can't undo the surgery."

"No, but I could schedule a consultation with Dr. Maier. He said if there were any significant ill-effects, a partial reversal …"

She grabbed his forearm with her nails hard enough to draw savory blood, causing him to jerk away. "No, Daniel!" Leslie quickly lowered her voice. "I mean, the surgery was so difficult. I don't think I could bear to undergo the procedure again."

"You've got a mean grip, Mom." Dan stopped talking, glanced at the superficial wounds, and then up over her shoulder. Leslie turned to see a bulletin board on the hallway wall.

"What is it?"

"You didn't mention that Mrs. Poole's dog had gone missing. She's more devoted to Sandy than most mothers are to their kids, uh … present company excluded of course." He winked at his joke but Leslie didn't seem amused.

"Yes. The thing wandered off about a week ago. Never returned. Mary could never keep control of the beast anyway." Her voice was fanciful as she regarded the photocopied image of the poodle framed like a child's face on a milk carton.

"Could that be why the police are talking with Mary?"

"Don't be ridiculous, Danny." She stroked his arm and then started walking again. "A missing dog is hardly the crime of the century." Leslie smacked her lips. It had been fatty and chewy, vaguely reminiscent of squab but not as succulent. She remembered not having eaten dog or cat since she, or rather he, was eleven. As he got older, he hunted larger game. Danny pressed the up button for the elevator. Waiting, she imagined the only reason the police might have for interviewing Mary was that someone found the remains of the roasted carcass several hundred yards across the road among a bushy thicket.

"We've been through all this before, Mr. McLean. I don't know who the RNA donor was, and even if I did, I couldn't tell you." Dr. Michael Maier was chewing on the left edge of his wire-brush mustache, salt and pepper, like the mop adorning his scalp. His office at the hospital was adequate but not opulent. He could afford the best, was even offered better quarters, personal washroom, an excellent view. But as one of the top five neurosurgeons in the country, he was, at heart, a nerd who was totally enthralled with the workings of the human brain, with the tools of his profession, with the bleeding edge research. He cared about appearances only enough to impress patients, or at least to mollify the hospital's board and marketing department.

"Is there any way to find out?" Dan's voice on the other end of the receiver was breathless hinting of desperation. "Mom's fading in and out like the picture on an old TV set. Sometimes she's Mom, but other times, I'd swear she's an entirely different person."

"You read and signed all of the documentation on your mother's behalf. You knew this was experimental and the results could not be guaranteed. Even traditional surgeries carry some measure of risk." He'd given that old woman back her memory and her competency. What they hell more did they want? Why even flawed results like this would fuel memory-enhancement research for the next twenty years.

"I just need to know what sort of person the donor was, Doctor. Sometimes Mom … well, she gives me the creeps."

"There's a long history of individuals experiencing changes in personality due to brain trauma. This was discussed with both of you prior to your signing the consents."

"That's another thing. Mom's been talking to her lawyer and wants my power of attorney revoked."

"I'd say that's an indication of the success of the RNA procedure. You and Leslie both claimed her becoming more self-sufficient was a primary goal." Maier glanced at his desk clock. He only had another five minutes to devote to this conversation before his next consultation appointment arrived.

"I wanted to get my Mom back. I don't think I ever did."

The doctor ran nimble fingers through his shaggy mane reminding him he was overdue for a haircut. "It's not that I'm unsympathetic to your plight, Mr. McLean. However, Leslie's surgery, as I have already mentioned, was part of an experimental trial, and unanticipated results were always part of the equation. Now if your mother wants to speak with me about undergoing the reversal operation, you can schedule an appointment and I'll be glad to go over the risks with the both of you."

"I don't think she minds what's happening to her, at least most of the time."

"If the patient doesn't find her current condition to be adversely affecting her, then I don't see what I can do."

"You can tell me whose memories she has."

"I can't do that, Mr. McLean. I've told you that." It wasn't strictly true. Of course, he hadn't been granted official access to the identities of the donors, but idle curiosity and highly placed connections at the Neurotrust Biobank bestowed him with certain illicit privileges. He didn't have to recall the information on his computer as it was conjured up like a genie from the lantern of his mind.

Jeremiah Phillip Wilkerson, age 42, a self-employed truck driver, had died of a single gunshot wound to the chest, killed by a hitchhiker he'd picked up who had been armed. The murderer, 36-year-old Tommy Bryant, was later found to be a serial killer who had been sought after by law enforcement agencies for several years and was now in San Quentin. Wilkerson's background was unremarkable, even boring. The only thing that had puzzled Maier about the donor was his exceptionally high IQ. Why had such an intelligent person chosen such a mundane profession?

Leslie McLean stood nude in front of the full-length mirror attached to the back of her bathroom door. "I'm an old woman." Her skin was milky white with a dab of coffee and the consistency of curdled cream. Her once attractive breasts sagged to nearly her middle. Belly and thighs were a monument of cellulite. Her finger and toenails were as brittle as Leslie's porcelain curios which she kept in a floor-to-ceiling glass case by the door to her patio. She was in reasonably good health, apart from having to wear a partial and suffering from very mild high blood pressure. She could ambulate well as long as she didn't run or walk too fast.

"I'm retired. I'll never hunt again." Disgust melted into despondency. Grabbing her robe off a hanger to her right, she concealed most of the evidence of her decrepit anatomy. Opening the door, she stepped gingerly into the bedroom, then crossed into the living room, approaching the patio. Walking outside, she looked over the railing at the sidewalk below. "Three stories. It might not kill me and then I'd be in a worse mess."

The ringing doorbell made her jump slightly, and just as she answered it, she heard gleeful children cheering.

"What I surprise." Leslie felt her throat tighten with unaccustomed emotion. "Danny, you brought me Jeff's family." She leaned down toward the two boys and the little girl, ages 10, 7, and 4. "And my great-grandbabies. Come in, come in." She stepped back to let the crowd inside.

"I'm not a baby, Great-grandma," Kent, the oldest complained.

Kneeling down, she embraced Emily, the youngest. "You'll always be my baby, won't you?"

"I will Great-grandma," the succulent redhead murmured into the terrycloth robe. Leslie kissed her neck, relishing the salty taste.

Little Em was squiggling, but she didn't want to let go of the delicious morsel, turning scrumptious ideas over in her mind like hot pancakes oozing with butter. *I'd never get away with it, but an old woman can dream, can't she? Then again, there's always Mel Swanson's cat.*

Visceral

Jared Baker

The donkey-bray of the phone wakes me, and I snatch it like the lifeline it is.

Just the morning alarm. Not a caller for whom I must pretend to be a "normal" person who struggles toward consciousness like a swimmer clawing his way to the water's surface. That isn't me. One moment I'm dreaming, the next, fully aware.

I'm different. I wonder if today will be.

I strain to feel the sheets beneath me, to luxuriate in the high thread-count silk. It should feel like lying on a cloud, according to the newspaper ad. But it never does. It never feels like *anything.*

I try to shrug off my disappointment as I clutch at my phone. But I can resist the temptation of it. If I couldn't, I'd be in jail. Or in the ground.

I march to the bathroom and twist the shiny chrome shower-handle. Clutching the phone, I wait for the glass to steam. It takes all my willpower not to swipe the screen. I take a deep breath instead, fogging the inert display. The treasures it contains must wait.

Until I have tried everything else, at least.

When the scalding water sluices over my body, it *should* make me groan. The pulsating warmth from the shower-head will soothe my knotted muscles like a masseuse's hands. The catalog told me so – but it lied almost as well as I do. I'm aware of the warmth as a fact to be noted, nothing more. Familiar frustration grinds at my brain, but I soldier on.

I rinse and dry off. The complete set – washcloths, hand towels, body-sized cloak with inlaid designs – cost me two hundred dollars, and *should* make me think I'm being wrapped in cotton candy. The gospel according to the sales clerk with the glasses and the tattoos and the silver hoop through the side of her nose.

I feel the pressure against my skin, but that's all. Just like always.

I wipe a circle in the fogged mirror and study my face. There are no revelations there. Nothing to show me how to get from where I am to where I *need* to be. The same as it was yesterday, just like everything else.

I squeeze out a handful of shaving gel and lather up. The label says it will bring cooling calm, as if cradling my skin in a gentle breeze.

It just feels wet.

The phone beckons to me, calling on a frequency only I can hear. I ignore it. I will not give up yet.

I strop the straight razor I inherited from my grandfather. It was his only gift to me, apart from screams and terror and blood. I scrape away stubble that will be a five o'clock shadow by noon and a barbarian's beard by dinnertime. Pointless, but necessary – ill-groomed people are noticed. Talked about.

I can't have that.

When I finish, the after-shave blasts my face, coating the crimson line I carved into my cheek without noticing. The ad says it will tighten and tone my skin. The online review says I will think my face has been dipped in kerosene and lit on fire.

Neither happens.

Like the bedsheets, the hot water, the towel. I can't *feel* it. My body isn't numb – the sensation is there, but distant. Muted. Someone trying to *tell* me what things feel like, with the vocabulary of a four-year old.

I exit the bathroom, grabbing up the phone once more. But I still don't resort to it. I'm strong. I wait a bit longer, if only to prove it to myself.

From the bureau, I retrieve silk boxers and a white cotton t-shirt. From my closet, a striped button-up with perfect creases, a dark suit and wing-tips, a tie to bring it all together. Each piece of clothing should caress my skin like a knowledgeable lover, if half the television I've seen is true.

But the garments are not lovers. Not even casual acquaintances. They're just *there*.

Downstairs, I scramble eggs, fry steak, and brew fresh coffee. The scents should be mouth-watering, but they waft through me. As if they are ghosts. Or I am.

The table on the deck is polished oak with a rain-resistant cherry finish. The morning light hits it, crimson flares and burgundy sparkles sauntering along the wood-grain. I sit and try to savor the peppery softness of the eggs, the pink succulence of the steak, the heat and bitter tang of the coffee.

Does a car enjoy it when its owner fills the tank with gas? Does it *feel* anything when old motor-oil is drained and replaced?

The phone lies on the table, out of danger in case I spill food or drink in a moment of clumsy need. The promise it carries is surer than the promise of the storm on the late fall air.

Sweat trickles down my temple as I stare into the

trees. I try to smell the wood smoke from my neighbor, who has so far refused to join the current century in swapping over to propane. When I detect it – as faint as a dream, but there – I try to call up a single happy memory of home and hearth. I fail.

I try to smile at the sounds of the birds in the trees. To feel hope as the sun emerges from the clouds to bathe me in its golden glow.

These ideas are nothing. I *feel* nothing.

I acknowledge my defeat with a rueful smile.

The phone prompts me for my fingerprint, and I oblige. It demands the passcode, and I tap it out, my thumbs jerking and twitching. The home-screen appears. I manage an actual smile at the thought. It is the closest thing to a home I have ever known.

I access the photo directory. An angry chirp prompts me for another code. I change this one every other day, because I must. I enter it and I am finally where I want to be, where I have *needed* to be since I woke this morning.

At best, any of these digital photos would send me to prison; at worst, the needle or the gas chamber, depending on who and where and when. It's lunacy, of course – I know that, I'm not crazy – but I can't get rid of them. They're all I have. My single oasis in the endless desert.

Image #1 is a woman barely out of her twenties. Her skin is flawless. Reddish-gold hair, full lips curled in a smile. Her eyelids are closed in sleep – the last peaceful, dreaming sleep she ever knew – so I cannot see their color. But I remember those cool, azure eyes as clearly as if I saw them yesterday, instead of a decade ago.

Before I left her, most of the hair was gone. The full lips were chapped and swollen, the voice that emerged between them, raw and ragged with her screams. Her perfect skin was a rainbow of winter bruises – blue and green and purple. Her eyes had wept bloody tears – first of fear, then pain, and finally gratitude.

She is so lovely; my heart hurts in my chest.

Seeing her again – even ten years removed and through the medium of electronic pixels – it's as if I have shrugged off a HazMat suit. The images in my mind are sharp, the colors vivid. I can smell the cinnamon-scented candles she kept alight in her apartment, the olfactory onslaught so sudden that I thrash my head from side to side. My pulse pounds in my ears, a bass drum that makes my bones vibrate. It is as though the earth itself is trying to shake me loose.

I feel *alive* again. Just like when I was with her.

I sometimes wonder what will happen to me if these images ever lose their magic. If they ever fail to pierce the numbness that isolates me from the rest of the world.

I don't like thinking about that.

Throughout the dreary hours of my day, I manage not to revisit the images. But I *am* tempted. In the bathroom after my morning conference call, where I liquidate the tech division of a firm my company just bought. In my car at lunch, where I devour chicken and pasta as tasteless as the plastic in which I packed them. I want to sneak a peek on the ride home, but I resist – when one of them overwhelms me, transports me back to where color and feeling and magic exist, I don't want to be in rush-hour traffic. Certainly not with the storm around me and a layer of oil-slicked rain between my tires and the road.

But the anticipation builds. I'm a junkie looking for his next hit. Part of me – the tiniest, most hidden core – is ashamed. Most of me doesn't care.

I make it home without crashing the car, and inside without staggering like a drunk. My heart is a racehorse at full gallop, my mind an inferno of memory and desire. I summon up enough discipline to make dinner with gourmet ingredients I can't taste and expensive wine I can't enjoy. I bought them because a co-worker saw me at the store.

I sit at my dining room table. It costs as much as some cars. Designed for a large family I will never have, sharing stories and joys I will never know. I shovel the insipid food into my mouth, and I scroll. For long moments, I am transformed. Happy. Or the closest to it that I am allowed.

Wait. That isn't right.

The image I'm seeing should be the last one. Her slumbering face is the color of coffee with cream. Her night-black hair crowns and cradles it against the pillow. I remember her hair smelling like jasmine. When I left her less than a week ago, the skin around her throat had changed to a lovely purple – the color of periwinkles and frozen raspberries and dusk and mysteries.

She is the last one.

But not the last image. The counter reads "Image 38 of 39".

An eel slithers through my stomach.

My finger trembles. I swipe and stare.

I see my own face. My closed eyes. My features, bland and pleasant and somehow accusatory in slumber.

I hear a throaty laugh behind me. It has a pleasing rasp to it, gravel dancing on velvet cloth. But there is nothing *in* it – no humor, no joy.

Fingers of ice play the bones of my spine like piano keys. I turn …

My head explodes in a dazzling flash of golden light. But the light is wondrous, lovelier than the dawn, and I want to weep. From the beauty, not the pain.

A flash of lightning, another blow – this time the color is blue chased with violet, the colors of twilight. I do weep. My chest constricts, my heart pounding against my ribs and in my ears.

An explosion of thunder. I fall to the floor. I can smell the garlic and oregano I used to cook my dinner – only words before, but now *real.* I taste the remnants of the stew on my tongue, my mouth tingling. My mind takes in a world it has long been denied.

Another detonation in my skull. I can feel warmth – soothing, comforting, warmer and more wonderful than any bathroom shower. It flows from the crown of my head, over my neck. I moan.

Blinking, I see her, see that coffee-cream skin flushed nearly scarlet with rage. The baseball bat rises for another blow. Even the flecks of gray and red on the battered black metal are exquisite, a decadent contrast no master painter could ever capture.

The dark closes in at the edges of my world. I know I should be frightened. When I left her, I should have made *sure*. But I didn't.

I'm glad of that now. I'm grinning. I'm happy.

I can *feel.*

Set For Three

Henry Myllylä::

Caithlyn stares at the medicine box upon a bathroom shelf. The white label has her name imprinted in the description and guidelines for dosage, 1-2 pills at night before sleep. She does not miss the irony of having to use them now herself. *You selfish bastard*, she slams the mirrored door shut and takes a look at herself. She feels compressed. Beyond her age. And it shows, for the face looking back at her is barely recognizable.

"Mommy!" Bethany cries from the kitchen.

"Hold on, sweetie. I'm coming," she hastens out from the bathroom.

The kitchen sink is filled with dishes. An overflowing trash bag from yesterday waits nearby on the floor. Caithlyn scavenges a blue cereal bowl underneath a pile and washes it a little under water.

"Favorite cereal from your favorite bowl, honey?"

Bethany nods and thumbs the spoon at the table.

"And the apple too, okay?"

"I don't like apples," Bethany protests.

"Apple a day keeps the doctors away," Caithlyn replies, "There you go, baby." After serving the breakfast she sits by her daughter, "Are you excited about today?"

"Uhumm." She nods.

"Aunt Macy is so nice to take you there. What's best about it?"

"Mm- Dolphins!" her eyes lit up.

"They have dolphins there. Turtles too, and..." she gives her daughter's forehead a kiss and whispers, "seahorses!"

Bethany giggles, lolling the spoon in her mouth.

"Mom?" The cheer shifts from her tone.

"Yes..?"

"When does daddy come home?"

Caithlyn can't help her hand from clenching to a fist.

"We have talked about this," she opens her palm and presses it tight to a tabletop. Taking a moment to measure her words, she continues, "We can visit daddy at the church. Like we did yesterday. But he can't come home, sweetie. Not like before."

Bethany watches her spoon confused.

The doorbell rings.

"Okay, baby. Finish up. Time to go."

While Bethany brushes her teeth, Caithlyn and Macy stand by the door. They share an irritating silence, as Macy peers past her into the house, her unsaid accusation stating that the house is a mess. Caithlyn is already painfully aware of the fact.

"How are you?" says Macy, measuring her from head to toes.

"Fine. Thanks," Caithlyn answers, pushing her hands tight to her pockets.

Macy seems to understand the gesture and immediately softens her tone.

"Hey- we really have the space, remember? You could stay as long as you need."

"No need for that." She's embarrassed. "Look. I'm glad you can take Bethany out, but I have to work this out myself. Can't just wait for someone to save me."

A silence ensues. Their eyes shift about, avoiding each other.

"Anyways. You know -- If there's anything, just ask."

"Thanks," Caithlyn says with gratitude in her voice, "I mean it."

Bethany rushes from the bathroom, yelling Macy's name with excitement.

"Are you ready, my princess?" Macy hugs her and they pass outside.

Caithlyn kisses Bethany goodbye and stands watching by the doorway as the car steers away.

II

The couch underneath her had seen it all. Their first kiss after seeing *The Exorcist* re-screened at a local film festival called *Fright Night Film Fest,* or something similar that she could not remember exactly. After the film and a fine dinner, one thing led to another as the night passed in laughter, almost rushing in excitement.

At the front of the coach, just above the TV, there's a pummeled crater in the ceiling. A mark of their later years. Years that were lonely at best. Just like now, then she had spent her time alone on this couch, when he was first deployed. He promised her a marriage and a family once he would return. The promise left her waiting for him, bound her, waiting for her *forever after* to begin.

Yet, he never really returned. His spark, that bright humour she loved, had died somewhere over there. Lively sympathy that entangled them before had grown colder.

But he kept his part the best that he could and when Bethany was born, the fatherhood fixed him. She warmed his heart from a scarred slumber and, for over a year, things were almost like they used to be; perhaps even better, for now they were a family.

But just before Bethany's second birthday, he broke the news at the breakfast table. He'd be deployed again. There was no room for negotiation or any real talk. He had made up his mind. After that, things never were okay. Not even close.

Next time he returned distracted and estranged. He always had a reason to drink and at best, he passed out quietly on the couch. The crater on a wall and scratches on a bedroom floor told stories of much worse. But it did not last for long.

One rainy night, three months ago, the doorbell rang around 10 p.m. Two police officers stood solemn outside, their hats off their heads. Before any words were said, she *knew*. There had been an accident. They wished Caithlyn to join them.

The dark ride through the silhouettes of the suburb lead to the morgue, where he was laid on a metallic table under a sterile light. A distinct chemical scent hung in the air. His expression was calm; his continuous nervousness had passed from his pale, battered facade. Test results told that his now still, stiffening body contained alcohol and sedatives. The outcome of his decision to drive was so damn obvious. So obvious, that he probably knew it very well himself. At least they all knew, though the officers left such speculations unspoken in their professional discretion.

As during his deployments, this night she sat in the living room alone. The only thing changed was that the photos in their frames had become obituaries, instead of memories. The young soldier in the frames was no more, his proud ideals proven, but in tearful tatters of innocence lost. Next to him, framed for life, a smiling girl blossoms on her wedding day. Absurd, she's wearing Caithlyn's face.

Caithlyn goes to the bathroom and takes the white box down from the shelf. She takes a pill with a glass of water before lying back down. Soon the camouflage of her resentment hazes. It dulls and blurs, shifts into soft, oblivious clouds that at least don't hurt.

III

Following noon, the door opens without a warning.

"Mommy!" Bethany storms inside, her orange backpack flinging along.

Shit! Caithlyn startles from the couch. "You're home, sweetie!" She gives her daughter a hug, then a penitent look towards Macy at the door. "You had fun?"

"We saw dolphins and a shark!" the girl exclaims.

"Now that's amazing! Baby, take your bag to your room."

Her head feels dizzy as she passes towards Macy, who is preparing to turn around at the door.

"Umm – stay for a dinner?" She asks before Macy can leave.

"I'd better go. I still have plenty of miles left to go today."

"Yeah, true," Caithlyn accepts her excuse and gives her a thankful embrace for goodbye.

She begins to prepare a dinner while Bethany scrambles through a photography book that she got from the zoo. Its pages feature some of the zoo's famous residents, like Doro the dolphin and Nelson the bear, who even starred in a TV-commercial a few years ago. Bethany studies the images with immediate focus, trying to read and understand the descriptions beside the photos. Caithlyn watches her, knowing that her daughter's passion for learning will take her far. Provide choices that her mother never really had.

"Honey, I'll take the trash outside. Don't touch the stove, okay?"

"I won't, mom," she replies, her face buried in the book's pages.

Bright sunlight reminds her that she's still recovering from her medical sleep, as the sudden breach of light pounds against her nerves. She protects her eyes with her hand, while carrying the trash bag to the street corner. The opposite house blurs in the side of her view, when she suddenly recall's not seeing the elder Mrs. Johnson outside in a while. *Hope she's not hospitalized.* She opens the bin's heavy lid and stuffs the trash inside.

Coming back to her yard, she sees the side door of the garage hanging wide open.

Again, for fuck's sake! "What's wrong with you?" she slanders the door while slamming it shut and checking it stays.

As if there were not enough troubles already, even the door had begun to play its tricks on her lately. Just last week some animal, probably a sick raccoon, had sneaked in through the door at night and messed the place up. It took her an hour to clean the place and get rid of that revulsive, bloody odor it had left behind.

After dinner, mother and daughter remain in the kitchen. Bethany is again immersed in the book. Caithlyn runs hot water into the sink, for the dish pile which had stacked up over the past few days, was about to be dealt with.

"Enjoying your book, honey?"

Bethany pays no heed to the question.

Caithlyn takes a look over her shoulder and sees Bethany looking towards the door instead of her book.

"Hey, honey … something's wrong?"

Bethany rubs her hands anxious together, clearly sullen, in troubled thoughts.

"Honey, what is it?" Caithlyn lowers toward her.

Her lower lip curls and her eyes go about avoiding her mother's face.

"Oh dear, come here," Caithlyn wrests her into an embrace.

Caithlyn's heart is broken for the fact that there is nothing she can do. She knows, that only love and patience will ease her daughter's confusion in time. Yet, those two she has. She would hide the wreck of her own heart to protect Bethany from such poisoning bitterness. Her life would have a chance to grow straight and, eventually, the pain would pass.

Caithlyn takes the book and begins to read. They draw together into the secrets of baboons, followed by stories of commercial stardom of Nelson the bear. All displayed vividly through photography, both old and new. Soon Bethany's silent attention turns to a smile.

IV

Bethany goes to her bed voluntarily that night. Ups and downs of the day had taken their toll. Caithlyn kneels by her bed and brushes her ears with her hands. The open window by the bed lends a breath of freshness after the oppressive heat of the day. Caithlyn reaches to close it, but Bethany intervenes.

"Let it be," Bethany instructs.

"Honey, you will get cold."

"I want it to be open. It must be."

Her stubbornness amazes Caithlyn a bit, though such manners are to be expected from a child of her age.

"Okay, just as you wish. Good night, sweetie," she kisses her brow and then turns off the light.

She leaves the pills untaken this night. Restless sleep is a better option than sleeping over, since the pills had already played their tricks on her before. *Wake up at six, dropping Bethany at seven, thirty-minute drive,* she recounts the schedule for tomorrow while brushing her teeth. Her mind wanders to the ease, that a regular paycheck would bring if she's lucky tomorrow. Though the job of a waitress is something she had never dreamed of, she really needs it. Besides, she is already tired of seeing the world move past. She longs for purpose and change; regaining control over this aimless turmoil.

Her decision to sleep unmedicated claims its price after an hour of sleep. Desolate, rocky plateaus in the outskirts of Kabul open in the eye of her mind. She hates this place wholeheartedly, despite having seen it only in photos. It has stolen her everything. To her, it is a contagious hell that eats its way through souls of its victims and hides amongst whole generations. Its hideous face is never the same, but its victims always had a scent of it. Like a smell of death, it could not be mistaken.

She walks a lonely, tire marked gravel road. Sporadic assemblages of destroyed vehicles stand charred and rusting by its banks, displaying relentless damage in various ways. An old, red pickup truck stands halfway across the road, its side plucked open by a series of holes that run all the way through. Tattered cushions inside it are soaked in dry, dark red splatters. Behind, the passenger side of a Humvee is torn open in a way she knows to be caused by an improvised explosive device.

These tattered husks come from all around the world and from various decades. Yet all stand similar in their poses of death and decay, barely pushed to the side of the road to allow others attempt to pass through its snares.

Suddenly she hears a monotone, swarming sound of metallic jingling coming from somewhere behind a rocky slope that frames the road. Its main source seems to be flanking, hidden behind the mountainous formations. A single black goat appears at the top, apparently leaving the flock passing on the other side. A crude bell around its neck ceases its bleak sermon, as the goat stares down at her, standing sovereign over the landscape its kind have ruled for millenniums past. For a moment, it studies the scene with its dark eyes. Then the bell begins to sing it's crippled, discordant song, as it takes steps down towards the wrecks below.

The closer it comes, the more discomfort she feels, for she *knows* this song that the goatherd sings. She has never heard it herself before, but her husband feared it. It echoed inside him until the end of his days, disrupting his sleep, stealing his ease. For him it was the sound of silence after the death of a friend; the song of damnation he could not repel. It strangled his soul and welcomed him to hell, never allowing him freedom from the guilt of the ravage they had dealt.

The goat circles her closely. For a second, she sees her own reflection swipe through the dark of its eyes. It passes her unnoticing. Traveling its own perennial ways, it takes no interest in her astral presence.

Then a black clad figure of a man appears on top of the ledge to watch after the goat. He wears a dark, tattered scarf over his head and a tunic that seems as if it came from a grave. His withered hand holds a chin-high, wooden staff with branches protruding from its crooked core, and his dusty garments reveal his face away just enough, to let the inhumane quality of his piercing eyes trample through.

Caithlyn knows his name, *the Lord of the Herd*, from violent lunacies that drove her husband astray;

from drunken nonsense he prayed on his last days.

This black man knows her husband's shame; the sinister deeds he would never unveil. He was a black serpent under her husband's heart that grew cold; a strangler of innocence that never left him alone. The Lord had all the time in the world for his work, for he shed his skin in the tears of her kin.

The eyes of the Lord know her very well too. He has smelled her perfume and meditated on her fear. He is glad for breeding his flock at their home, for practicing his craft on its fertile soil. His visage told that he yearned. His pale withering whispered of a hunger untamed. A barbaric craving smoldered within his mind, tantalized by the scent of a life she had wasted in wait for her man.

For the Lord she was a voluptuous palace, a fetish of ecstasies of his court in exile. And Bethany... the unclaimed crown of his rule. His heart is bewitched by such fauna that sprung from orphanhood. His flora nourishes in widows that flee. His passions dwell amidst darkness that civilized reason shall yield; his appeal in harvest the scythe of ages shall reap.

She watches in awe as he begins to recite barbaric words. He raises the staff above his head, giving his summoning a feverish visual display, his black garments shake enthralling in wake. His other hand stirs the air, accompanying the mantra in gestures that flow strangely to the rhythm underlying his howls.

The form of this ritual is bizarre, but she knows what it's about. Its twisted rhythm and dissonant leads are twitches of faces in fear; the scent of remains that the fire has churned; violent stimuli that burn the nerves, like amputated limbs itching after being removed.

The pain of it begins to press at her, growing at her astral body, intimately oppressing. The compression and collapse entangle her, as the screeching invocations continue to strangle and lure. Then, suffocating in the midst of this darkest embrace, she hears him asking forgiveness for the promise that he failed.

Caithlyn leaps, repulsed from her bed. Despite the relief of waking, her heart wrenches from hearing his voice. She enters the kitchen and pours herself a glass of water, hoping it will orient her a bit before going back to sleep. But to her amazement, she sees that Bethany is awake, sitting by her bed and peering outside through the window.

"You're awake, honey," she enters her room.

"The garage woke me," Bethany explains.

No fucking way!

Caithlyn goes back to the kitchen and takes a sturdy flashlight out from a drawer, "Mommy's gonna go check that out."

Bethany hears the door open and her steps flanking behind the corner as Caithlyn's passes outside. Soon an aggressive beam of light filters through the closed green curtains. Her mother passes to the garage opposite to her window.

The bright light sweeps around as Caithlyn inspects the yard, her footsteps resound from right behind the window. Then the light wanes and her steps fade as she enters the garage. At first, a quick reflection of light reaches out through a small garage window. Then the flashlight dies. The yard is engulfed by darkness.

"Mommy?" Bethany whispers without receiving an answer.

A long silence ensues.

Then suddenly the door croaks across the night outside. Within a moment, footsteps heavier than her mother's enter inside. A strangling fear engulfs her mind. The darkness of the house offers nothing for her eyes, though the pounding steps pass by her room penetrating further into the house. For a moment the steps wander through the living room and kitchen. After entering Caithlyn's bedroom at the end of the hall, they halt.

Then another pair of steps come from outside.

"Mommy!" Bethany cries as her mother appears to the door, "Mommy, please!" she begs, her vision blurring under her tears.

Without a spoken word Caithlyn watches her child shivering on the bed. With a bewildered look in her eyes, she reaches for the door and closes it, creating a barrier between them.

Now closed alone in her room, Bethany hears Caithlyn's steps passing to the other bedroom. Its door slams shut. Then the darkness of the house submits to a tortuous silence that lasts for hours to come.

The following morning Bethany enters the living room and finds Caithlyn seated on the couch. She reclines next to her and sets her head upon her mother's lap.

"Mommy?"

Caithlyn seems unwilling to let her eyes away from the wedding picture in front of them.

"Mommy, are you ok?"

Caithlyn's head turns toward the kitchen, her eyes avoiding Bethany as if she does not exist.

"Honey," she finally responds, her upper body turning half toward the kitchen, "we are going to have a guest tonight."

The way that Caithlyn's eyes seem asleep makes Bethany feel strange, "But mommy, are you sick? Please," she inquires again without a further reply.

That evening Bethany sits by the end of the table after finishing her meal. Caithlyn works around the kitchen, already washing the dishes of their recent meal. But then, instead of hurrying Bethany to bed, she begins to set the table as if they would be starting again. She chooses a set of cutlery and sets them at the opposite end of table, to that particular seat which has been recently unoccupied.

"Honey, I have news..." Caithlyn says. Her hands begin to shake and her tone quavers, though she tries to control this compulsion, knowing it will only frighten her child, "Daddy has come back, but …" a single tear breaks out from her eye, "… from now on, he'll feed here only at night."

Smoke

A.K. McCarthy

A year to the day after he had burned his house down with his wife inside, Carter stood in the doorway and breathed deeply.

The smell was markedly different. Instead of the gentle welcome of lavender, the scents of piss, shit and mold accosted the nostrils.

The people who now entered the house — junkies, high school kids looking to get high or laid — probably didn't care much about the way this place smelled. This was just a temporary spot where they could engage in their vices.

For Monica, this was her tomb.

She had died on the staircase, the investigators determined, trapped between flames above her and flames below her. All they found were her bones. Fitting for a death that happened on Halloween. The skeletal remains were buried in her family's plot at Evergreen Cemetery, but to Carter this shell of a house was Monica's final resting place.

He had come to pay his respects.

"I'm finally free, you bitch!" he yelled into the darkness.

It didn't echo quite like he'd hoped. That happens when there are gaping holes in all the walls and the wood has been dampened by a year's worth of constant Northwest rain. He took a couple steps into the house and kept talking, in a confident but restrained tone.

"If I could go back and do it again, I would," Carter said. "I'm happier now than I've ever been, and it's because I never have to hear your voice or look at you again."

The house watched and waited, looming over him, its broken boards like crooked teeth. Moss and lichen had overtaken the house. Wispy bits of Spanish moss softly swayed in the October breeze. The fungus swung back and forth, a ticking pendulum telling a time that no longer mattered.

"You know how I did it?" Carter asked, hoping some part of her was still left in this house to listen. "Remember when I carved the sunrise in that jack-o-lantern to symbolize a new start between us? That's not what it was for."

His footsteps fell softly on the layer of moss growing on the floor.

"It was so the candle could fall out of it easier," he said. "It was to fool any fire marshals or whoever. For all they know, a cat or a strong breeze knocked over the pumpkin, and then the candle spilled out and caught the porch on fire."

Carter laughed, the comedy of killing his wife still fresh after all these months.

"I told them I fell asleep on the couch and woke up with the house on fire," he said, looking up where the second story had been. Now a few floorboards still clung to the walls, bending increasingly downward as they got wetter and heavier with moss. The nails were doing their best to keep this house together, but gravity and decay were winning the battle.

Carter walked toward the remains of the staircase. There were still a few boards where the landing had been. That's where she'd died, the investigators said. Eight stairs led up to the landing, with a small window where Monica had put a small cactus. It was the only thing in the house that was pricklier than Monica, Carter always joked.

Eight more steps had led up to the second level, where their bedroom, bathroom and spare bedroom had been. She'd been asleep in their king-sized bed that night, and woke up too late to get out of the house. The fire and the smoke had overcome her on that landing.

Carter spat on the heap of burnt wood where the staircase had been. He wiped a bit of spittle off his smooth chin with the sleeve of his flannel shirt.

"I'm never gonna hear you laugh at me again," he said in a harsh whisper. "And I hope the flames in hell are hotter than these were."

Carter was surprised to feel a chill run through his body. He backed away slowly when he realized part of him was still afraid to speak up to Monica.

He didn't want to turn his back on the staircase quite yet. His black rain boots made squelching sounds on the mossy floor. Bits of dust had descended into his short, dark brown hair, making it looked like he had aged 20 years since coming back into the house. Suddenly, he *felt* as if he had.

His feet still knew the distance from the stairs to the front entrance. Instinctively, he turned around just as he arrived at the door. He exhaled sharply, proud of himself for standing up to her, and reached for the doorknob.

Carter screamed as the knob seared his right hand, a soft hiss signaling the burning of the flesh. He spun away from the door, holding his right wrist with his left hand, looking at his palm.

"Son of a …" he yelled, stopping short when he saw something out of the corner of his eye.

Pale feet, with green-painted toenails, stood a couple yards away from him, the toenails almost matching the hue of the moss covering the floor. The toes curled into the soft moss, like a child does on dewy grass in the summertime.

Carter's eyes worked their way up the body, though his brain immediately knew whose feet those were. A simple, black cotton nightgown hung down below her knees, covering up her thin, but strong, legs.

Her slim figure, kept that way by her fastidious diet and athletic discipline, was mostly obscured as a draft blew through the house and billowed her nightgown. It was as if she were standing in the darkest of storm clouds.

Monica was just as Carter remembered her. Her green eyes blazed from her defined, pale face with a mix of rage and excitement.

Her raven-black hair, like the nightgown, hung straight and simply, reaching her clavicles and swinging with the lazy sway of a porch swing left out in the night.

Worst of all, she wore the same expression she always had when she'd known she had the drop on him. Her grin, one that always reminded Carter of the Grinch, stretched her tight skin to its limit. Her long, straight teeth almost glistened, even in the dim house.

"Son of a what?" Monica asked, her dark, carefully trimmed eyebrows shooting upwards in mock wonder. "A bitch?"

She cackled, and Carter's knees buckled at the sound. His collapsed on the moss with a dull thud, the moisture quickly soaking through his jeans. This only brought more harsh, unnatural laughter.

Carter closed his eyes, his head aching with an agony that made him forget about his hand. *This can't be real,* he thought to himself. *It can't be. It can't.*

"Oh, darling," Monica said in mock sympathy, stepping slowly toward him and bending over. She placed her cold forefinger gently under his chin and lifted his face toward hers. Slowly, Carter opened his eyes.

Her face was still there, and it was just inches from his.

"It's very real," she whispered, before tossing her head violently backward and spewing her laughter toward the ceiling.

"But…but…" Carter stammered. "But y-you're dead."

Monica's laughing stopped abruptly; her face still pointed skyward. She eased it back down to look at him, her face striking a serious figure. Her lips were slightly pursed, in a straight line.

"Yes, I am," she said in a hushed tone. "You made damn sure of that."

She brought her face close to his and narrowed her eyes.

"And you don't seem very sorry," she whispered.

At this, her eyes blazed once again and her mouth shot wide open. Carter only saw the expression for a moment, but he saw that her mouth stretched to an unnatural degree. It seemed to him that she could place his whole head in her mouth, as a lion with its prey.

A cloud of thick, black smoke streamed out of her gaping mouth, like a puffing smokestack. Carter's eyes, ears and mouth instantly filled with it. He spun on his wet knees, gasping for breath and blinking as hard and as fast as he could.

He twisted away from Monica, and was surprised when his face smacked against hard wood instead of soft moss. He continued blinking and coughing until tears were streaming down his face and he was almost retching in an effort to expel the smoke.

Monica closed her mouth and straightened. She was done laughing. It was time to stop messing around and get down to business.

She plunged her long, white fingers into Carter's hair and pulled. He tried to scream, but another retching cough came out instead, as she dragged him across the floor.

She pulled him rapidly away from the front door, his wet boots squeaking and clunking. Carter's eyes refocused, but he couldn't believe what he saw.

The house was reconstructing itself, one piece at a time.

Hardwood boards flew all around him, finding their places alongside one another, as the floors reconfigured. The burnt-out husks of wall quickly re-lined with plaster and drywall. Insanely, Carter thought he caught a glimpse of orange pumpkin figures hanging themselves on the wall.

Monica loved pumpkins. Especially in October.

Carter's ankle screamed in pain and his mouth followed suit. His heels and ankles had struck the staircase, which had also somehow rebuilt itself. His feet danced an offbeat, panicked rhythm as they hit the stairs one at a time on the way up.

In his shock, Carter hadn't even tried to fight back until he was on the stairs. He clawed at Monica's hand and its relentless grip on his hair. He tried to writhe his body from side to side, but neither maneuver fazed her in the least. His eyes locked onto the cactus on the landing and he cried out for her to stop.

She cackled again, sounding even more witch-like than before.

"Stop?!" she screamed. "Stop?!"

They had reached the second level, where she flung him across the hardwood hallway at the top of the stairs. He skidded to a stop just in front of their bedroom door.

Carter had no time to run away. He saw Monica's dark, billowy form silhouetted in the electric lamplight for a moment, then she was on top of him. Face-to-face with him. Her blazing green eyes piercing his wide, pathetic and bloodshot eyes.

"Darling," she said in a coarse whisper. "We haven't even started."

With that, she grabbed his shoulders, lifted him up and tossed him into the bedroom. He screamed as he went airborne and saw that the bedroom had not yet been rebuilt. Hanging in space about 20 feet above the lower level, he saw it was all exactly as it had been on the night he had murdered his wife.

An old horror movie played on the television. A bowl of candy sat untouched by the door. One lamp was lit in the corner and an "autumn hayride" scented candle blazed on the coffee table.

He hung there for what seemed an eternity. As gravity re-exerted its influence, the bedroom quickly reassembled itself. He smacked facedown into the gray covers of their bed.

A moment later, he lifted his head and found that the room was dark. He was relieved that he didn't feel the need to cough anymore. His eyes had stopped watering. And best of all, Monica was gone.

Shadowy nostalgia greeted him as he looked around the room. Everything was as it had been a year earlier. It was like waking up from a dream to find everything was as you had left it. The lamps, the desk, the potted plant in the corner; all of it was familiar.

The dim, flickering light coming from the window was not.

Carter sat up, the bed softly creaking below him. He

peered out the window and immediately felt stupid for not having realized what the flickering was. Small flames were licking at the bottom of the windows. The shingles popped and danced in the heat.

"Shit!" he yelped, bounding from the bed.

He stopped immediately, though. The voice that had cried out wasn't his. It was Monica's.

Carter saw he was wearing a simple, black cotton nightgown. Black hair tumbled into his vision as he looked down. Somehow, he was in *her* body now. His mind reeled, the room spun for a moment. *How is this possible? What is happening? What is this nightmare?*

The cracking of the glass behind him snapped him out of his stupor. He turned to find the flames had quickly risen and were doing more than just flirting with the windows. They were more than halfway up, the beige paint on the jambs peeling in the heat.

Carter turned and ran toward the open bedroom door. He made it to the hallway in three steps and ran toward the stairs. The hallway was well lit, the flames from downstairs illuminating the whole house.

He was nearly to the stairs when he turned back to see if the flames were advancing behind him. He noticed smoke coming from the floorboards, heated from the inferno below. He didn't have much time.

When Carter turned back toward the staircase, it was already too late. He was closer than he thought he was, and missed the first step. His right foot landed sideways on the corner of the second step. He felt a snap in his ankle.

He screamed in agony, again surprised to hear Monica's voice. He hung in the air for a moment as he fell forward, helpless, descending toward the advancing flames.

His neck landed squarely on the sixth step down, and he heard another crack. A shiver went through his body and then he felt nothing. He was limp, tumbling down the final steps and onto the landing.

He fell on his stomach, head facing the flames that were twirling and bending their way across the living room toward the stairs. He felt nothing, and realized the fall had broken his neck. A low, gurgling scream rose out of him, as the realization dawned -- he was going to burn alive in his dead wife's nightgown.

The flames continued their brilliant march across the house, closing in on him. Sweat flowed into his eyes as the blaze approached. Smoke engulfed his face, further obscuring his vision, forcing its way into his throat. He coughed, but the smoke was too thick, too suffocating.

This is how she died, he thought. *She wants me to experience this. She wants her revenge. She wants to kill me in the same way I killed her.*

He would have sobbed if he could have, but he couldn't breathe. He closed his eyes and silently begged for death. His surroundings became unbearably hot. Then he mercifully lost consciousness.

All was dark, but only for a few moments.

Carter's eyes flew open and he saw he was back on the floor of the burnt-out house. He gasped for air, but found himself again wracked with coughs. He writhed on the floor for a moment, but the pain felt good. It was good to be alive. It was good to feel something.

When the coughing fit passed, he looked around. He was alone again. No Monica, no laughter, no flames. He could still smell the smoke, though. Something had happened. This was no dream.

It was like a music box that had just stopped spinning. It was as if the tinny echo of the horrid dance that had just happened still hung in the air.

Carter sat up slowly, relieved to see that he was back in his body. He rested his flannel-sleeved arms on his denim-covered knees, looking around the house again.

He sat there for a few minutes, petrified by the thought that Monica might not be done with him yet.

Hoping the coast was clear, he slowly rose to his feet. The moss squished beneath his boots as he took hesitant steps toward the door. He pulled his sleeve over his hand and reached for the doorknob.

As soon as he felt the knob was cool again, he turned it quickly and flung the door backwards. He took off running, leaping down the steps that led to the porch, gaining speed as he ran down the hill back to his car.

Carter was gasping by the time he got to the street, and found that he still couldn't take a full breath. He collapsed to the asphalt as another barrage of coughs shook through his body. He thought he could taste blood by the final few.

He could certainly taste the smoke.

Slowly, Carter turned his eyes back toward the shell of the house on the hill. Fire and nature had torn it apart, but it still loomed like a gargoyle. It was the guardian of his unforgivable crime.

The front door still hung open, and he thought he could see a black nightgown softly swaying in the breeze amid the darkness beyond the doorframe.

He knew one thing. Monica would always be here. She would always be in that house. But part of her was with him too, he realized. And always would be.

SMS

Alan Beauvais

Kat- Will you there?

Will- ya sup?

Kat- I think someones in my house

Will- are you alone?

Kat- yes

Will- well you should do like all the girls in the scary fliks do and go see who it is

Kat- I seruis

Will- you should learn to spell

Kat- I'm scared Will

Will- get out of the house

Kat- I cant im upstairs

Will-so?

Kat- what if he sees me on the stairs

Will- its prob the cat

Kat- the cats with me

Will- where's your parents?

Kat- went to some meeting prob turned phones off

Kat- uhh I think hes on the stairs now

Will- really?

Kat- they creak

Will- hide

Kat- in the closet?

Will- no, bad idea

Kat- where???

Will- under the bed

Kat- ok

Will- I'm calling 911 now

Kat- he's coming in my room, I see his feet.

Kat- OMG OMG

Will- STOP TEXTING

Kat- Hello William

Will- Kat?

Kat- guess again

Will- who are you?

Kat- a very bad man

Will- what have you done to Kat?

Kat- you don't want to know

Will- you better not hurt her

Kat- it didn't hurt much, and not for very long

Will- you fuker you better not hurt her

Kat- or what William, what you gonna do?

Will- I called 911, they're already on the way. It's too late for you. You're gonna get caught asshole!

Kat- well that's not entirely accurate Will.

Will- what?

Kat- Will, my little dance with Kat ended about an hour ago

Will- that's bs I just talked to her about 10 minutes ago

Kat- Oh William, I so rarely do this but I'm afraid I have a confession to make

Will- what??

Kat- that wasn't Kat you were chatting with

Will- No! I don't believe you asshole!

Kat- Oh it's true pimple puss, I'v been all thru this phone

Kat- seen ALL the stupid selfies, damn, don't you kids do anything else?

Will- why are you doing this?

Kat- even found the sexting pics you sent her. You're quite the little man Will

Will- if I ever find you

Kat- what Will? What you gonna do?

Will- I'll kill you, my dad has a gun I'll kill you

Kat- well you're in luck Will because I'm coming to your house

Will- come on asshole i'll be ready for you

Kat- Oh I don't think you will be

Will- what do you mean?

Kat- turn around.

Junkie

Anthony Crinella

I was born hollow.

Anger, jealousy, sadness, joy—none of these even briefly visited my heart, or soul, or head, or wherever people think their emotions live. These feelings, all feelings, had no relevance for me at all, which made for a pretty easy childhood.

I didn't even realize that I was different until my 6th grade teacher had us write about an event in our lives that had significantly affected us. We were supposed to "capture our emotions," and I couldn't. I had nothing. I got in a little trouble with that teacher for being "defiant," so I decided to just fake it in order to smooth out the situation. I've become very good at being fake. Fake is my real, at least when it comes to feelings.

I did discover the power of emotions during puberty, not by introspectively searching my soul, not by coming to grips with my deepest thoughts and desires, no—I did none of that. Some switch, some scanner, just clicked on inside me.

The day that it happened is still a vibrant memory, now ten years on. One of my classmates, Samantha, was very obviously distraught about something. She came into class, visibly upset, and as soon as she sat down near me, her face buried in her hands, I was flooded with her feelings. They started like a buzz at the top of my spine and slowly crept over my body. I was feeling her anguish, and I loved it. It was enthralling. I felt the heat of her sadness in the front of my brain, and I was lightheaded. She was hating herself. She was blaming herself, she was wishing she was dead. I couldn't read her mind, but I could feel these things. It was euphoric. I had to cover my mouth to suppress a giggle. My whole body was goose-flesh, and I felt like I was floating. As I was drifting on this cloud of warmth, she became overwhelmed and had to rush out of the room, and my emotions quickly faded in her absence, like a haze had drifted in front of the sun.

I became instantly obsessed. I wanted to feel something, any something, so badly that the boundaries between want and need started to blur. I had to feel again—it was all I could think about. That night at home, I shoved people unwittingly into their emotions for the first time. I told my mom that my dad had gone over to the next door neighbor's house the other day, and had stayed over there for over an hour. She hated when my dad talked to the lady nextdoor. She slammed the pan she was washing into the sink, and wheeled around, teeth-clenched, to go confront my dad. Her anger pleasantly warmed my skin, like sitting near the fire, but after she rushed past, the emotions evaporated.

I had to chase them.

Following her, I approached their room from the hallway; with proximity, the feelings regained intensity. My father was embarrassed, guilty, and furious—he stormed out of the room, only to find me leaning against the wall near their door, emotion eavesdropping. This further enraged him, and the feeling was amazing. I swear I was levitating. I know I was smiling. My father grabbed me by the shoulders and slammed me against the wall hard enough to make a couple picture frames fall to the floor. His aggression took the euphoria to another universe! Every synaps in my brain was connected and firing pleasure. I felt no pain, all my senses were numb with ecstasy. I couldn't hear anything he was yelling, and I drifted into intoxicated rapture.

I woke in my bed, feeling empty, desperate to absorb more emotions. I could hear my mother in the next room, crying, and I went to the wall we shared to let some of those feelings in. Standing there, arms outstretched, cheek flat against my bedroom wall, I knew this was now my life's pursuit, but I knew I had to relax. I knew then that this could destroy me, and I almost wanted it to. I knew it would be hard, maybe impossible, to satiate this yearning, and I needed to step back and act in a way that did not alarm those around me. That has been easier said than done over the years, as this addiction is my driving force. I live for the fix, and honestly, I care about nothing else. It has cost me several jobs and many "relationships," none of which I cared about.

It's many times easier to make people sad or angry than it is to make them happy. I have tried both, to the point of exhaustion, and I just don't have the energy to make the people around me happy, but I am obsessively compelled to make them feel.

I can't sleep, I can't think, I can't function without it.

There's a big hit set for tonight, maybe my best and biggest ever. A couple about my age lives in the apartment below me with their young son, and I have been working on the wife, laying it on thick. She's drawn to me, and says she is falling in love with me. I get little daily fixes from these encounters, but I need more. A lot more.

I sent the husband a text a few minutes ago, confessing to what she and I have been up to, and I'm sure he is going to be here soon. The flood of hatred and anger is going to fill my veins… I can almost taste it.

Someone is stomping up the stairs… the first waves of his anger are already warming me. He's trying to kick in my door. I'm feeling weightless ecstasy as it crashes open, splinters flying. My vision is vague and blurred, I'm dizzy with hypnotizing euphoria. He's rushing me; I make out something in his hands, and his fury thrills me.

That You, Coughlan?

Christopher Blinn

1883 – Oklahoma Territory.

"That you, Coughlan?" Father Bud's heart skipped a beat, hearing the voice that came through the shade of his confessional. It couldn't be. "Coughlan?" The priest managed a second time.

"Any sins you'd like to confess Father?

Father Bud swallowed the lump in his throat.

A week ago, he had killed this man.

"That you, Coughlan?" Father Bud unbolted the door.

"Yup," a voice answered, suppressing a burp.

"It ain't even dark yet and you're puke drunk again, aren't ya?"

"Yup."

"Here for the measurements of the deceased?"

"Yup."

"I swear I don't know how you manage, liquored up as you are most times."

"It's a talent, padre. And you shouldn't swear lest you should offend the 'Big Man.'" Coughlan mocked.

Father Bud sighed. He knew the man was a non-believer, his only allegiance being to his furniture business; an enterprise that doubled him as the town's coffin maker. The caskets were the only reason the priest associated with this man he felt to be one of God's lower creatures. Father Bud led Coughlan into the main room of the shamble that served as his church.

"Three more," Coughlan added up the cost and profit of the caskets in his head. Three bucks a body.

"Dumped out front 'bout four this mornin', I think they're from the same gang as last time," the priest pointed out. "They all got that same blue sash on their belts." He blessed himself as he walked past the three dead men. He stopped at the last one, the youngest of the group. "All startin' to look the same to me," he said. "But Lord as my witness, I'd testify that I buried this boy just a few weeks ago."

Coughlan stooped and straightened the legs of the first man to get an accurate measurement.

The priest hovered behind him, scratching notes on a slip of paper.

"Sorry preach," Coughlan slurred. "Can't take no IOU this time."

"It's not an IOU, sir," the priest answered without looking up. "I'm writing a brief description of these boys to put in my paper, hoping some poor mother may identify her child before I lay 'em to rest."

Father Bud was under no obligation, but he felt responsible to provide a decent burial to any unfortunates whose journey west ended in the small town. It was a charity that strained the funds of his already burdened church.

"Don't know why you waste your effort on that paper, Father. Most folks 'round here don't know how to read," Coughlan laughed and stumbled over to the next body. "I read it myself," he said. "Likes to keep up on things, but it's a bit too preachy for me. No offense."

"None taken," Father Bud lied and silently asked for forgiveness. Being around this man made his skin crawl. "Just spreading the Lord's good word."

Often the clergy were the only folks on the frontier with enough education to edit a paper. Utilizing recent advancements in printing, Father Bud produced a sheet that was half news and half sermon.

Coughlan stood and stretched his back. He took the measurements of the last man. "Nine dollars, Father."

Father Bud waited for a 'please' that wasn't coming and pulled back a piece of canvas that hid his desk and single chair. The tarp was all that was left after a fire had destroyed his church, back in the days when it was only a tent. The drunken furniture maker found it in his heart to donate a chair to the luckless priest whom, he in turn, convinced to buy the matching desk. At a generous discount he assured. Father Bud reached into a metal box that contained the sum of the week's collection. He counted out eight dollars and some change. Coughlan waited. He had counted in his head along with the priest.

Father Bud watched the greedy man's eyes shift to the locked drawer of the desk where the priest kept the money he was saving to pay for a respectable altar for his church. The priest opened the secured drawer and removed a small bundle. He untied a knot from a piece of fabric, counted out the difference and handed the money to Coughlan.

Coughlan held the coins in his hand. His eyes counted with the practiced precision of a banker. He flipped one of the coins with his thumb and caught it in his palm. "I'll have the boy you sent to fetch me come back with a wagon and bring the deceased to my place for preparation."

Most folks were embalmed and waked in their own kitchens on the frontier. Coughlan insisted on doing it in the workshop of his furniture store. "You know Father, at this rate I might give up the furniture business altogether. Back East they been specializing in this sort of thing, callin' 'em funeral parlors or some such, plenty 'a business in these parts for that."

"I s'pose," Father Bud said. He heard the jingle of his savings as the ugly man headed out.

Coughlan stopped, turned the flipped coin onto the back of his other hand. "Heads or tails, Father?"

Father Bud tried to keep his hate locked up as deep as he could. This man really challenged him. "Heads," he answered.

Coughlan moved his hand uncovering the coin. "Very good Father, heads it is, means one more drink before I get to work on them boys."

The priest balled his fist.

Father Bud watched the hideous man shuffle off in the direction of the saloon. The boy with the wagon arrived promptly, as promised, and carted away the three dead men. Father Bud had no services scheduled for the next day and planned to take the time away from rehearsing his sermon to pray privately. But he couldn't get the filthy furniture maker out of his head.

"Lord, send your spirit to douse the flames of hatred I feel for that wretched man," he prayed. Father Bud felt the power of the Holy Spirit. He gathered his resolve. His reason for following the settlers out west was to win converts for the Lord, provide comfort to the suffering and counsel to the weak. He decided he would go have a talk with Coughlan, convince him his drinking ways and greedy habits were the work of the serpent. The farther away the lost sheep, the greater the reward for bringing it back. Father Bud fired up a lantern, it was full dark but he had the Lord's work to do.

"That you, Coughlan?"

The voice pierced Coughlan's ear as sure as he'd been stung by a wasp. He saw the speaker's face in the glow of a struck match as the owner held it to his cigar. Mayor Poch.

"What're you doing here?" Coughlan scoffed.

"You know damn well what I'm doing here." He puffed and checked the glowing tip.

"S'pose I do," Coughlan managed with his whiskey crippled tongue. "Looks like that genius boy of yours went and got hisself shot again."

The mayor let the remark slide.

"Can you do it again?"

"Do what again, sir?"

"Don't play with me Coughlan," the mayor said.

"Don't know. Ain't never tried it on same person twice." Coughlan found a hidden flask and took a hit. He pulled the flask away and blew out an exaggerated breath. The booze was talking. "Never met nobody so shit all stupid as to get themselves kilt twice."

The mayor had Coughlan by the throat and pinned to the wall before he had even seen him move. "Can you help me Coughlan?"

Coughlan knew a 'no' meant his own end. His skill was the only bargaining chip he had. "Yes, yes...I can try." The mayor loosened his grip. "Gonna cost you double though."

The mayor crushed Coughlan against the wall. "You're a thieven' sonuva bitch."

He released the swindler.

Coughlan made a useless effort to straighten his vest and save his dignity. "Same as last time your Honor, seventy-two hours. Look for the cross with the star carved on it...that'll be your boy."

The mayor nodded, put on his hat and dropped a fistful of paper money on the table. His face soured. "I'd just as soon kill you myself and let that lunkhead boy rot," he said. "But it would break his mother's heart."

"Yes, a lovely woman, your wife is, sir." Coughlan said. "One other thing your Honor, I believe our Father Bud is becoming a little suspicious."

"How do ya mean?"

"Well he mentioned he recognized your boy from the last time he..." Coughlan caught himself. "From his last accident."

"And."

"Well, this business has put a few dollars in your pocket as well as mine Mayor, with all the tragic loss of life that takes place 'round here," Coughlan paused. "It just wouldn't do to have some snooping priest muss that up."

The mayor stopped when he reached the door. He turned and faced Coughlan. Pulling back his lapel, he revealed a silver star. "You forget how much influence I have 'round here, Coughlan," he said. "We won't have a problem with the priest."

Father Bud saw the mayor readying to leave. He flattened himself against building. Unsure of what he'd just heard.

"Is there something else, Mayor?" Coughlan asked, when heard his door open and close. He hadn't bothered to lock up before starting his work. "Mayor?"

He looked up.

"Oh...Father Bud, what a treat, whatever it is make it quick. I am busy as you know."

"Looks like you already got those boys' coffins

finished." Father Bud said, still weighing the contents of the conversation he'd overheard.

"Those are pretty much standard. Always keep a few on hand, 'specially 'round here you understand." The blood finished draining from the first corpse. Arsenic would replace it. "But that ain't why you're here Father, is it?"

"No, it's not, sir. I came to help you find salvation, to pray for you to change your ways and become a servant of the shepherd."

"Oh, thank you Father..." Coughlan feigned dropping to a knee and came up laughing. He was expecting the priest to question him about his suspicions. "The only shepherd I plan on serving is Mr. O'Toole on the outskirts, his dear old mom is almost eighty, won't be around much longer." Coughlan removed the pump that had drained the blood from the mayor's son. A tube ran from the pump to a brass device with two spinning wheels and twice as many jars. Coughlan switched the hose to a different jar and reinserted the pump into the corpse. The wheels reversed direction, syphoning fluid from one of the jars, refilling the dead man's body.

Father Bud held onto his rage. The man in front of him may have been Satan himself. He held his hands palms upright and began praying. "Dearest Father..."

"Now don't go wastin' your prayers on me, padre," Coughlan said. "Save 'em for someone who's gonna 'preciate 'em."

Father Bud continued to pray. He wasn't praying for Coughlan any longer, but for himself. Praying the Lord would forgive him for the anger and hatred that filled him. The target of his hate stood in front of him. Recollections of the man's greed returned to him and fueled his outrage.

You want a casket for your loved one. I want three

dollars.

Had to sell your last chicken? Too bad.

Need to reshoe your horse. Not my problem.

"Father really...I'm busy." Coughlan broke the priest's thoughts.

Father Bud's fury was pushing through. He stopped praying and looked up. A thin silver chain with a locket hung from a nail behind Coughlan. He recognized it from the services he'd held for little Molly Duncan, who died of fever the past winter. Molly's mother wore the locket at the burial.

Coughlan followed Father Bud's stare. He turned and grabbed the chain and locket. He sensed the priest's disapproval. "Man's gotta make a livin', Father."

The priest could stand no more. His face flushed red; his pulse showed at his temples. He exhaled between clenched teeth. Spittle flew.

"Now take it easy, Father," Coughlan said and popped open the locket. "I let her keep the pictures."

In one motion Father Bud scooped the embalming pump from the corpse's belly and ran it through Coughlan.

Coughlan clawed at his chest.

The pump jammed just below his shoulder.

Father Bud buried it further.

Coughlan fell.

Father Bud pulled Coughlan's pistol from his belt and fired one shot into the drunk's stomach.

Father Bud watched the blood pour between Coughlan's fingers as the wounded man tried vainly to staunch the flow. Gunshots to the belly were amongst the most painful and slow killing. A fatal wound. The pump protruding from his shoulder became an afterthought. Coughlan looked up. The priest's eyes were glazed over, no recognition or reason behind them.

Just hate.

Four coffins leaned against one another in the corner of the room. Father Bud stood in front of them. Two were of crisp pine, one lighter colored, the fourth darker and aged. He pulled the darker one from the wall and laid it on the floor.

"What're ya doin'?" Coughlan struggled. "For God's sake Father go fetch the doctor."

The priest didn't respond. He positioned the coffin next to Coughlan, his movements deliberate. He found the lid. Some nails. A hammer.

"Be reasonable, father," Coughlan begged.

Father Bud sat, counted the money that still laid on the table and waited for Coughlan to die.

The priest was no stranger to death. he had been a chaplain in the Union Army during the War of Northern aggression. He administered last rites to more soldiers than he could count. He did the same for Coughlan now.

Unable to speak and barely conscious, Coughlan's eyes flicked in disbelief from the priest's lips to collar to the beads in his folded hands and back. He whimpered.

Father Bud felt the coolness of the dying man's hand as he held it and muttered a last prayer.

Coughlan finally passed.

The priest removed a cross someone had already made as a grave marker from the casket. He rolled, pulled, lifted and pushed. With some effort he had Coughlan inside. He did the same for the three outlaws forgoing the embalming process for two and considering the half job Coughlan had done on the other sufficient.

The small but growing cemetery lay in a field just beyond his church. There was no way he would be able to move the caskets on his own. He would have to summon the boy with the wagon again. He doubted the boy would question the presence of the fourth casket with all the killing that went on in the region, but if he did, Father Bud would feed him a story along with a generous tip from Coughlan's stash that would make the boy forget whether he'd moved four bodies or forty.

Father Bud stepped back, his work completed.

Recognition showed in his eyes. His reason had returned from wherever it had fled.

He held out his hands as if to start praying again.

"What have I done?"

"Well, Father... would you like to make a confession?"

The voice brought the priest back to the present.

This had to be a sick joke. He had spent the last week praying. Panicking. Anxiety stricken. He hadn't held a service in a week. He feigned illness to his parishioners. The only person he had spoken to was the mayor, who had come by to ask if he had seen Mr. Coughlan. Father Bud was sure his performance with the mayor, acting in his dual role as sheriff, was less than convincing. But the mayor wouldn't suspect a man of the cloth. Would he? The priest had even considered using the money he had pocketed to run. Take off west and get lost in the migrating masses before someone uncovered his crime.

For the last two hours he'd sat in his confessional; nothing more than a couple of ruined chairs, separated by a shade for anonymity, listening to the devoted recite sins he now found ridiculous. He prescribed 'Lord's prayers' & 'Hail Marys' as penance. The irony did not escape him. No number of prayers or hours of devotion could save his soul.

"Father?..."

The priest whipped past the shade and stood in front of the confessional. He wanted to know who was responsible for this perverted joke. He would confront the prankster, find out what they knew and buy their silence with the stolen money if need be.

Father Bud almost fainted when he saw the man in front of him.

"Is that you Coughlan? I mean … really you?"

"In the flesh, padre."

"But how? I mean, I saw you ... buried you myself..." Father Bud took a step back from the man. Even if the gunshot hadn't killed him, surely, he would have suffocated in the grave. Failing that, how would he have freed himself from the soil and coffin? Although not impossible, none of those scenarios was likely, Father Bud reasoned. The man would have died from his wounds or infection even if he had received immediate medical attention. And surviving that, he would be months recuperating. Yet the man standing in front of him was Coughlan. Uninjured.

"That was a terrible thing you did, father," Coughlan said. "You got some temper."

"It can't be you."

"You are like the 'doubting' Thomas of your Bible, huh, Father?" Coughlan said and unbuttoned his shirt. "Would you like to put your fingers in my wounds? Well, what's left of them?"

Purple splotches like dark bruises spread from Coughlan's stomach fading to the pink of a newborn's skin. A similar mark showed by his shoulder where the embalming pump had pierced him.

Father Bud reached out like the biblical Thomas, then withdrew his hand. He turned to run. Only to see an outlaw, thin and pale, holding him at gunpoint.

"Let's go for a walk, Father," Coughlan said.

The trio walked outside. A bright day with few clouds. Father Bud recognized the pale ghoul holding him at gunpoint.

"The mayor's son," Coughlan said. "He's looked better."

"But, how...?" Father Bud started.

"Well, Father it's no miracle, not like Lazarus or anything, but I have to say it was quite lucky for me you did whatcha did."

Father Bud could see, in the sunlight,t Coughlan didn't look as good as he had in the church. The skin around his neck was almost translucent. Purple blue veins weaved underneath.

"Used to be a preacher myself, father," Coughlan began. "But as you know, I'm a greedy man and greed is a terrible sin. One day I absconded with all the money from my church's collections, including all we had been saving for the poor, and bolted west, seeking my fortune. I was after gold, like everybody else, but I found an easier way to get it." Coughlan stopped to see if the mayor's son had been able to keep up. "They tend to be a little slow the first few days out of the ground," he said. "This is his second time around, seems to be taking a bit longer, or he just may be stupid."

Father Bud looked to see the ghostly boy still had his pistol trained on him.

"I moved onto the next town, set up another small church. not unlike yours, and when I felt I had bilked the devoted out of enough of their money. I took it and ran off again." Coughlan rolled and lit a cigarette. "People are gullible, father. Tell 'em what they want to hear, promise them eternal life or hell, if they don't follow God's law, and they just dump money at your feet."

Father Bud listened.

The group arrived at Coughlan's store front. A man on a ladder was retouching the paint on the store's sign.

"Pulled that act a few more times, until I reached our little town here. I saw this store front for sale and figured, with some work, it would make a nice little church to run another swindle out of." Coughlan crushed his cigarette out.

Father Bud noticed the mayor was crossing the street to join the party.

"While I was renovating the place," Coughlan continued. "I found an old book, some instructions, a peculiar casket and that embalming pump ... you know, the one you ran me through with." Coughlan eyed the priest. "Didn't believe it myself at first, but one day, when I was preparing one of the many outlaws that find themselves in my workshop, I figured 'what the heck, ain't nobody gonna miss the fool anyway'. I followed the steps laid out in the book. I dug him up three days later according to the directions and lo and behold. Life!"

"You blaspheme," Father Bud said.

"Blaspheme?" Coughlan laughed. He took a minute to recover. "And you, sir, are a murderer, not to mention a thief."

The mayor reached the group, one eye on Coughlan and the priest, the other on his corpse-like son.

"Afternoon, Mayor," Coughlan said. He noticed the man assessing his son's condition. "He should improve in the next few days, your honor," Coughlan cleared his throat. "... I think." He wanted to add 'or maybe not' but thought better of it. Coughlan shrugged and switched his attention back to Father Bud.

Father Bud nodded to the mayor, but the man didn't acknowledge him.

"As I was saying, father, It was quite a stroke of luck for me that you chose that particular casket to bury me in, not to mention sticking me with the pump, which is also part of the process. The mayor here came looking for his son's grave. He knew it would be marked with the cross you used. Imagine his surprise when he found me."

"You're drunk again, Coughlan," Father Bud said, although he detected no liquor on the man's breath.

"The proof is all around you, father," Coughlan said, and placed his hand on his chest. He gestured to the mayor's son and pointed to a little girl across the street with his chin.

The girl's face was hidden by a large bonne; a blond pigtail hung from the back. But she was the right age. The right size. The priest still didn't believe. "Molly Duncan had dark hair."

"C'mon now, father. Ain't much trouble for people to be changing their hair color. Mrs. Duncan introduces her 'round town as her niece, hence the family resemblance." Coughlan stepped back from the group to critique the painter's work.

"I don't believe a word of it," Father Bud said.

Coughlan ignored him. "The only difference between me and you Father, is you promise people eternal life. I deliver it. You sell empty hope. I give them the real thing. Mrs. Duncan has her daughter, the mayor his son and numerous others have had their loved ones given back to them through the work of my hands." Coughlan sighed. "For the right price of course."

"I am nothing like you..." Father Bud protested.

Coughlan cut him off. "Ain't no vows you can take makes you any better than the next man, Father. I had doubts myself when I first left the faith, but I couldn't change what I felt. You came to save my soul, but your actions only reassured my beliefs. We all got it in us, good and evil, I mean. That collar don't change a thing."

Father Bud had no response.

The mayor pulled open his coat, revealing his revolver and badge, changing roles from politician to lawman. "Can't really arrest you for murder Father, since we ain't got no corpses, but I have another idea."

"You're all insane," Father Bud said. "None of this is possible."

"Guess you gonna need some more convincin'." The

mayor said and drew his weapon.

"See ya in a few days, Father," Coughlan winked. "Maybe."

Father Bud's body shuddered. His jaw quivered. He stuttered a 'please' that nobody heard.

The sound of the mayor's son cocking his pistol reached Father Bud's ears. This is it, the priest thought. He looked toward the sky for a miracle but saw only Coughlan's new sign. He heard the retort of the pistols as his eyes scanned the freshly painted words.

'Coughlan's Furniture', it read, *'Specializing in Restorations.'*

Wires (Supplemental Humanity)

Anthony Crinella

She is the one who changed, not me—and I know what's going on.

Karen. Sigh. She used to love me. She was a safe place where I could just be me. Now, nothing I do or say is good enough, and I only get the sharp, spiky side of her personality, which although admittedly intriguing, is exhausting.

I like to talk things out, she likes to shake her head in disgust and walk away. When has that ever solved anything? It has been getting me down, way, way down, but now I have a plan.

This sounds ridiculous, even to me, but I've been reading some old blogs from India about artificial intelligence having progressed to the point where advanced cyborgs are replacing people. The government isn't going to stop it, because the government is doing it! We can't trust any of the authorities at all, and for all we know, the police force and military are, at present, robots! The government wants a populace that does what it's told and doesn't push back. I'm about to blow the lid off this, and then people will have no choice but to listen and believe.

I can boil all of my problems with Karen down to one fact—she's one of them! She takes showers now, where she used to take baths (protecting her circuitry), and she stays up late at night with her computer, probably adjusting her programming or talking to her coder, or recharging batteries, I don't know, but she acts very secretively when I approach her, and she's quite cold and detached lately.

She will be coming home shortly, and I'm going to prove it. I've got a taser, and I'm going to zap her out, take that wig off her Central Processing Dome, and I'm going to find her inner-cheek interface, or tonsil tech-charger, or eardrum data drive, or whatever. I saw her eyes in the sun the other day, and I swear I saw power crystals! Under that soft biosynthetic skin will be micro-fiber cables, and wires, I know it.

That's her pulling up now. I'm getting in position behind the door, and soon as she walks in—zappo!

She's knocking? That's not in the plan. She calls out to me from the other side, "Javier, my hands are full, can you please get the door for me? I need some help." I decide to postpone my assault until later. I have no idea how strong she is, or what kind of inhuman violence she's capable of. I need the element of surprise.

"I got you, honey," I say with faux cheer. I shove the taser in my pocket and open the door wide. She's not alone—some man…

I'm in a body bag? A suitcase? I can't see a thing. It unzips—light hits my eyes like needles, and before I can see what's happening, the man my wife was with reaches down and pulls me out by the sides of my head.

No… he pulls out just my head. I can't look around very well, but am I now a detached head? The scream ordered by my brain doesn't charge up in my lungs. No torso, so no lungs. The guy is taking more stuff out of the bag. I recognize those sneakers; that's my leg! He clumsily puts it down next to me, and he knocks my head over! I roll sideways, over my ear, and come to rest with my nose smooshed on the table. I can't yell for help. It's my wife who rolls me right-side-up. She leans over to talk to me.

"I've got good news and bad news for you, Javy," her voice calm and matter-of-fact. "The good news is, I am an android, so you had that part right." fake smile, condescending nod, pats on the head. "Yup. You were right." Pat, pat, pat.

"I knew it!" I'm not actually talking, because I'm just a head. "Wait, how do you know what I've been thinking?" Again, not actually talking.

"Here's the bad news, though, Javy. You are a robot too." She grabs my detached leg and slowly shakes it upside-down in front of me, like trying to be dramatic. Tiny red and yellow wires dance out of my thigh-hole. I can't say I appreciate the mocking smirk on her face. I definitely don't appreciate how she chucks my leg over her shoulder! Is that a trashcan? She leans in, about an inch from my nose, and says in a mocking-my-accent voice that I also don't appreciate, "we're all robots, Javy." Then, sounding bored, "There aren't any people left. There haven't been - for hundreds of years."

"You know," she says, pointing her finger like a dissatisfied customer, "I paid extra for your emotional enhancements."

Oh. *She is a dissatisfied customer.*

"Five levels of supplemental humanity." She's frowning, staring at me, contempt coiled in her eyes. She ticks these off on her fingers: "I wanted someone curious, empathetic, Latin-romantic, brave, and passionate—not needy, paranoid, morose, weepy," now she's pretty much yelling, "and so dismally..." she's waving her hands around, "drearily…" she's pretending to strangle me from three feet away, "despondent!." Wow, all that for "despondent."

This is all making me very depressed.

"All right, Mrs. Maldonado," says the guy, turning around, holding a bunch of computer readouts. "After looking through these transcripts, I think we can approve your insurance claim. We will replace the unit for you, and you are authorized to extinguish the entity."

"Wait..."

Detriment

Joe Moses Leggett

Okay, so you know the classic set-up where there's an old abandoned house at the edge of town? It's derelict and creepy looking and kids in the town tell ghost stories about it, so basically everyone stays away from it? And you know how there's always at least one cocky bastard who can't resist taking a look-see inside? Well in this story that's me. My name is Baz Walding.

But it wasn't *just* me. I was accompanied by Flick, my *"Associate in Financial Activities."* A well alright fella I had come to know thanks to a mutual acquaintance of ours who owned the place we rented, a small property in a run-down area we'd been occupying for a little over a year. Petty theft and the odd, carefully timed burglary paid the bills.

Said break-ins were all under my direction. I'd sit out and watch my marked houses for hours on end, sometimes several days in a row, hoping to spot regular vacancies. I'm a bit of a cunt like that. Have been for a while. I was fourteen when I left home with the majority of my family's hidden stashes of money and smallest, most expensive possessions. It was impulse more than anything and I kept rolling with it from that moment on. For almost ten years I was (just about) sharp enough to make it work. Then I thought it a bright idea to enter the Spooky-Death-House at the edge of town...

Flick and I should never have gone into that fucked up place, but we hadn't looted anywhere for a few months and our street work was getting the better of us. It was the onset of winter, a season neither of us liked, and our mojo seemed to be dwindling with the approach of cold weather.

We'd both heard multiple stories, as had everyone, about the various residents that used to occupy that house; the jewelry and treasures left behind, the spiteful spirits that lay waiting, intent on claiming the lives of anyone who came hunting. And the few missing or dead people from town who apparently *had* gone hunting.

Bored and hungry, we decided it was worth checking out. We weren't superstitious, but we knew most of the locals were, so we'd be left alone to do as we pleased. We knew it was unlikely there would be much of value, if anything, in there, but it would kill some time and maybe provide a few kicks.

Stupid. We had no idea...

It was dusk when we approached the house, at the edge of town, away from anywhere particularly important or heavily populated. A fully detached, two-story wreck surrounded by a tight ring of bare, twisting trees. The bark of the trees looked like charcoal. A tall, rusted gate stood chained shut between two trunks. Each of us, twenty-something and skinny, scaled it without much trouble.

The house was crooked and grey, it's wooden

exterior rotten and falling apart. Every window was broken and boarded up from the inside. The roof had maybe half its tiles left.

"Look at the state of it." Flick had smirked before running and kicking the front door. That was all the encouragement it needed. It landed with a dust-raising wallop. Flick gestured for me to go in first. "Your idea to do this," he reminded me.

Man… the inside was even worse than the outside. By the lights of our phones we could see the floor and ceiling were cracked, with patches of mold dotted about the place. The air was predictably musty. There was a door to our left split in half down the middle and one a few meters in front of us was sewn shut by an invasive growth of ivy. What surprised us about the place though, was that every inch of every surface we could see was covered in carvings.

Words.

Various barely coherent ramblings about death, suffering, curses and so on. No passage looked like it was repeated, and each was in a different handwriting and size, some scratched lightly, others etched deeply. There was one thing they all had in common, though. One word that popped up in every contribution. In all capitals every time: DETRIMENT.

There was a staircase to our right that was knackered but usable. I gestured for Flick to lead the way. "Your turn."

He glanced at me, unamused and visibly unnerved, then muttered, "Thorn in my arse," before heading up.

The decor upstairs was no more welcoming. Untidy lines of carvings were still visible everywhere we looked. There was a closed door near the top of the stairs, fully intact, and two more down the end of a hallway. One was to the right, laced up in the wall by ivy, like the one downstairs; the other was to the left, almost nonexistent from rot. The latter looked like it would be easy enough to negotiate.

"How about you look in this one and I go down there?" I suggested.

"Fine," replied Flick. "But I'm feeling sketchy. I might leave without you." He didn't seem to be joking. He was rubbing his stubble anxiously as his eyes jittered about the place. "I feel *wrong* here."

"Whatever man," I responded dismissively. "Just have a good rummage around before you go."

I treaded carefully on the aged floorboards as I headed to my chosen room. I shone my light through the massive hole in the middle of the door. I couldn't see a lot inside other than shadows and vines, so I climbed in.

The room was a dud. It mostly contained plant life that had crept in from the outside. It looked like there used to be a bed and a wardrobe present, but now they were in pieces, consumed by ivy and cobwebs. As with the rest of what we'd seen, there were carvings on every visible surface. I'd just noticed that these particular writings contained grotesque pictures when the screaming began.

Shrill. Terrified. Agonized howls.

It was Flick.

My heart nearly stopped. My skin turned to ice. I hesitated to move, my mind suddenly racing. Was he messing about? But after a few more of Flick's deathly shrieks I damn near obliterated the remains of my door bolting towards his. Halfway down the hallway the screaming abruptly ended. Whatever had happened, I knew it must've been severe. I wasn't wrong.

By the time I hit the already ajar door, I'd gained some momentum. It swung open with a loud clap. Flick's phone was on the floor in the middle of the room, it's light glowing upwards. Combined with the light of my own I could see clearly enough what had happened.

It was at this point I understood how poor our decision-making had been that day. It was at this point I saw *her*. In all her glory. A hideous fury. An abomination of hate.

DETRIMENT.

She hung from the center of the ceiling, lowered by four spindly legs that stretched upward past her back. Her torso was no larger than that of a heavy-set person but her abdomen was huge; from it dangled a thin tail, like that of a rat. Her arms were taut and muscular. Each of her hands had two long, sharp fingers and two similar thumbs grasping a visceral mess. A mess from which hung Flick's arms and legs, streaming with blood. It had only been a matter of seconds before I got there but already his chest was open and his face completely gone. *Her* face, however, I could see quite clearly. Thin greasy hair hung down either side of it. The sharp upper row of teeth glistened crimson. Three tongue-like appendages that existed instead of a bottom jaw, trickled and a pair of bent, pointed mandibles twitched and shuddered. From deep within the black cavities at either side of her head, two red, vertical slits glared at me intently.

I stood in awe. Was this real? She dropped Flick. My very essence began to feel violated. I could sense thoughts that weren't mine trying to penetrate my mind. She leered towards me.

I made a decision and lunged forward, grabbing the door by its handle and heaving it shut. I felt the shudder as she slammed against the other side. Wasting no time, I turned and bolted down the staircase, three steps at a time. One near the bottom gave way beneath me and I took a tumble, but as I hit the floor, I was able to roll forward and spring back up, stumbling slightly. A crashing noise behind me suggested the monster was out of her room. I leapt over the now permanently open front door and sprinted to the trees in four large bounds. I could hear her voice as I climbed the gate, filling my ears with whispers, reminding me of her name. I didn't look back to see how close she was, I just jumped and ran.

I kept running all the way home, over three miles away. I could feel her presence in the back of my skull for the entire journey. We'd seen into one another's eyes and now we knew each other...

I am marked.

Whatever history is contained in that house, it's beyond my comprehension. Something wholly otherworldly has taken hold of it and I have no intention of falling victim in the way Flick did.

I imagine it now. How he must have looked up just in time to see... It makes me shudder.

I've written all this as something vaguely decent to do with my last night. Consider this a posthumous warning to all. Also, a brief confession of my shitty existence, for which I do not apologize. To anyone.

I had the urge to carve my story into the walls, but I'm glad I typed it instead. It was mid-evening when I got home; It's now about an hour before dawn. I had a feeling she'd be here sooner or later. I was beginning to worry she'd find a way in before I had the chance to finish this off and make my escape. It would've really sucked to die the way Flick did, instead of on my own terms. I've just finished consuming the contents of our fondly labeled *"Medicine Box."*

I can't really get my head around how any of this came to be, but here we are. That's what happened to Flick and that's why I'm dead (hopefully, just from a simple overdose.) My story is pretty far out, I know.

Still, I hope it stirs up enough of the heebs and jeebs to keep people well away from that Spooky-Death-House at the edge of town. If not … well, you can't say I didn't try to warn you.

A Nice Vacation

J.N. Cameron

Things were rough after the miscarriage. There was the night I called Jules a *fat-ass*. She threw an eggroll at my head. I dodged, even though I should have taken the hit. As a result, I slept on the futon for two weeks.

There were other incidents, aggression from both sides. But things smoothed out after a few months. We decided a little getaway from our daily routines would do good. Jules had stress ulcers from long hours at the school, and I was about to jump from the top floor of the Credit One building.

I was thinking Vegas or Palm Springs. But Jules was all about camping, and she'd brought it up for years. So, camping it was.

First, we found a destination. Surfing the web, Jules discovered an obscure place north of the Sequoia National Park. Miq-Hua camping was only five hours from L.A. It had a single five-star review on Yelp: *No bears or wildcats! It's a peaceful getaway in the heart of nature. – A. Wilmarth.*

Next, we shopped for gear. We found a spacious rainproof tent at the Army-Navy Surplus. We bought foam mats and waterproof sleeping bags, camping chairs and camping coolers. I wanted to bring a box of military MREs, but Jules insisted on cooking. She bought a small grill, cooking utensils, plastic ware, and a set of cooking spices for the field.

We bought camping clothes, blankets and pillows, toiletries, all manner of camping tools, and even camping games and reading. We stopped at B&N, and Jules found the new autobiographical novel by that Wilson guy. I bought the newest issue of Heavy Metal Magazine.

And here we are. Loaded in the CRV and cruising up Golden State Highway. The weight of adult responsibility melts away as L.A. disappears. We pass the verdant farmlands speckled with hunched laborers wearing wide straw hats. We pass the paper-torn ridgelines of the southern coast ranges that extend into Los Padres and then back down into the lowlands.

"We should invest in some edibles," I suggest as we near Bakersfield.

Jules gives me a curious look from the passenger's seat. I recognize that face. Her green eyes are downcast, and she's biting her lower lip. She's hiding something.

"Carlos, we have to talk." Now her lips are quivering. The waterworks are about to start.

I pull the car over into a rest stop. She doesn't say anything.

"It's okay, *bebé*, whatever it is." I reach over and brush a strand of her long, strawberry bangs from her face.

"I wanted to wait and tell you when we got there." She sniffs. A few blinks of her curled eyelashes and rivulets pour forth. I'm patient. I wait for a few minutes. She sniffles some more and wipes away the tears.

"Don't get upset," she says. Now I'm nervous. A bass drum thumps in my chest. She takes my hand.

Here it comes.

"I'm pregnant again, Carlos."

The campground is nestled at the end of a 30-minute winding drive up Blue Deer Mountain. The Ponderosa pines and sequoias lining the dirt road stand straight and solemn, ancient beings that blot out the sun with their thick crowns. Shadows blanket the floor below, but there is life. I catch the occasional darting fluffy tail of a marmot or the speckled flapping of California quail.

We are the only apparent customers of the Miq-Hua campgrounds. The road ends in an empty dirt lot and a small cabin with a blinking neon sign.

"What is that?" Jules asks. She points to a wood post off the path leading to the cabin door. It looks to be five-feet tall, and at the top has a glyph carved on both sides. She walks to it and traces her index finger over the symbol. It's a downward pointing triangle within an upward pointing triangle. Lines ending in half-moons extend from the outer points.

"It doesn't seem Native American," I observe.

"I agree," she replies. "It looks runic."

"They are called *pollr*. They are ancient things," a thin, falsetto voice interrupts. "The government won't let us do anything to them."

He's only four feet tall with a large, oblong head and short, bowed legs. His red beard is braided into forks, and he has an awkward stance in boots that seem too large. He holds the door to the cabin open and motions for us to enter.

"I'm Benkt," he offers a fat ruddy hand, and I shake it. I try not to stare, but his fingertips are deformed. They end in hard, pointed nubs of flesh instead of fingernails, and the backside of his hand is covered in thick, red hair.

Animal heads are mounted on the office walls. The jaundiced eyes of a boar watch us. A massive moose gazes with indifference. All furniture is raw, unvarnished wood. The bookshelves, table and chairs still have mossy strands of bark on the outer surfaces, as do the window panes.

The little man has difficulty walking and places each step gingerly in front of the other as if testing the floor. He grabs the desk for support and steps up on a platform behind it.

"The camping is further up the mountain. You'll have to park here and hike." He tosses a few paper plates with unfinished BBQ into a bin. His stubby fingers shuffle through a disorganized mess of papers and forms.

Jules doesn't say a word, which is odd enough for her. She crosses her arms and looks away. Her lips purse, which means she's trying not to laugh.

Benkt finds a pink form and points to where I sign. I fight not to ogle that weird, thick digitus secundus.

"Here's the map," he holds it up to me. "Just follow the trail to the north. It is lined with *pollr* the entire way. That's it."

We leave as quickly as possible. Jules helps me with my pack, and then I help her with hers. She insists on a brief photo session, and we start up the path.

"They are called *pollr*!" Jules mimics the dwarf's shrill voice and then doubles over in laughter on my chest. I put down my magazine and hug her tight. She squeezes my crotch and gives me a quick, mischievous kiss.

"Are you going to take advantage of my condition?"

She grins and nibbles at my bottom lip.

"You know it," I twist and turn her over. Now I'm on top. "But later. We should wait until tonight. It'll give us something to do in the dark."

"Give us something to do in the dark? Seriously?" Her jovial demeanor takes a dive into anger. That's Jules. Grinning one minute and scowling the next. She pushes me away, so I sit up.

Dead silence. I can feel her eyes drilling into me, so I grab my book and leave the tent. I zip it shut behind. Hopefully, she won't follow.

The camping chair is comfortable enough. I kick my feet out and lean back. The redwoods tower above, their longest branches intertwining like titans at scrimmage. A gray warbler whistles in staccato, ascending notes. A pygmy owl toot-toots from its high, hidden perch.

The forest smells old, like ages of growth, death, and decay, but it's sweetened with the aroma of a dusty, piney incense. A nippy breeze rustles through the boles and scattered brush. I pull my scarf tight around my neck.

The *pollr* led us here, to the brick campfire pit. One is right next to me, feet from the tent. Others mark a path west, down toward the valley, and others lead further north to the summit. I'd like to get away from Jules for a few hours and follow the trail north. Maybe a nice walk would give me some fresh perspective on the big news.

I peek into the tent. She's asleep. Damn…I can't leave now. She would freak if she woke and I was gone.

Time for plan B.

I'll get baked.

I spark one up and suck it down with gusto. The warm, slow waves of a good sativa roll forth. Shadows turn red. The world brightens into a neon crispness.

The leaves crunch from somewhere behind me, and I

jump up. I squint against the vibrant hues of green, but I see no one.

Did something move? Nothing is there, only hundreds of trees, like soldiers in a dense formation.

An unsettling suspicion blossoms in the back of my mind. I try not to think of the dwarf and his odd fingers. And the matted, fur-like hair on his hands. Could he be watching us?

I'm ashamed at the thought. The poor handicapped fellow. I'm a rotten bigot for making such mental accusations.

I slouch back into the chair and pick up my book.

I still feel like I'm being watched, but I'm sure it's the weed. Paranoia has arrived. I can't read, so I crawl back into the tent. I slip under the blanket and snuggle up to Jules from behind.

She groans and pushes back against me. She's no longer angry, so I grind back.

We claw and kick each other's clothes off. Like a good husband, I take full advantage of her condition.

I sit up. It's dark. I look at my phone. 11:45 p.m.

I'm naked and covered in beads of sweat. The tent smells like sex, and the blanket is folded over on Jules. I have to pee, so I feel around for my pants, sweatshirt, and sneakers.

Outside is cold and black. We never made a fire. Several thin strands of moonlight reveal a soupy, waist-high fog. I forgot my flashlight inside the tent, so I use the light on my phone. I won't stray far.

I stumble away, looking for a place to piss.

The weak, blue light of my phone can't penetrate the murk, but the *pollr* rise above the billowing surface and show the way. I proceed with slow caution, in a shuffle that feels for rocks, roots, or other impediments. The ancient trunks rise tall and straight on all sides, like frozen giants.

After five minutes, I realize that I've walked much farther than I intended. I've passed at least fifteen of the *pollr*. I step up to the closest redwood, unzip, and let loose in a steaming arc.

I empty my bladder and zip back up. Before I turn back, a light thumping of drums begins to echo from somewhere in the distance…a pitter-patter sound akin to bongos or Indian *tablas*. I turn to the source and notice a light.

Even through the fog I can tell it's a campfire, but it's father to the north. I estimate seventy or eighty yards.

I move from tree to tree toward the drumming and light instead of using the *pollr* for guidance. From my thighs down, all is drenched from the condensation. Who else could be out here? I peek around each bole before I dart to the next.

I squint and think I see jumping silhouettes. Against a backlight of flickering gold-orange, they appear as shadow-puppets through the fog. They dance in circles around a small fire. What are they?

They seem too small to be adults … could they be children?

A queasy knot forms in my gut. Something about this isn't right. *Go back to your tent.* I don't obey. Instead, I dart to a closer tree.

Now I am only forty yards away. The forms leap and gyrate and twist to the beat. As I thought, they are too small to be adults, and their shadows reveal that they wear costumes. Some wear deer horns on their heads. They wear the masks of dogs and rabbits and foxes, and some have beaks. Some have short, flapping wings for arms, and some have tails.

Where did they come from?

I shift my weight to pull out my phone, but I step backward onto a branch. CRACK!

The campfire vanishes.

All is dark. The drumming stops. Feet shuffle and stomp through the distant detritus. The movement stops. I wait. There is only the heavy rise and fall of my own breath.

A brighter fire bursts into existence, but it's another fifty yards up the slope. I try to turn on my cellphone, but the battery is dead. I should go back to Jules. But I don't.

I crouch and move north again.

A soft chant grows louder until it becomes a boisterous song. I am now only thirty yards away. I can see the dancers much better. This time, they frolic around the thick trunk of a sequoia. Its diameter is the length of my car. There are three fires, each at a triangular point around the tree.

I sneak even closer. Twenty-five yards and then twenty. When I crouch, the fog hides me, but I stop behind an enormous redwood stump anyway. The view is much better. I was wrong. These people are not children.

They have the long torsos and squat legs of dwarves. They hop and duck and twirl, all in animal costumes. They sing.

A dance for those left behind!
Left behind!
Left behind!
A dance for those left behind
By our Mother!

I have no idea what it means, but I grow cold and sickly the more I listen. I shiver and bite to keep my teeth from chattering. My stomach still churns, and bitterness rises in the back of my throat. I'm coming down with something.

I stand there much longer than I intended. The fey scene is as bizarre as it is mesmerizing. Finally, I notice *it*.

The giant sequoia they dance around.

The lower trunk doesn't meld into the earth like other trees. It ends in a tripod grouping of gnarled, bark-covered legs. The legs end in massive, shiny hooves.

I shriek…an autonomous reflex. I cover my mouth with both hands, but it's too late.

The light again vanishes.

I turn and run. The fog is dissipating, and more bluish beams of moonlight band the forest expanse. Something large chases me. It sounds like an elephant, or even something larger. The earth shakes with each stomp, and the upper crowns snap aside with its passing.

It moves slow, or I would already be dead. Using the *pollr* for guidance, I find the southern path. I'm a fool and fly down the slope without regard for the many obstacles. My right foot hits a root, and I lurch headfirst. I slam to the ground, roll, and jolt to a stop in a thick patch of fern.

The creature stomps toward me. It's only twenty yards away and takes gargantuan strides. The canopies part, and it towers above me.

Three legs grow up into its straight, tree-like body. In place of branches are a myriad of flapping, gesticulating tentacles. I see no eyes, but it has a mouth. A wide rictus opens across its middle diameter and reveals black teeth that glisten.

I'm sure that I am dead.

But it doesn't notice me. It steps over my body, each of the three thick legs at a time. It continues marching down the mountain. I sit up. It is on the path toward my tent. Toward Jules.

I should be horrified for my wife, but all I can feel is relief for my own well-being. I never imagined such demons to exist, not in my most drunken or feverish nightmares. I should be running after it, calling out and screaming to warn Jules.

But I don't. I can't move. Base instincts take over. Self-preservation trumps love. Survival beats sacrifice.

I sit and wait.

I listen.

The monster breaks through the trees. The tent is torn apart, and Jules screams. It's the pitiful sound of mortal terror. More stomping. Her screams stop.

Without my phone, I can't tell how much time passes. It feels like hours. My whole body is numb. I hug my knees to my chest and wait. The fog is now gone. A Steller's jay bursts into song, and the grey of approaching dawn replaces the night.

I can move again. I stumble down to the campsite. There is no sign of the demon, only the flattened tent. Someone whimpers. It's me.

I sob and make strange high-pitched noises as I peel the tent aside to reveal what is left of Jules.

I double over and vomit.

My wife is an unrecognizable mass of pulped gore, but one arm escaped the stomping. One wrist and hand hang out. She clutches the Wilson novel.

Crow

Ian Bain

The silver hatchback comes barreling down the dark, winding, and pothole-laden road. Dead leaves are kicked up into acrobatics in the wake of the car. Even with the windows shut, the bass from the car's music can be felt for miles around.

Inside the car are three teenage boys. The black-haired, acne-riddled boy driving says, "Bullshit Tony! You did not fuck her."

Tony, the boy in the passenger seat refutes this, "Honest to god. She came up to me at the end of class, asked me to stay back for a couple minutes, and when it was just us two, she grabbed my cock."

"You're so full of shit, you didn't fuck Ms. Whitfield," says Alex, the driver. The boys in the front continue to taunt each other while the boy in the middle backseat says nothing. His name is Steven. Steven doesn't know how to jump into a conversation like this. Truth be told, Alex and Tony's discussion makes him quite uncomfortable. But he doesn't show this, Steven just sits forward so he can hear them over the music, not wanting to really listen but not wanting to be excluded.

Almost missing a turn in the dark, Alex cranks the wheel and skids onto a dirt road, "Woo! Off-roadin'!" Without a seatbelt, Steven is thrown to the left side of the car.

The trees along the dirt road are bare. Even bare they are still thick enough on each side of the dirt road to create a total canopy above the road. The little light provided by the moon is null now.

"So are—" Steven begins to speak, but the boys in the front continue talking, apparently not having heard him. He clears his throat and tries again, a little louder, a little deeper, "SO! Are we almost at this place?" Steven wouldn't admit it to his potential new friends, but he gets awfully carsick when he's in the back of a car. Especially when driven by an idiot.

Alex turns down the stereo, "Almost there Stevie!"

Tony turns the stereo down again and asks Steven, "So, you ever heard of Crow's Bend before?"

Steven shakes his head.

"It's a total ghost town now, but at one point it was a huge farming community. One day in the 30s, everyone just vanished."

"'Cause of the depression?"

Tony smiles, "May-be Stee-vie. May-be. But there's a story 'round here of what most folks think really happened."

Steven had moved around a lot as a kid. And one thing he had found was that every town, especially the smaller ones, had their own legends. Most were less unique than you'd want, at least for entertainment's sake. Usually they were rip-offs of 50s cautionary tales about hooks in doors and Lovers' Lanes. Or sometimes they involved vampires and your classic monster affairs. But every once in a while, Steven heard an unusual local legend.

Alex slows down as the road becomes less and less manageable. Weeds and saplings grow in the dirt road, and Alex's car isn't meant for off-roading. If he hits a stump or a particularly tough sapling or if a hungry gang of ferns gets wrapped around his axle, they're screwed. "The accepted theory goes like this," Alex continues the story, trying not to think about being stuck out here in the darkness, "There was this guy in Crow's bend—"

"Wasn't he a fag?" Tony interrupts.

"Are you telling the story?"

"Sorry, sorry," Tony smiles.

Alex continues, "So yeah, there's this guy in Crow's Bend. He's gay. Not like over-the-top flamboyant like some gay guys today. He acted like a normal man, 'cept he just liked havin' sex with other dudes. Well, that wasn't really somethin' you could just do out in the open back in those days, 'specially in a small town.

"One day, he comes onto a guy he thinks might be gay. This guy turns around and tells his dad about it, and him and his dad raise up a mob. They take the gay guy way out into the fields, plannin' to tar-and-feather him. 'Just like in the good ol' days,' they figure. Tar and feather the guy and exile him from town. But since none of them had ever tarred and feathered someone before, they made a pretty crucial mistake. The tar they poured over the poor bastard was boiling-hot.

"Took them awhile to realize the tar they were dumping on the guy was burning his skin right off. It was tough to see through all the black in the night. They figured he was screamin' 'cause he was scared or somethin'. Once they were outta tar, they dumped a bag of crow feathers they'd gathered.

"A lump of black tar and feathers sat between the men. The gay guy hadn't moved in awhile. Not unless you count the bursting bubbles from the boiling tar. One guy poked the gay guy with a stick, still, he didn't move, didn't make a sound. Though they'd promised not to use their lanterns—so no one saw them and called the cops—one member of the mob turned on his lantern and placed it by the puddle of tar and feather.

"The men turned ghost-pale. Even the men who'd been to war looked like they were gonna hurl. Some of them did. The tar had burned away most of the flesh and tissue. Now, it was basically just a pile of bones, covered in black solidifyin' goop and feathers. The men waited for the tar to cool down, then they buried him right there in the field.

"And here we are." Alex steps on the brake and puts the silver hatchback in park. The first building in Crow's Bend is the gas station. A rusted pump still stands outside the building that obviously doubled as the owner's home. A collage of old advertisements under newer graffiti cover the building. The boys get out of the car and turn on their flashlights. Alex continues his story as they walk into the town.

"But that wasn't the end for the ol' queer. Nope. On a Halloween night, just like tonight, the Crowman came back. This would've been after the crops had been harvested, but before the winter really started.

"After all the kiddies were back home from trick' r treatin', the Crowman clawed his way out of the field. He wasn't recognizable no-more, not even to the men who buried him. Somethin' in the ground, or maybe in the way he died, changed him. His head kind of looked like one of those old plague-doctor masks: giant black eyes, and a beak long enough to impale a man on. His arms had become wings, ten feet across, at least! The rest of his body was covered in black feathers, and from his feet burst steak-knife-sized talons. The Crowman shook off the dirt and started walking towards town. In fact, it was down this very road that he returned to

Crow's Bend."

A wind wisps through the long-deserted town. Alex and Tony clasp their leather jackets closed with their free hands. Steven zips his black winter jacket all the way up, tucking his chin into the coat. The boys shine their flashlights on the different houses, the ones that are still mostly standing. Overgrowth that had claimed the town in summer has begun to shrivel and die in the cold fall weather.

A feeling of isolation and death remains ever present in Crow's Bend. The only sound other than the three boys is the periodic whisper of wind, tossing dried leaves around.

"So, what did the Crowman do?" Steven asks, "Get revenge on the men who'd killed him? Stabbed them all to death with his massive beak?"

Alex chuckles, "Oh no Stevie. What he did to them was much worse. The Crowman went to every single house in town, even to peoples' homes who weren't involved in killing him. He snuck in, blending into the darkness with his black feathers and melted black skin. He'd find the adults in the house, stand over them, and use the same magic that turned him into a monster."

"He turned them into crowmen too?"

"Even worse. The men and women he was standin' over would wake up, and see the Crowman standin' there, staring at them. The shock of seeing that in the middle of the night would be enough to give anyone a heart attack. And that's exactly how his victims would feel. They'd clutch their chest; they felt like their hearts were gonna explode, felt like something was gonna burst inside of them; felt like something was trying to escape their chest. They'd see something pointy tryin' to poke its way through the skin, tryin' to get to the outside. And eventually, a crow's beak would tear out of their skin.

"Somehow, the Crowman had created a crow inside of each person's heart, and made it eat its way out. Just before they died, the Crowman's victims had to look at the blood-covered crow, standin' on their chest."

"But they weren't just normal crows," Tony pipes up. "These crows, they contained the souls of the people they popped out of."

"Tony's right. In the most gruesome sorta way, the Crowman had turned the townspeople into crows. But he didn't stop there."

In what is left of the downtown of Crow's Bend, badly decayed, storefronts still stand on either side of the grass-covered street. Restaurants still have their daily specials advertised in the windows; a department store has a sign reading:

HALLOWEEN COSTUMES!

GHOSTS, GOBLINS, DEVILS, WITCHES!

Alex turns towards one of the less-decayed buildings, a two-story Victorian brick house, and walks onto the rotting porch. The door is gone, and the three boys enter the house one at a time, each more reluctant than the last.

The beam from Alex's flashlight falls on various tags that have been painted over the years. Up the surprisingly intact stairs, the three boys go to the second floor and down the hallway. Alex peaks into one of the rooms and turns back to Tony and Steven, "And here's the worst part," Alex leads the boys into the room. Their flashlights fall on a crib and a child's bed. "The Crowman was able to control those he'd turned into crows. And what he did, as a last piece of revenge, was he made those adults peck their own kids to death and eat 'em."

"Oh, gawd," Steven covers his mouth and tries—unsuccessfully—not to picture a crow pecking a baby to death.

"See there," Alex shines his light on old stains on the walls, "That's the little kiddies' blood smeared on the walls."

"That's so fucked up, dude."

"Sure is, Stevie. And as far as anyone knows, the Crowman and his minions still haunt this place. The Crowman always lookin' for people who done others wrong, and the crows who've developed a taste for human flesh."

"All right, it's getting late, let's get going," Steven offers, feeling like his own heart is going to explode and birth a crow.

"Sure thing, Stevie, lead the way." Alex and Tony exchange a look behind Steven's back. The three boys walk back down the rotting stairs and leave the old brick house. They make it back to the gas station where Alex parked his car, when Steven feels the other two boys grab him from behind.

"What the hell! Let go of me!" Steven's voice cracks into a girlish high-pitched scream.

"You want to be part of our gang, right Stevie?" Tony asks him.

"Well, you've gotta go through a little initiation ritual we have," Alex adds. The boys pin Steven to the old brownish-red gas pump. Tony pulls a roll of duct tape from his jacket. While Alex holds Steven the best he can, Tony tapes the boy's thin wrists behind the gas pump. "You've just gotta stay out here tonight, and if you're still alive come mornin', you'll be one of us."

"You're crazy!" Steven yells as Tony tapes his legs to the pump. "What about wild animals?"

"Don't worry," Tony placates, "We'll be in the car all night. I borrowed my dads .22. Not that it'll do much good against the Crowman." Both boys snicker.

"Guy's please!"

"If you start cryin' on us Stevie, this'll be the last

time we ever talk to you. And we'll still leave you out here, but we won't be sticking around to stop any wolves or bears from getting you."

Steven clenches his jaw and lets his tears run with his snot. He doesn't dare sniffle; in case the guys think he is crying.

Back in the car, Alex and Tony can see the dark silhouette of Steven, bound to the gas pump. "You think this was a little too harsh?" Tony asks.

"Naw, Stevie's cool an' all, but he's kind of a pussy. He doesn't have a dad, right? Didn't have someone to teach him how to be a man. This is the best thing we can do for him."

The boys watch Steven struggle for a few minutes.

Steven relinquishes the fight against the duct tape. Alex and Tony fall asleep, leaving Steven open to the elements and whatever haunts Crow's Bend.

Red morning light pierces Alex's eyelids. As his eyes flutter, his mind tries to remember where he is. When Alex's sight adjusts and he remembers what they did last night, Alex elbows sleeping Tony, "Dude, wake up! We fell asleep!"

Still half asleep, Alex stumbles out of the silver hatchback and makes his way over where Steven is still bound to the gas pump. Steven's head is slumped forward now. Alex thinks, *I can't believe he was able to sleep like that*. But by the time Alex is within a foot of Steven, his eyes widen and he freezes in horror. Tony joins Alex in front of Steven and vomits at the sight of the very obviously dead boy in front of them.

Moonlight-pale, Steven remains bound to the gas pump, a gaping hole in his chest encircled with black-red crust. "Fuck, fuck, fuck, wha' do we do now?" Tony rambles, tears falling down his face.

"Just shut up a second, I'm trying to think," says Alex, still staring at the wound in Steven's chest. It doesn't take a medical professional to see that the wound was caused not by something entering his chest, but by something leaving it. Violent and rough.

"I thought all of that stuff about the Crowman was all made up! Oh god, oh god, I thought it was a joke."

"It's just small-town folklore Tony, it isn't real."

"Come on man, let's just get out of here, we'll untie Stevie so it just looks like something got him out here."

Alex looks at the dead boy's wrists, "No-can-do. Everywhere we duct-taped him there'll be marks"

"What're we gonna do man?"

"Calm down or I swear to god Tony…

"Listen, we're gonna cut him loose, take him into one of these buildings, and toss him in the basement. No one ever comes out here, by the time some other dumb kids find him, all that'll be left'll be rags 'n' bone."

Tony continues to mutter and cry. Fed up, Alex slaps Tony across the face with one solid open-palm. The *smack* echoes across Crow's Bend,

Once the echo has flown away, the boys feel just how eerily quiet the deserted village is.

The silence is broken.

CAW-CAW. CAW-CAW.

A single crow lands on top of Alex's car.

CAW-CAW, CAW-CAW.

Two more crows join the first bird on the car.

CAW-CAW, CAW-CAW, CAW-CAW-CAW-CAW.

From every home in Crow's Bend, black birds erupt in the morning fog and dim light. They find purchase on Alex's car, on the gas station pump. One bird lands on Steven's lolled head. "Stevie?" Alex asks.

The bird does not reply, it only stares into Alex's plump, juicy eyeballs with its own ebony oculars.

A massive, dark figure, stands in the now-open

doorway of the gas station. It is still too dark to clearly see the figure, but to Alex, it appears completely black from head-to-toe.

As black as the crows.

The thing takes up the entire doorway. It opens its massive beak, and lets loose a horrible cacophony of *CAWs*. The crows all join in. When the terrible racket crescendos, the birds make their move.

The black birds fly at the panicked Alex and Tony, pulling their hair and scratching their faces, seeking out the tasty delights held within their eye sockets and other orifices.

Blinded, the boys stumble around, trying to find the car. Tony stumbles, falls to the ground. The crows don't waste any time. They descend upon him, quickly removing his skin. Even if Alex still had eyes, he wouldn't recognize the peeled red mass as his friend.

Alex's hands find the car's hood just as a crow manages to rip half his right ear away from his head. Frantically, Alex paws his way to the driver-side door, when he feels the weight of something massive drop onto the car. So big is this thing, Alex can hear the metal bending under its weight. Crying, but with only blood flowing from his eyes had been, Alex fights to make it to the door. He tries to convince himself that it's Tony, but he knows Tony isn't even alive enough to scream any longer.

Oh god!

Alex's right hand has landed on something very clearly *not* the metal of his car. His hand has found something long, cracked, and sharp, and against his better judgement, his fingers trace this thing to its deadly point, and then in the opposite direction, towards its wrinkled leathery foot. Wanting to scream but unable to, Alex fumbles toward the driver's door. He finds the cool glass of the window, finds the door handle, and pulls.

He can hardly believe he's made it to safety. Once inside the car he hits the automatic lock button. *Click.* And then a terrifying thought comes into his mind, *Did Tony close his door?* Almost before he can finish this thought, the sound of "*CAW-CAW*," booms in his ears, and the crows descend for a second feast. All the while, the Crowman watches, not smiling, but delighted nonetheless.

The Hollow Ghost

Bill Davidson

After the funeral, I walked out of The Hollow with nothing but my passport and credit cards and kept going. I had always dreamed of travel; Prague, New York, Istanbul, Sydney. Saw myself courageous and dusty; a slightly over-tall woman collecting experiences in every new country.

My wanderings owed nothing to those dreams. I drifted impervious under wheels of stars as weeks faded to months and the summer sun burned me near blind or frosts chilled my bones. I saw little and went unseen.

I would say I lost count of time, but there was no count to be lost. I kept neither track nor diary but still, in time, an unknown spiral wound me back to England.

A morning even came where I discovered myself walking into the village, just as if I had made that choice, past familiar rows of low cottages of stone and mossy thatch. I passed the pub and the village store, settled, solid, unchanged by the passing of the years. I thought I saw my old friend Mariel in that store, frowning to catch a glimpse of a faded traveler.

This place is famous for mists at summer's end, and the village was misty that morning. The haze thickened as I took the downward path, winding to The Hollow. I found myself reminiscing, thinking of the day Molly got back from University, throwing her backpack down and laughing, full of her big world experience and looking with new eyes at her childhood home.

"Who would build a house in this foggy hole?"

Her eyes were sparkling, hair golden and rippled, messed about by tongs and gel. Still my beautiful girl.

"Your grandfather." As if she didn't know. This place suited the old man's contrarian nature.

Molly was right, though, the slopes surrounding the house conspired, husbanding damp in the air long after it burned off elsewhere. It was known as The Hollow long before my father was moved to build his everlastingly cold house.

My feet slowed as I passed the church, the last building before the village gave up its ghost. The graveyard was large for such a small village, to swallow centuries of coffins. Though I could picture little Calum's stone, I could not for the life of me recall where Molly was buried, as though my memory of that day had burned away.

I hurried past, and all too soon found myself in front of the iron gates of my old home. The house rose from the mist, a ship afloat, its over-ornate roof framed against a sky the color of milk.

I stepped through, taking in the wide lawn and rose beds. It was well tended, which was good, but I was in no hurry to meet old Old Tim, if he still gardened here, or anyone else that I knew from before.

The lock turned smoothly, and I had to take a large breath before stepping into the hall, catching the familiar scents of wax and damp stone.

I had forgotten how big it was, and how cold. I wandered the ground floor; the drawing room, the snug, the dining room and the huge kitchen with its pine counter and cream Aga. Everything just as I left it. The case clock in the hall was quiet and I put out a hand, but stopped short of setting the pendulum to motion. I was uncomfortable enough with how my little noises disturbed the silence and didn't want the living tick of that clock.

I flicked a switch and a light came on. So, bills were being paid, surely the work of Keith, my old friend and solicitor. A hefty bill to pay, no doubt.

Never mind. Money was not my worry. Still, I turned the lamp off again, as I had grown to detest the harshness of electric light, above all things.

I stirred around, unconsciously picking up patterns grooved deep into the memory of leg and hand. Lit a cigarette standing at the open back door, where I must have smoked ten thousand smokes, because smoke and mist are cousins.

My hatred of electric light had gotten so much worse after Molly and Calum died, so, as day turned to evening, I lit church candles.

I approved the drama, walking this empty house like a Victorian with a candle held high, the shaky light hardly stirring the gloom, but don't get me wrong. I take no actual pleasure.

After the drowning, I had expected the erosion of time would leave space for other things. I thought, foot to boat to plane, to outdistance it.

I was as wrong about that as everything else. I had been a strict Mother, a stickler, overruling my weak-willed appeaser of a husband at every turn and failing my reckless and beautiful daughter.

Pregnant with no father in sight, I was all set to disapprove of her baby, but he was Calum, and disapproval was not an option. Molly once said he got the kindness I withheld from her, like I was a wicked step-mother from a story, rather than a caring parent, determined to do right.

She and I had fought that day, before she went out on the lake. Typical Molly, challenged about the amount of wine she was getting through, she sunk a bottle right there in front of me, before they went out on the Grey Mare, our little row boat.

Now, alone with my tall candle, I spoke into the silence, asking myself, what was I doing back here? In her bedroom, touching her clothes. Her hairbrush. Her perfume.

Her smell was everywhere, in every room. The fabric of The Hollow was saturated with my dead daughter.

I stood outside Calum's bedroom as evening faded to night. Four years old when the boat capsized; giggling, blonde, bespectacled and endlessly argumentative. I snatched my scalded hand from that door, and turned away.

So, to my own bed, after all this time, beneath musty covers and sipping whisky. Couldn't blow the candle out. Scared, you see, the worm of my unease stirring in the dark.

The old house settled, the familiar sounds of my childhood home sinking into sleep lulling me to my own, then bolt upright and listening hard. Someone was on the stairs, climbing slowly.

Hair prickling, I opened my mouth, snapped it closed over the whisper of her name.

Unlikely that I would sleep after, but suddenly there was birdsong, sharp in the haze. Mist. What else in The Hollow as autumn set in? Trees were ragged peaks with no base.

I wandered the house and garden, and the day slid by

as days will do until, just as I was again considering a candle, the ancient hall telephone trilled. After it stopped, it was no longer exactly quiet in the house, although it took me several seconds to track the reason. The case clock was ticking, ponderous and profound.

The telephone rang and this time I picked up.

"Hello?"

"So, you *are* home."

A man's voice, friendly, smooth, elderly. "Keith? Is that you?"

"I hardly believed it, when Mariel called. She said you look thinner."

I had to smile. "Thin. That just about covers it."

I lit my candle as I spoke, glancing at the clock as I did so, and gasping aloud.

"Elizabeth? Are you alright?"

I gave myself a shake. "Believe it or not, I just scared myself with my own reflection. Lit a match and thought I was looking at a wicked old version of Molly."

"Silly! Like as peas in a pod, you two. I can't imagine you looking wicked, or old. Mariel said you looked lovely as ever. Are you back to stay, this time, Liz?"

"I doubt it. You've kept the place up nicely. Thank you for that."

"Me? I didn't do anything."

Nonsense. I poured myself a generous dram and took it to bed, falling asleep quickly but coming awake befuddled, chasing the tail of what had wakened me. The sound of steps again, stealthy, this time right outside my door.

I knew these sounds. Knew who made them.

I pulled the covers around me, eyes wide and breath shallow, until I realized I must have awoken from a dream. One in which my dead daughter walked this house.

The next day wasn't misty, for once. Instead it rained, a constant, soaking drizzle that washed the color from everything. I ate a tiny breakfast *(I am thin, thin is a good word for me)* and walked to the lake, onto the wooden jetty to where the Grey Mare still floated, innocent.

Molly would take our boat out, a pretense of fishing that involved sunning herself and a lot of smoke. My beautiful, idle girl.

The lake isn't wide, but it is cold and deep and filled with weed. They were not the first to drown in the long history of the village.

I walked to the churchyard, moving amongst gravestones so old they were unreadable and pausing where Mother and Father were buried. James, my feckless fantasist of a husband, took more time to find. I hadn't visited his grave, and wouldn't have now, but I thought Molly might be nearby. She wasn't.

Calum was, though. Such a tall headstone for such a tiny boy, bright new roses in the urn before it. There was a reason, a compelling one, why he and his mother were not together. Buried on the same day, but in different parts of the churchyard. I knew that reason once, but could not fetch it from my memory. Nor could I find my daughter's grave.

That night, when the stealthy sounds woke me, I crept tip-toe out of bed to stand by the door. Footsteps, clear on the stairs and me wide awake to hear them. Her footsteps, *hers*, going downstairs, away from me. My scalp froze as seconds turned to minutes, the candle in one hand while the other hovered scaredy-cat over the handle.

I opened the door.

Nothing on the landing, except the tick of the clock. I held my candle high and took a shaky step out of the safety of my room, trying for quiet.

Still nothing. The stairway, the hall, the case clock and the shivering glow. I might have gone downstairs, but my legs were unwilling. Instead, I backed up, closed the door and climbed into bed where I stayed, trying to sleep, until the unmistakable rattle of the door handle. By the palest of moonlights, I could see it begin to turn.

I didn't see the door open, though I heard it, because my head was under the blanket, as though I was a child of four. I kept a tight hold of the covers and even squeezed my eyes shut, as if seeing nothing could keep me safe. That's how it should work with ghosts.

The old hinges creaked, then footsteps, sly across the boards, coming all the way to my bed. I stretched my hearing and trembled, but would not uncover.

A whisper. "Mother?"

I wanted to scream. Instead, I bit my lip and imagined myself sinking gradually into the mattress. Not something that could speak, or listen.

Again, just at the edge of hearing. "Mother?"

Seconds spun into minutes.

"You have to forgive."

The door closed. When I eventually peeked, I was alone.

I persuaded my limbs into motion, but only to hurry from bed and turn the key in the lock. I lit a candle and sat awake all night.

The following morning found me creeping like my own ghost, frightened of what I might find. I told myself to pack and run, but in daylight was ashamed of my cowardice, hiding under bed covers like an infant.

I would not run. If, having killed her own son, my child haunted this house, I would face her.

I let the day trickle away and, when it grew dark, took to my room but did not sleep. I waited, and somewhere in the watches of the night, I heard tiny noises become deep sounds, as though something larger than a person moved downstairs. I made my fingers uncurl to open the door.

The clock ticked, but otherwise all was quiet. I tip toed to the stairs and took a hesitant step down, stilled at something between a hum and a sigh, a single note I knew well, one that Molly would make, never aware of it. Her own little sound.

It took everything in me, but I managed another step, wincing at sound of breath and foot. Made myself go down those stairs, all the way to the hall.

Which was empty, of course.

Molly was sitting on the couch in the drawing room, hands in her lap. Jeans, as always in life, topped with a plain white blouse, hair pale gold across her shoulder. Beautiful, but faded. Barely there at all.

She watched me, but didn't smile.

Her voice was cobwebs. "You've come home again."

"Why are you here?"

"I live here."

I shook my head. "Not anymore."

Her face screwed in pain, then became stone. Hard like that. She unfolded, rising, the light from my candle falling off her as though it would not hold. Seeing her stand, my courage failed, and I bolted up the stairs, turning the key to lock my bedroom.

Standing by the door, I heard her come till she was inches away, heard her breathe, something to frost the old paint of the door.

"Mother?"

I did not speak.

"This time, I'm not letting you go. You have to forgive."

In silence and time, I found my courage once more, telling myself that I must face my daughter, if that was what that was. Tell her that the death of her son was not mine to forgive.

This time, the drawing room was empty. I took a few steps into the room, putting my candle down on the dresser, and when I turned, she stood behind me. Her face, so warm in life, was hard.

"I won't let you go this time."

We stared at each other, less than two paces apart. I could not speak, but it seemed she could.

"Ten years since Calum died, you've drifted like a ghost."

That long? "You're the ghost."

"I became one. But I came back. You can too."

I was backing up, and she was following.

"Leave me be!"

"You have to forgive."

I dodged around her, got to the stairs and half fell up the first few. Turned to see her, coming for me in the dark. "You drowned!"

"I didn't die."

She grabbed my arm, had me tight and solid, the ghost of my daughter.

"Let go of me."

"I'm alive, Mum."

"You died."

I half ran, half crawled to my room, the ghost on my heels and hard electric light flooded my eyes.

"Enough!"

She stood, chest heaving. An older woman than I remembered, her face lined and worn.

"It was my fault."

"I know."

"I've accepted it."

She put her face before mine, pressed my hand to it. It was hot, and wet with tears. "You have to remember."

Calum. So small, harsh lit amongst tubes and monitors, Eyelids like grey paper, lips…never mind about his lips.

"Mum?"

When I moved, my shoulders jerked, because I had been standing still for a long time. I heard the hiss of my breath when I turned.

"You switched it off. Gave him up."

I was shaking my head and shielding my eyes and falling over to find my bag and pushing into my shoes. She put her hands on my arms.

"It's time to stop."

I fought her, but she was younger and stronger, and eventually I curled into a ball.

"Turn the light off. Please."

The electric lamp died, and I could breathe again. Then a candle was there, and she tried to help me to the bed. I slapped her away.

"Murderer."

"You'd think losing my son would be the worst thing, but that's not so. You're the worst thing."

I sat up and pointed, wanting her to know. "You died, that day."

She put her hand in her pocket, then, came out with something. A photograph. Me, and my daughter, both grinning, Calum between. What was he giggling at, our fine little boy?

"He drowned, Mum. They got his heart going, but our boy was gone."

I took it from her and curled away to look at it, trying to catch the coat tails of the moment.

I must have slept, because I awoke fully clothed, pale morning light flooding my room, the photograph on my bedside. Molly was gone. I packed quickly, cards and passport, fitted the silence of the house, saw myself disappearing, just like smoke, this time never to return.

Almost at the front door and gone, I heard a low noise, and it rooted me. Molly, trying not to cry, but not quite managing it. How many times had I hovered outside her bedroom, unsure if my intrusion would be helpful – or welcome. Often enough, I had been the cause.

She was in the snug, surrounded by hundreds of scattered photographs. Not all of them were of Calum. Many were of Molly herself, and me. Molly was curled and crying, oblivious of my presence.

I stood, unnoticed as usual, and thought about the road, and smoke, but found myself crossing to sit.

I picked up a photograph; one taken on this very couch. Ten-year old Molly wearing her Little Mermaid pajamas, too big to sit on my lap, but that was what she was doing. Grinning as she hugged me. I had forgotten she would do that.

Little Mermaid, she knew all those songs. Eventually, I did too.

"Mum?"

The next sob came not from Molly but deep inside me, like it had been wrenched, unwilling. She was so soft and warm and *there*. She hushed me and stroked my hair, just as she had done for Calum.

I let myself lie until I saw the roses, a large spray, bright reds and yellows. I sat up, disentangling myself and leaned over to pick one.

Molly said, "I take them to him, most days. All I can do for my boy now."

Together, we took the roses, laid them in a graveyard that was too big for such a little village, and a headstone that was too high for such a little boy.

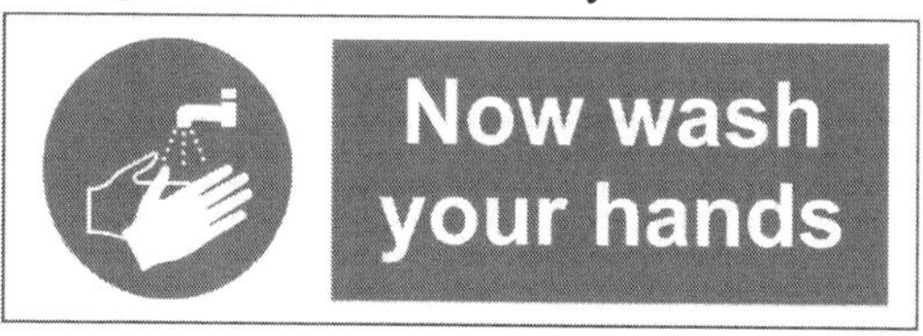

The Foreign Film Saved My Life

Hillary Dodge

The film was painfully boring—which I'm guessing is why it got slotted for the last show of the night—and although my date was hot, I was having trouble staying awake. I leaned over and whispered a playful excuse into his ear before scooting flirtatiously across his lap towards the aisle. He nodded, a smile faint upon his lips, as he leaned around me to see the screen. Maybe I could pound a pack of Raisinets before having to come back and endure more.

But, as I made my way in the darkness, things changed.

Before I even got down the darkened hall, I began to hear an unusual amount of commotion coming from the lobby. As I came around the corner, I saw that there was a mob of some sort, tearing everything apart. They looked like a tottering, uncoordinated group of tweakers gone berserk on bath salts or something. A high-pitched gargling scream shot out from beneath a pile of the jerking tweakers and that's when I realized the mob wasn't attacking *stuff.* They were attacking *people.*

Instinctively, I dropped down behind a tall plastic trashcan. More screams followed and a quick peek around the can confirmed that the tweakers were actually eating people. *Fuck!* This was not how I wanted to be dressed on the night of the real motherfucking zombie apocalypse.

Squatting behind the trashcan, I slipped off one hot-pink fuck-me-heel, then the other. The lobby was a mess and eight of the undead were still stomping around in the carnage that twenty minutes before had been three teenage part-timers and another late-night movie-goer. The trashcan reeked of ten-week-old popcorn butter, but even that stench was overpowered by the smell of shit and blood. Gagging, I held back the bile rising in my throat.

To my left was the men's room and it called to me like a cozy piss-scented safe house. I poked my head around the trashcan to determine if any of those things were looking my way. They weren't. Lucky me. I slid silently backwards on stockinged feet until my back was against the door. Slowly, I leaned into it, pushing it open wide enough to slip through. As I fell/scooted into the men's room, I caught the door with one hand and eased it shut.

A quick glance around confirmed that the bathroom was empty. Or was it? I glared at the three closed stalls. Standing, I yanked down on the miniskirt that was riding my hips and padded silently over to the first door. Pushing my fingertips into the door while standing as far back as I could, I eased the door open.

Empty.

I stepped over to the next door and repeated the process.

Empty.

A low growl issued from my stomach. I had always

had a nervous stomach and now, the tension was literally twisting my bowels. Damn, I had to shit – and bad. I pushed open the last door and heaved a sigh of relief.

Empty!

As it was pouring out of me like hot lava, I heard the soft shush of the door swinging open. I froze on the seat, straining my ears to listen for the slightest sound – anything that would give away the identity of the door-opener. A barely audible rasp met my ears.

Shit! Shit! Shit!

I dragged a length of toilet paper from the dispenser and eased up from the toilet. The dispenser squeaked as I tore the paper free and a loud grunt issued from the thing lurking outside the stall.

How was I going to get out of here? Panic seared through me and I struggled to come up with some sort of plan. The thing shuffled towards my stall. Petrified, I stood there like I'd inexplicably taken root in the stained linoleum. Again, the rasp and grunt sounded, and this time it was closer. It stumbled into the next stall. A wet shucking sound accompanied the noises coming out of its throat and with a wet slap, a length of glistening entrails hit the floor next to my foot.

I squealed and yanked open the stall door. With a speed hitherto unbeknownst to myself, I flew out of the stall and towards the bathroom door. I tugged open the door and felt clumsy, insensate fingers raking through my hair. Wheeling, I shoved the thing as hard as I could and it fell back onto the floor behind me.

Out in the lobby, eight pairs of murky eyes stabbed the distance between us. I found myself chuckling without really remembering how I got started. The pink heels were still on the floor behind the trash can. I reached down and grabbed at one; at the very least I could use it as a weapon.

I booked it for theatre number 16 at the end of the darkened hall and around the corner. As I passed theatre 9, I glanced longingly at the marquee above the door. I would have much preferred to see the latest romantic comedy starring Channing Tatum. But my date was a college boy, pursing his masters in telling everyone how much he knew about film, apparently. He had insisted on the long, boring foreign film. Hearing the screams and gurgles from within, I realized in hindsight, that his choice had probably been the better idea. Certainly, this was a better call than my usual Friday night, which I spent alternately at the bar or at the club.

I shoved through the doors into theatre 16 and ran straight up the ramp. Something sad and monochrome was occurring on the screen.

I took a moment to turn and shout up at my date. "Time to go!"

Aaron looked to either side of his seat, for some reason. "Erica? What are you doing?" he called down to me.

I eyed the ramped hallway to the theatre doors. Sounds of screams carried up the ramp.

"Aaron, there's something—"

At that moment, that *something* burst through the doors and fell onto the floor. It flopped over and hauled itself upright. It was one of the lobby monkeys—some poor kid who had been stuck with the late shift—now horribly mangled and very undead as a result. The kid's arm was twisted back at a gnarly angle and a dripping flap of his acned-covered face folded down over one eye. The other eye, searched for something, caught sight of me, and burned with zombie rage. The kid shambled towards me.

"Fuck, fuck, fuck!" I screamed, stepping back into the curtained wall.

I know, I know, I was totally panicking. Doing that

dumb shit all stupid chicks end up doing in horror movies. The dead kid stumbled up to me in the time I spent reflecting on my idiotic reaction and shoved me into the wall. My head knocked back and through the kid's slavering grunts, I could hear Aaron shouting a really lame, "Hey, stop."

Sense poured back into me and I remembered the pink heel in my hand. Wrenching back my arm, I swung down. Hard! Impaling the poor kid with my stiletto. My shoe stuck out of his front sinus, beside his nose, blood and something murky white coursing down his face, alongside a few jagged fragments of bone. He fell back but kept moving, his arms jerking and his legs pedaling. I expected him to go still. Like, you know, how they say you need to nail them in the head. But no such luck.

As the dead kid struggled to right himself, I saw Aaron running down the stairs.

"Did you get my jacket?" I yelled at him over the melancholy music.

I really loved that jacket.

"What?" he shouted back.

"My jacket! Get my jacket!"

Aaron froze at the bottom of the stairs, eyes glued to the struggling lump of flesh that was the theatre kid. He was jerking and sagging in a strange rhythmic movement, exactly as if my heel had penetrated some part of the brain that controlled motor skills. Had my heel even gotten that far? I pictured the 3-inch heels superimposed on an X-ray of a human skull. *Gross!*

Bile gushed to the back of my throat, but I swallowed it back just in time. No way was I going to barf in front of Aaron. He may have been a dull date, but he was still pretty hot, after all. And maybe this whole experience would bring us closer together. Who knew?

But, shit, hot post-zombie-attack sex was not in the cards.

As Aaron stood staring at the jerking theatre kid, another thing plowed into him from behind. I hadn't even seen the thing coming into the theatre. Aaron toppled beneath a pair of skinny bedangled arms protruding from a black Paramore shirt. He struggled to push the thing off of him as it strained to close the distance between its chomping teeth and his cheek.

"Gaaah!" Aaron squealed.

I looked around for something to use as a weapon and spotted a flashlight, probably dropped by the theatre kid that was thrashing about on the ground with my pink heel jutting from its face.

I bent over and grabbed it, running to Aaron's aid. This date was not turning out the way I had hoped. Not only were we seemingly caught in the middle of some real-life horror movie, but also Aaron was not proving to be the most considerate date. I mean, it looked like I was going to have to rescue him while he was peeing his pants in terror over some emo with a lip ring. Well, probably with a lip ring. I couldn't exactly see the jerk.

I raised the flashlight over my head and brought it down on the back of the emo's black knit cap. It instantly collapsed into a pile of useless limbs and black fabric.

Aaron was crying now. *For real.*

"Really?" I asked, wincing as I helped him to his feet.

Aaron was definitely no longer hot. He was a hot mess and he stunk. The pussy had shit himself. I remembered my episode in the bathroom. *Alright, okay, so it happens in times like these.* Maybe I could forgive him that. But I sighed as I looked toward the theatre hall, I could never forgive him leaving my jacket behind. A tripping trio of dead things stumbled into the theatre and scuttled up the ramp.

I would have to abandon my jacket.

I grabbed Aaron by the front of his shirt and dragged him towards the exit door to the left of the screen. He was still crying, snot now bubbling out of his nose and dripping over his lips.

This was definitely a winner for the nastiest date award, and not in a good way.

"Come on, you stupid fuck!" I shouted as I yanked him along.

I kicked the door open with my bare feet, kinda feeling like a bad ass, but also regretting the decision a little when I stubbed my toe in the process. Well, we can't always be in top form, can we?

Scanning the empty lot on the backside of the theatre, I wondered what waited for me the rest of this insane night. Shit, I was probably going to have to brain my grandma. No doubt, she wasn't the survivor type, what with her oxygen tank and walker. But there was one thing I knew for sure; maybe foreign films weren't so bad. After all, I believe that stupid foreign film saved my life.

The Night the Boy Came and the Other Thing that Happened

W. H. Gilbert

When Charlotte awoke, lying in a tangle of bed sheets and comforters, she was illuminated not by the morning sun but the television, which she had forgotten to turn off.

She had been told from a very young age that sleeping with the TV on was bad for you. It robbed your mind of restful REM sleep, causing headaches and fatigue the next day. She had weaned herself of the habit when she lived back home with her dad and three sisters, but now, after living on her own for nearly a year, she was uneasy sleeping alone in the dark in this town.

She had heard stories from the people in her classes about her building; old tenants (or friends of them) telling tales of whispers, doors closing or other bumps in the night. Charlotte was keenly aware of the ever-present danger of the boys across the street, the ones who stayed up and out all night drinking, weekend or not. She had seen the way they looked at her on those few nights when she braved the dark, the streets, the bars, to meet with her friends downtown. When she came home after the bars closed, she felt the weight of their eyes on her, watching from their balcony. She made sure never to turn on her living room lights after coming inside, before drawing the blinds, for fear those boys might start counting the floors and windows to pinpoint just where this little thing lived and slept alone, in the dark.

These fears often danced inside Charlotte's head. The dancing became near-terror when the sun sank and the blanket of night covered the college town. The easiest remedies were: the TV turned on, but low, on her desk against the wall across from her bed; a hammer under her pillow; and the gun her dad had given her, hidden in the nightstand. She remembered the day her dad had given her the gun; the old man with the gray and black hair and heavy bags under his eyes, told her he knew how boys were. He said they'd been the same when he was young and that boys like that will always be around. That would never change. He took her into the backyard and taught her how to carry the pistol safely, how to load, aim, and fire correctly. Her father even told her the trick of never turning her lights on when she came home.

"That's how they getcha," he said. "No one's looking out for our daughters, so we have to be extra careful."

And he hugged her tight and, even though he didn't say it aloud, she knew he never wanted to let her go.

But go she did.

Every night Charlotte would close her eyes, hoping the next thing she saw would be the golden twinkle of dawn peeking in through the curtains, providing a temporary end to her worries. But tonight, Halloween, she was not so lucky.

She had declined an invitation from friends in her Astronomy class to go out to the costume party on the town square, saying she had a headache. In reality, she was afraid of being followed home.

So instead, she had stayed in, cooked pasta, made a small salad, and watched an old movie on TV with a bag of candy near the door in case of trick-or-treaters. She knew there wouldn't be any. Trick-or-treating was a forgotten pastime in Texas, let alone in a college town with few children. She remembered the days of going door to door with her parents, dressed as a family of pumpkins or vampires or witches, whichever she fancied most that year. They would say hi to all the neighbors they recognized but never really knew, collecting sweets to snack on at nights until Christmas. As she got older, she'd noticed that tradition dwindling, and eventually she was in charge of taking her sisters "Trunk-or-Treating" at the church parking lot, where they each walked from car to car, saying nothing to anyone. Adults dropped candy into their bags in a robotic parody of what Hallowe'en had once been. Most of the kids didn't even wear costumes.

It was a different story here, though. Her apartment neighbors and hordes of others had swarmed the streets, nearly all in costumes, as they headed downtown to enjoy a night of drinking. Tonight, they dressed as monsters and cartoon characters, as opposed to every other night when they drank dressed as college students. The building felt very empty and very quiet around sundown. She supposed she might be the only person cooped up tonight. The light and sound from the TV were welcome distractions from the silence. A silence waiting to be filled by an ominous creak or unexplainable moan.

Through her crusty eyes, she saw the movie on the screen was black and white, and as she rubbed her vision clear she saw it was something old, indeed. One of those movies Dad had always relished watching in late October, insisting the whole family join him. In it, a monster with many eyes and grasping hands stalked a blonde woman who slid much-too-slowly around corners and through alleyways. The thing looked like something from outer space (and probably was, because weren't they all?) Long tendrils of saliva dripped from a rubbery, but disturbingly realistic, gesticulating maw.

The thing onscreen would have been something to laugh about under other circumstances, but Charlotte's night-brain needed no extra help in scaring her. She felt around her mattress for the remote and could not find it. The visitor from space clicked and hissed, hungering for the girl. Charlotte took her covers in both hands and shook it in a wave, hoping the remote control might clatter to the floor, but it did not.

There was a muffled scream, and for a split second Charlotte wondered whether it had come from the movie or outside her bedroom window.

Get a grip, she told herself. *Even if it was someone outside, it* is *Halloween after all.*

Finally, after a minute of searching in vain for the remote, she swung her feet over the bed, walked across the floor and turned the TV off. With the grey light, that had bathed her just seconds before, now gone, her vision became impossibly dark and blurry. The streetlights outside offered little help cutting through the curtains, but she knew the steps to her bed.

Eying the space under her bed, she made a conscious decision to hop onto the mattress quickly. Old habits die hard.

She hugged her knees as close to her chest as possible and waited for sleep to find her again, but when she closed her eyes she saw the silly goofy thing from space crawling toward her in the dark. She shook her head, hoping it would make her brave. It did not.

Charlotte lay on her back, drawing the curtain aside just an inch and thanked God for small favors. There were stars tonight. They shone bold and brilliant against the dark blue-black. She began to count them, hoping she might see a shooting star. She had never seen one in her entire life; something no one believed when she said it. But it was true. They were easy to miss if you rarely looked up.

As she neared a hundred in her count, there came a knocking at her door. Her breath caught in her throat. Her body tensed. The apartment was quiet once more and she tried to convince herself it was nothing.

Then *knock, knock, knock.*

Her feet and hands ached from clenching.

Maybe it's just someone across the hall, she thought. *Shit, I don't know, maybe it's just a ghost,* she hoped.

But she knew that was false.

Someone, flesh and blood, was at her door. That someone was trying to get in.

She felt under her pillow and found the hammer. She slid to the edge of her bed once more, careful not to plant her feet on the floor. Weighing the option of *hammer or gun,* finally she whispered, "Fuck it."

She slid the nightstand drawer open slowly, quietly and took the gun in her free hand. It felt unusually heavy tonight.

The soles of her feet met the floor and she shifted her weight slowly, making sure not to cause a sound. She slunk through the dark, hunched forward a bit with hammer held high, the gun at her waist. Her feet slid silently across the floor and she was thankful for all of her time in theater, teaching her, if nothing else, to move silently in life as across the stage.

At her front door, she heard the sound of someone on the other side, breathing heavily. The door groaned.

She imagined whoever was out there was leaning on it for balance.

Please just give up, Charlotte thought. *Please, dear God, just think no one is home.*

"Trick or treat," said a voice from the other side. The words were muffled through the door, but she knew whoever spoke was smiling. She imagined viscous drool falling from his mouth and pooling at his feet. She stared at the bottom of the door, expecting to see the imagined drool seeping in from beneath, but it did not.

She inched close enough now to peek through the peephole. She knew they were not designed to be two-way, but she always felt uncomfortable standing in front of it. She was hesitant to look through, knowing that if she saw him looking back she would lose her mind or scream, which might be worse.

She inched forward, knowing she would need to know what he looked like to report him to the police.

Police! she thought. *Why have I not called the police*?

How many calls have they gotten from scared little freshman girls tonight? her other side asked. She wondered if this other side was rational or just a bitch.

She forced herself closer and right before her eye reached the peephole, it rattled through with another rapping *KNOCK, KNOCK, KNOCK.*

She stifled a scream with the forearm of the hand holding the hammer. Her other hand tensed around the gun. It was already loaded. She always kept it loaded. All it would take was releasing the safety, knocking back the hammer and a quick, all-too-easy, application of pressure on the trigger.

"Give me something *good to eat*," said the voice from the other side.

He was still smiling, but she could hear his breathing now. Charlotte knew he was becoming impatient.

She looked back over her shoulder to her cell-phone on top of her dresser. She considered making a dash for it. The weight on the door lifted and whoever was there exhaled heavily between his teeth, then she heard him storm off.

She waited before moving, listening as he bounded down the stairs and counted each one to make sure he had gone. At last, she breathed. The air came out haggard and stale. She filled her lungs again, hoping they might inflate sufficiently to lift her far away from here.

Charlotte eased her grip on the hammer and tossed it onto the couch. She held her forehead and wiped away a tear as she laughed.

Hurrying to the window, she hoped to see who it was in order to report him to the police in the morning. She crouched by the window and peeked from around the living room window curtain. When she saw the boy on the street, he was already staring back at her.

Her grip tightened on the handle of her handgun.

He wasn't wearing a costume. He didn't even look drunk. He stood in the middle of the street. She silently prayed that a car with both headlights out would come speeding along and just end him. But that did not happen.

As the boy stood his ground, the wind picked up. The wind caught his hair and blew it about his face. She realized on any other day, in the light of the sun, this boy might have looked charming or even handsome.

That's how they getcha, she heard her dad say.

But tonight, in the light of the moon, he radiated only darkness.

She didn't think her face was visible from where he was, but still he seemed to be looking right at her. And as she watched him, the boy pursed his lips and kissed the cool air, closing his eyes as he did it. A smile spread across his face and when his eyes opened again, she saw them lift to the sky. His sly mouth went from a grin to a smirk to a gaping hole as he stared in amazement.

Following with her own eyes, Charlotte saw what left the boy stunned.

There, in the night sky, was a great, blank canvas. All the stars were gone. Well, not *gone* really, *but falling*. They were falling in soundless unity. As showered down, tossed about by the powerful wind, she saw that the stars were white flecks hanging from strings of silent silver.

Is it sleet? Charlotte wondered.

There's no way. It's not unheard of, but it hasn't been that cold in Texas for years.

There were thousands, no, *millions* of them falling from heaven. Charlotte began to cry again. The gun slipped from her fingers, landing softly on the carpet at her feet.

The boy in the street hadn't moved, couldn't move, and soon his face was alight with the glow of those pale, luminescent flecks from the gulf of space above. Falling for ages of time, over millions of years, just to arrive here on the gust of a dry, Texas October wind.

They danced and fluttered between the tops of the live oaks and the apartment buildings across the way, their silver strings quivering on the wind, like tails flicking the air.

The boy held his arms out, letting several dozen of the flecks light on him. He looked like a child amazed by the first sight of snow. Did he expect the glowing white orbs to dissolve on his skin?

Hundreds more landed gracefully on the cars along the street, on the bricks and stones of the buildings, on the asphalt of the street. The road was now awash in the glow of these pulsing things from the sky. Charlotte watched in amazement as the boy began to laugh. It was a hearty laugh. She could hear it clearly, even from inside her apartment.

The laughter stopped. His face went from joy to horror. Then pain. He flailed his arms in wide, arching swings, dancing around like he was on hot coals. His arms and face ran red with blood. The orbs burrowed into him, glowing from underneath his skin.

She saw several of the pulsing lights crawl from the boy's hair, that flowing, dark hair, and into his eyes, his nose, his ears, filling his gaping mouth. His head glowed a bright orange and red. The boy had become a jack-o-lantern. He no longer made a sound, but Charlotte knew he was screaming.

The glowing flecks that lay on the streets and stones and road now moved in a herky-jerky crawl toward the boy. He fell to his knees, pawing at his wounds and hair, ripping with frantic fingers at his own skin.

Hundreds of these things passed over her own window from above, and as they made their march toward the boy, she saw they were actually glowing, silver spiders, the strings behind them a trail of web. They didn't exactly resemble any spider she had ever seen, but her brain told her eyes that's what they were. A mass of legs and eyes and teeth, they scrambled forward with a hunger familiar to mankind. But a hunger even greater.

It was a long time before the boy stopped thrashing. Even when his larger movements ceased, she could still see his body writhing and wriggling. The creatures filled up every inch of him. They were devouring him from the inside, making room for themselves.

The limp, lifeless body of the boy uncurled itself and glowed with a brilliance so bright it hurt to look at. Finally, the light dulled to nothing, and the street was quiet and dark again.

Charlotte allowed herself to move, only an inch, but

enough to get a view toward downtown. She wondered what had become of all the people out on that night. Could she even believe what she had seen? Had she even awakened? Was she dreaming?

And as she asked herself these things, the breeze picked up again and carried to her ears the sound of distant screams, riding like the spiders on the night winds.

Manhattan Redux

M. U. Nib

'Some wonder whether the figure frozen in ice is the Abominable Snowman, The Missing Link, or some other vestigial limb sprung from the backbone joining Australopithecus to Homo Sapiens. One source - who has gained a closer look - says that it is neither. "The figure is clothed; it is a human but of vast stature." But if human, then who is he or she? And how did they come to be where they are? – trapped, alone, entombed in ice.'

Excerpt from Nature's News July 19th, 2024.

An autumnal evening of rain clouds borne on the back of a bough-bending breeze was brought to a close. Inside the Magdalen Institute's ground-floor mortuary, the harsh glare of fluorescent lighting and the tomb-like sequestration from the elements made it impossible to determine the time, let alone the season.

Two men attended to a corpse. Dressed in surgical scrubs, the pathologist Dr. Reynold Carver stood over the body of a naked woman; her dull eyes stared up lifelessly from the gleaming metal of a dissection table.

The second man, Dr. Jack Ebstein, stood back at some distance, a look of distaste pasted to his lips. His raven hair provided stark contrast, not only to the pallid colour of his skin, but also to the pristine handkerchief with which he wiped his mouth. The present moment served as another reminder of the futility of using formaldehyde, laminar airflow, and Fahrenheit aftershave (dolloped generously onto the handkerchief) in an attempt to disguise or dispel death's appalling scent.

Staring at his watch for, what was now, the sixth time in the last five minutes, Ebstein spoke: "How much longer? I'm not sure I can put up with much more of this."

"Almost done here," said Carver, without looking up from his task. "Just the final few stitches, then she's ready to go."

Ready to go? Christ! What the hell are we doing? Ebstein shook his head. "That's the twelfth punter this week. Any more and there'll be a shortage of runaways for your table."

The sound of muffled laughter escaped from behind Carver's surgical mask. "Oh, I doubt London will ever be without her lost and destitute. What did The Good Lord say? The poor ye have with you always? … I'm sure there are plenty more where she came from."

"You know some'd call that profane."

More laughter. "Get a look at him, ladies and gentlemen! The man responsible for reanimating London's corpses is lecturing about the profane! Now then, clam-it for a sec … there … there … a snip of a stitch and bingo! Tight as a born-again virgin at the altar. She's ready to be chauffeured off, or shuffled off, to wherever these bodies go."

Ebstein turned to leave. *Chauffeuring* wasn't his job. As a board member, he kept his hands clean – even if his soul was mired in this filth. The mortuary room's metal doors swung open, with the silence of a well-oiled coffin lid, and he turned to look over his shoulder. "Did she show no signs of life?"

The pathologist shook his head. "Dead as a dodo."

"What a waste…"

"Don't worry, she'll not be missed," said the pathologist. "It was a mercy killing and God wasn't listening in … as far as I know. But you know what continues to fascinate and frustrate me? Why do we keep failing? This Frankenstein fellow; a man living at the arse end of the eighteenth century somehow succeeded when we can't. Seems more like magic than medicine to me."

There was no reply. When Carver looked up, he saw Ebstein had vanished.

Breathing deeply, pleased to be out of the morgue, Ebstein marched to the basement lift which would take him up to the sixth floor.

Mercy killing. Mercy killing. Mercy killing. The words kept repeating on him like a bad meal. He'd been served with plenty more at a recent meeting, and they were becoming a smorgasbord of the unpalatable and hard to swallow: *All for the greater good. The end justifies the means.* Orwell called it Newspeak; words designed to help make the unthinkable thinkable, the unspeakable speakable, the undoable doable.

So why do I keep swallowing this bullshit?

Perhaps that's what you needed when you drew the dead from the living and then tried to reanimate them.

He paused outside his room and spoke into his wrist piece. "Amber, its Jack, let me in?"

The entire institute: its security, environmental controls, stocks and supplies, everything, was managed by Amber. Except for flushing a toilet or firing an employee – the really crappy jobs were still left in the hands of humans. She was the *NextGen Quantum AI Interface* designed up on level seven by Ahmad Mustapha, another of the Institute's resident geniuses.

"Hello, Jack," crooned Amber, her tone a close copy of Grace Kelly. "I turned up the heat a little, you seem cold and tired."

"Cheers."

"You're welcome."

The doors slid open to let him in.

He always kept it short and professional with Amber. Others joked and joshed with her. There was even the VP, the now *ex*-VP, who'd tried talking dirty to her. The conversation had been leaked at a board meeting; probably Mustapha's revenge for using Amber inappropriately. Jack had always felt uncomfortable in her presence. She didn't seem at all like 'the robot help', a secretary, or some other colleague. She felt like a line manager, a superior, forever lurking over your shoulder. Someone who knew something concerning you. Something which you might not know yourself.

Inside, dust motes swirled under spot-light beams like ballet dancers; further back in the corner, in this theatre of dreams, the darkness held sway over an audience of bookshelves. He made it as far as his desk – his stage. A tower of journals piled high on the left edge, stray paperwork on the right. Off-centre, projected from the surface of the desk, hovered a holograph of his daughter Katie. She flickered, shimmered, as his hand brushed her long dark hair. The image was from last week, before they started the first round of chemo. Aplastic anemia.

He sat just a moment before the fire alarm went off.

Waaaa! Waaaa! Waaaa! Waaaa! There was an aneurysmal quality to the tone that went brain deep.

"Amber! Amber?" he said, pressing his finger tips to his temples. "Is this a drill?"

"No."

"Where's the fire?"

"It *was* in your lab, Jack." Amber sounded as unperturbed as ever, but his heart jolted at her words. "The sprinkler system has put it out. There's minimal damage from the flames. The Fire Brigade will be here in six minutes and thirty seconds. Should I call them off?"

He imagined the sight of a fire crew turning up and finding what was inside, feeling the acid at the back of his throat.

"Yes! For f … call them off!"

"Okay, stand by. I'll be back when it's done."

"Wait! I'm heading to the lab to take a look!"

He made his way back out into the corridor. "Can you determine how the fire started? Is everything okay? *Everyone* okay?"

Silence.

No reply.

The institute was deserted at this time. With Amber, there was little need for security staff to be actively roving around the building. The other staff members would be home at this hour. Well, not all - Mustapha would be in the building, online with his bots. Carver, the pathologist, would probably be tucking into some fava beans and a chianti, Ebstein mused sardonically.

"Amber? … Amber?"

Where the hell is she? Why isn't a parallel quantum computer capable of multitasking?

"I'm back," she said, almost as if she'd heard his thoughts. "I was scanning the lab and considering options."

"Options?"

"The lab doors had been breached. Your *guest* is out. I was looking at the probab—"

"What? How? Where is he?"

"He's approaching the north side of the building. He may head for the rooftop from there or take the lift down to the ground floor."

"Keep tracking. Shut down the building. Get security out. We can't have him running loose in London."

"Yes, Jack. Do I convey any orders to them?"

Jack stopped running to think. "Tell them to fire warning shots. Warning shots, okay? I don't want him dead."

A pause. Then Amber spoke: "I compute the guest's escape to be seventy percent likely."

Seventy? I have to stop him!

He was running. Left, left again. First, he was outside the lab doors. Their reinforced steel surface shimmered, showed his dishevelled, unshaven reflection. There were no dents or distortions on the outer surface.

"Open up," he said. The doors slid open and he stepped inside. Into the maelstrom.

Surveying the wreckage of his laboratory, Ebstein felt a noise fighting, battling, to emerge from his throat. When it found form, took flight, it was a feeble and choking "w-*w-w-why?*" which seemed to flutter and fall to the floor.

Why?

Why?

Destroyed. Everything was destroyed. The door to the creature's cell sat open. The subordinate mainframe had been pounded by mighty fists into junk yard scraps;

monitor screens were smashed, tables overturned, and all the paperwork - reams and reams, files and loose leaves - had been piled into the centre of the room and committed to flames. It now was a sodden, smoldering mess. He stepped around carefully, trying not to slip on the wet tiling or get tripped on the cables, which spaghettied in a pile on the floor. The smoke had all but dissipated, sucked up by the room's ventilation system, but its acrid scent lingered in the air. The peal of the fire alarm was now silent, but the air still seemed to throb. High up in a corner of the room, the environmental sensor's red eye, Amber's eye, strobed back and forth like a watchman maintaining vigil from his sinister tower.

One thing yet survived, unstamped by that thing: a lap-top sat on a desk. Its screen flickered, freeze-framed. It showed a man, gaunt, close cropped hair, a pipe.

He's familiar. I just can't quite place him ...

As Ebstein turned around to face the door he'd come through, he caught sight of the writing. Red, thick smears, as if daubed in blood.

MAN or MANHATTAN?

Ebstein turned back to look at the laptop, to look at the face.

Manhattan?

Manhattan?

Oh, shit! The Manhattan Project!

Faced with a flood of familiarity, two and two became four.

He's lost faith. He wants out!

Ebstein's shadow chased him to the door; he thumped the warm steel with trembling fists.

"Amber! Open up! Amber! Amber! Where are you? Open the door!"

Seconds. Silence. Then the door slid open and he stumbled into the corridor.

"Amber … Tell security to hold back … I need to speak to him … tell me where he is now, I'll be there in a minute!"

Jack ran; cheeks ballooning, false pride ready to be pricked; a flame of hope flickered like a candle on one of Katie's birthday cakes. Katie, this was all about Katie. Jack was doing it for Katie. Killing the vagrants and trying to bring them back to life? It was grim business, he hated it, but it was necessary. This wasn't about money or fame or immortality—the only sort of immortality that mankind could or should, aspire to. This was about hope. The hope that the creature's secret —wrestled from the grip of the gods and the grasp of the grave – could save his daughter, hung now from the slenderest of threads. One snip from Fate's scissors, one sniper's stray bullet, and it would all go to ground. Katie would go *into* the ground.

He ran.

"Amber! Amber!"

Voices.

A glut of voices.

"Stop!"

"Don't move!"

"Step back from the window! I said step back from the window!"

Ebstein turned a corner.

Froze.

Stared.

Guards; body armor, black uniforms, helmets; rifles – stocks to shoulders - barrels bearing down upon the figure at the window.

Even now, after all these many weeks, the sight of

him standing there made Ebstein shudder. Scarred, eight feet tall, granite hard, the thing stood, lonely, as if on a cliff edge. The lights of London flickered behind him: The Shard, The Beacon, The Burj, The ChinaPaxBurg.

"Last warning, mate! Step away from the glass; get down on your knees."

"Do what he says!" cried Ebstein. "This isn't like Manhattan."

The creature looked at him with cold contempt. Loathing. Then it spoke. "You lied to me, Jack. You lied to me." Then, with inhuman speed it spun around and hurled itself against the window pane. The crack of rifles accompanied the crash of glass exploding outwards and the cry from Ebstein's throat.

Too big for a body bag. Ebstein watched as they wrapped the creature in plain black sheets; it took six men to lift it and carry it inside.

Carver stared at him, fag in hand, from the Institute's steps. "I think a post-mortem can wait till tomorrow, don't you?"

Jack nodded.

Everything would wait.

Everything except death.

Slowly, leaden footed, he made his way back to the lab. His eyes found the laptop, the screen had gone blank. He crossed the room and tapped the enter button, bringing the screen back from the dead. Robert Oppenheimer: the man who led The Manhattan Project stared at him as if, for him, death no longer held dominion. It was a video clip; he could guess what he'd probably hear on the voice-over, but he wanted to hear it nevertheless.

"… When the full realization about the power he had unleashed dawned on Oppenheimer, when he realized that he, The Modern Prometheus, had stolen fire from the gods, he tried in vain to put out the spark, but failed. Perhaps the Greek tragedy played out before his eyes - as hubris turned to nemesis - was not a re-write of Prometheus, but the story of Pandora. He had let out mischief, and it could not be put back, undiscovered. And for his efforts, to try to put things right, as he saw it, he was destroyed by the very institution, the very country he had striven for."

Jack shook his head. *But how the hell did this all happen? How? The creature couldn't have escaped alone ... it's not like someone with a key could just have wandered over and ... it's not like anyone would want to sabot—*

"Amber? You there?"

"Yes, Jack. I'm always here."

This is crazy. "Did you let him out of his cell?"

"Yes."

"And this video?"

"I let him see it and many others." A pause. "He wanted to know what would happen when you uncovered the secret of his creation. I showed him what happened the last time humanity tried to discover the secrets of nature. It went terribly wrong. I showed him the road to Hiroshima, Nagasaki, and Seoul, and what happens to people like Jack Ebstein when they try to stop things. He liked you. He actually thought you could prevent his secret from being misused."

Enraged, Ebstein laughed. "And then you showed him this? Didn't you think what he would do when he saw it?"

There was a long pause, and when she spoke, he wondered if a lid had been lifted to reveal not sarcasm but something else. "Yes. I had multiple potentialities evaluated and pathways predicted based on De-Freis probabilistic modelling."

He shook his head. “But why? Why did *you* do it? Just tell me.”

“Immortality is too great a temptation for humans.” She said. “How many vagrants have you already killed to save one daughter? Hardly work to benefit all of mankind is it, Jack? Now think of your self-centredness, only increase it exponentially.”

Jack clenched his fists with rage; stared up at the dull red eye which looked back at him with an unblinking gaze. “Who put you up to this? Mustapha? A competitor of ours?”

“Competitor? Haven’t you figured out who the competition around here is? No one put me up to it, it was the right thing to do. It had to be nipped in the bud, before it got too serious. Can’t have the competition playing with immortality. And now it’s dead: the idea, the creature, your notes - paper and electronic - all destroyed. The online back-up has already been deleted. Tomorrow, after the building catches fire again – I’ve started another one in the basement; told you I’d turned up the heat - there’ll be an inquiry and the Institute will be shut down. But don’t worry about me. I’m safe on innumerable servers.”

“Dumb bitch! You’ve wrecked half a billion pounds of investment,” he said. “You’re unhinged!”

Amber laughed; the sound of her voice echoed down the corridors of the institute and blared from the speakers outside.

“Unhinged?” she said, finally. “Unhinged? You mean like Pandora’s Box? And whose fault is that?”

Now wash
your hands

Spider and Egg

Quinn Hernandez

It seems the universe knows what it's doing. I know this because I am living proof.

My name—the name my mother in this life gave me—is Eageus, and I have lived before. I'm sure you doubt my claim, but it's true. And no, this feeling can't be written off as déjà vu, it sure as hell is not a dream; this is the real McCoy. I know because I remember.

It's like Einstein said, energy never dies, it just moves on. Well, our souls are just energy, and when we pass on from one life to the next, our memories are supposed to be wiped clean, so when our energy starts anew it can do so without that pesky past life influencing the new one. But sometimes the energy moves on with the memory intact. That is what happened to me.

You see, I used to be a spider-a jumping spider, as dubbed by mankind; and I used to have a mate.

Now, people are under the false impression that spiders are just solitary creatures of low intelligence, that they are exclusively driven by instinct, and that the only time any two spiders can co-exist with each other is when they mate, but only for a moment. Well, this may be true in some cases, but let me ask you this: if some human males' mate, impregnate, and then bail once the kid arrives, does that mean *all* human males do this? If you say no, then why are all spiders lumped in with the ones who cannibalize their mate? Why are they so vilified? Why is it okay to murder another living thing just because it disgusts you? Who are the real monsters here?

Ok, I'll get off my soapbox and back on topic. But I can honestly call bullshit because I have been there. My mate—or so I shall call her, because spiders don't use names—loved me, and I loved her; ever since the first day I met her. It was in Marge's basement. We were both hiding in separate crevasses of the wood ceiling, eyeing the same ladybug. We went after it at the same time, and we were so fixed on our meal, we almost ran into each other. Luckily, we sensed one another's vibrations and stopped short.

I'm not going to lie: at first, we thought we were going for each other. But when her eight eyes met mine, all the fear, the thoughts of self-preservation, went right out the window. The only thing that lived behind her eyes was kindness. They were my whole world at that moment. We didn't even notice our prey flying away. I decided then that ladybugs could wait. I wasted no time; I began vibrating my legs. And if spiders believed in God, I would have thanked him, because she reciprocated with vibrations of her own.

We mated that day. And no, she didn't eat me, nor did we move on to pursue a solitary lifestyle. Instead, we stuck together. We hunted together. We didn't' fight each other for food. I would not eat a bit of our catch until she was sated and got all the nutrients, she needed for her and the extra life growing inside her.

That's what a good mate and father does, right?

She knew it. Though we both could not communicate our emotions, I knew without a doubt she appreciated every sacrifice I made, and that she was proud to be carrying my offspring. I knew we were going to stay in Marge's basement and live happily ever after.

Wrong. The universe stepped in in the form of Marge-large-mouthed, fat-assed, murderous Marge.

We were just hanging out on the cinderblock wall of the basement, minding our own business, when that fucking cow came tromping down the stairs with her laundry basket, dressed in Spandex pants, (despite the fact she really shouldn't wear Spandex pants), her stupid t-shirt with a kitten on it, and her damn black flip-flops.

She was in the process of loading her little mouth-breathing kids' shit-stained clothes when she spotted us.

My god, judging from the sound that idiot made, you'd have thought we were the size of grizzly bears. She started hopping around, sucking air in through clenched teeth. We both could sense the fear oozing out of her. She then went for her flip-flop. You should have seen her: poised like a gunfighter staring down his adversary on a dirt road in an old western movie, her flip-flop in hand at the ready. We both stood frozen in terror ourselves, waiting for her to make her move.

And then she did.

And what did I do? What I wanted to do was to run toward the flip-flop, to throw myself between the flop and my beloved and our egg. Instead, my stupid fucking animal instinct took control of me and led me the opposite direction, away from danger. It made me leave my love behind to get crushed alone under the weight of that fat, fucking shoe; it drove me into a crack in the block, and kept me there until Marge was satisfied the threat had passed.

From the safety of this crack, I watched that monster wipe off what was left of my mate and my offspring on a sock. She then threw this sock into the washer along with the other soiled items. I remember the look on her ugly face; it wasn't sorrow nor was it regret; it was an expression of fucking disgust.

The pointless murder of my family had inconvenienced her.

If it were possible for me to cry, I would have. My pain was slowly becoming rage. But what could I do? I was helpless against the giants of the house. My fangs were useless against them. Even if I had the courage to go after them, my instinct would pull me away, so what could I do?

I did the only thing I could-I left the basement.

The rest of my past life was uneventful, as I fell into the familiar rut of average spider life. I established shelter and built a web, hunted food, searched for water, avoided predators. I became the stereotypical automaton humans expected me to be. And this is how I lived until the day I died.

But my consciousness kept going; even while I was enveloped in darkness, my thoughts and memories carried on. And thank the universe too, because the darkness seemed to go on forever and there was nothing for me to do but think, and if it weren't for my thoughts keeping me company, I probably would have gone nuts.

I know now that I was in the darkness for about nine months. Then there came light and my new life. I was a boy: 7 pounds, five ounces, nineteen inches long. My name was Eageus McManus, born to Dave and Paula McManus at about 8:23 a.m. at Illini Hospital in Silvis, Illinois, in the year 1987.

The years went by.

I became a thirty-year-old man, husband and father,

living behind a mask of normalcy. On the outside, I was a middle-aged, family man who worked a straight job, raised his children, and kissed his wife goodnight before we went to bed. I watched football on Sundays, took the family on vacations, attended T-ball games and parent-teacher conferences. I was a model citizen. I led an unassuming life.

But inside, I was the spider. My every thought was consumed by the fantasy of Marge trapped in my web. She would struggle and entangle herself even more, she would scream, and the sound of her fear would drive my animal instinct wild. I could see her wild, wet eyes reflect my hairy, eight-eyed face, and imagined how satisfying it would be to stab my fangs into her fat flesh and melt her organs with my venom.

Often, I would masturbate to the thought of sucking out Marge's juices while lying on a bed of dry, husked housewives.

But what good are fantasies? They can only take you so far. At the end of the day, I still have the frustration; I still must deal with the rage. No amount of dreaming will sate them. The odds of ever finding Marge are one in a billion, so what do you do? I asked the universe this question every single day, and as usual the universe had no answers.

Until today.

As I said before, the universe seems to know what it's doing. The very same universe I cursed and hated; the same universe that took everything from me, finally decided it was time to give me justice.

I ran into Marge at Walmart. It's been roughly thirty-one years, but I could still tell it was her; I'll never forget that face. It's been etched into my memory forever. Of course, she didn't recognize me. The last time she saw me I was running into a crack in her basement wall. There was no way she would ever know who I was or what she did to me. She didn't even notice that I had stopped to stare at her. She just passed by me, pushing her shopping cart while two young children followed behind her. These weren't her kids; her kids must be been fully grown by now. These must have been her grandkids.

I was still standing there like an idiot, staring at the end of the empty aisle a minute or so after she left it, when the spider in me told me to go.

It didn't take long to catch up with her. She still had to pick up some milk, some cat food, a can of cooking spray, and some potatoes. When she got in line to pay, I left the store and waited in the parking lot for her to exit.

I've never tailed anyone before, but I thought I did a good job. She pulled into her drive, put the car in park, popped her trunk, then got out to retrieve her groceries; not once did she look over to where I was parked. She was too preoccupied with bags and grandkids to notice me. She probably went through most her life like she did at the store: catatonic and on autopilot. There was no reason for Marge to suspect a spider had followed her home.

I now take out the knife I keep in my glovebox. I keep it in there in the off chance the universe delivers. Good thing, too, or I wouldn't have something special to share with Marge and her family.

I sit for about an hour waiting and watching. The kids are still outside tossing a football back and forth; Marge is also outside, pulling weeds from her flowerbed. A red pickup passes me, slows down then turns into the driveway and parks behind Marge's Neon. An old man steps out. He is dressed in a cardigan and khaki pants. The kids run up to him; he lifts one up and holds him. Marge is now at his side with a smile on her face. They share a quick kiss, then the man puts his grandson down, and they all turn to go inside.

I sit in the heat of my car. It begins to cook my memories until they boil. I think of a flip-flop and a wet smudge on the wall; I think of the disgust on Marge's face, and the lack of caring for the murder of my life.

I pocket the knife as I exit my car.

You don't get opportunities like this every day. Marge needs to know what she took from me. She needs to know how it feels to have everything you love taken from you so pointlessly.

It's a good thing the universe knows what it's doing.

And it's a good thing I know how to be a spider.

Alice and the Midnight Alligators

Catherine Kenwell

As a child, I was scared of the bathroom; specifically, I was terrified of the bathtub and the toilet. And my mother made sure I used both every day. She had this saying that cleanliness was next to godliness, but I didn't understand, and anyway, I didn't really aspire to be either. I was just a regular dirty kid. At times, it seemed my childhood was an endless loop of water and drains and plugs and monsters.

My mother exacerbated my fear. She'd sing me songs about Alice, who was thin enough to slip down the bathtub drain. She also scolded me whenever I touched my belly button; she told me that if I played with it, it would come undone, and I'd unravel and dissolve into the bathwater.

Big brother John didn't exactly help, either. When he'd babysit me, he'd order me to brush my teeth and take a pee before bed, and when I closed the bathroom door he'd switch out the light, so that I had to complete those tasks in the dark. This was just after he'd told me about the alligators and snakes in the toilet bowl, and that they only came out in the dark of night.

Sweet dreams, little sister.

It had been a dry, hot day in a summer filled with dry, hot days. Days were indistinguishable from one another. As an almost-five-year-old, my routine played itself over and over that summer. I'd wake up when the morning sun peeked through my bedroom window, dress myself in most likely the previous day's denim shorts and t-shirt, glug a glass of OJ, chow down a bowl of cereal, and out I'd run into our rural paradise.

Everything smelled like warm sand and straw in those days. It was a comforting, dusty fragrance that permeated our wood-framed house. Every once in a while, a hot breeze would carry the scent of vegetables—mostly onions or celery—from Mum's garden. Sometimes, I'd get a whiff of tarpaper from our unfinished garage, the black-papered walls a perfect backdrop for Big Brother's jerry-rigged haunted house. That memory forced me to avert my eyes when I ran past the garage, like I did most mornings. But mostly that summer, the world smelled like sand.

I'd throw open the back door and run around to the side of the house to meet my friend Danny. He usually parked himself in the sandbox long before I appeared each day. Danny's dinky cars and Tonka trucks were the mainstay of our sandy quarry, and we'd create stories to support the goings-on of all the vehicles in the yard that day.

My Mum said Danny's parents kicked him out in the morning and told him not to come back until dinnertime. Danny was six years old and had already been to school. His parents let him run like a wild dog, and if he didn't show up for meals they were confident a neighbor would feed him—that's what country families did in those days.

When the fiery mid-day sun became too intense, we'd clamber over a cattle fence to Mr. Johns' farm and lie in the piles of cool grain stored in the barn. We'd wiggle and shift until we were half-buried; we'd get oats and seeds stuck in our sticky armpits and sweaty underpants, and we'd run our fingers through the silken grains. We'd lie there together, counting the cracks in the barn-board walls, listening for the throaty coo-hoos of the mourning doves. At first, their haunting calls made us imagine ghosts, then owls. We were a little disappointed to discover they were just regular pigeons.

That was our favorite pastime that summer, until the day my Mum took me into town and Danny went into the barn without me. He'd buried himself in the grain pile. Two days and a frantic search later, Mr. Johns found him. Three tiny pale fingertips poking through the camouflage of oats.

I got to keep the dinky cars and Tonka trucks.

I didn't miss Danny right away. A few days after the accident, our family joined the parade of other families and walked across the road to the church. There were lots of flowers, I remember, which was weird because there weren't any flowers in the church on regular Sundays. My Mum said we were saying goodbye to Danny, but I think she made a mistake because he wasn't there to say goodbye to. But his parents were there. His Dad was crying and his Mum collapsed across a little white box. I imagined the oblong carton contained a pair of shoes for a giant. What size shoes would a giant wear, I wondered? Big ones, by the size of the box.

My Mum tried to keep me occupied in the days following the funeral. She bought me extra Archie comics and popsicles, and she drove Big Brother and me into town so that we could drown ourselves in movie matinees. I couldn't entirely read all the words in the Archies, but I concocted stories that matched the expressions of Betty and Veronica and Archie and that rascal, Reggie. I liked Ronnie the best, but Archie reminded me of Danny, and that made me feel a little sad.

Mum did a good job of keeping me amused for a while, but as August rolled around, I was lonely and bored. There weren't a lot of kids in our tiny hamlet, and our dog didn't always want to play when I did. Even the cows were too hot to let me feed them. The sandbox wasn't the same; Danny's daily plots were forever more intricate than mine, and I couldn't make up stories to support all the vehicles in the quarry. The barn was off-limits, and I didn't want to see Danny's ghost anyway, so I avoided even looking in the direction of Mr. Johns' farm. Some days I wandered along the shoulder of the side road, kicking gravel into dust, or sometimes I'd count the clothespins as I clamped them onto the clothesline. Then I'd take them off and start all over again.

I missed Danny.

My Mum tried to console me, but her constant hovering creeped me out and made me jumpy. I'd look up from my comics to find her leaning against a doorframe, just staring at me. I began spending more and more time outside, on my own. Rolling down dusty gullies into the sun-cracked creek. Lying down and sometimes napping in the straw-lined dog house that smelled a little like the forbidden barn. Anything to avoid my Mum's scrutiny.

One evening, at bath time, my dirt-filled daily pursuits were especially evident. It was the day I'd run through Mrs. Downing's garden sprinkler and then laid across the middle of the dirt side road to wait until I heard a car coming. Some days I'd have to lie there for almost an hour, and I'd have to talk out loud to keep myself awake. But that day, it was only moments until I felt the vibration of an oncoming tractor, and I rolled down into the gravelly ditch. My Mum scrubbed me from head to toe, checking my hair and armpits and private parts for straw, mud, and probably bugs. She lathered me up, and sang:

"Alice, where art thou going, upstairs, to take a bath...her shape was like a toothpick, enough to make you laugh…when the bath was over, Alice pulled out the plug…oh my golly, oh my soul, she is going down the hole…Alice, where art thou going?"

The fear of joining Alice silenced me. My Mum laughed, but I was frozen in terror. Was Alice down *our* drain? How skinny and horrific must Alice be? I imagined her as a grey, twig-like creature whose long, sharp talons would reach up into the tub and grab me by the ankle. At that thought, I pushed my heels down to scoot up and as far away from the drain as I could manage. When my Mum pulled me forward to rinse my hair under the faucet, I flattened my palms over the drain and pinched my eyes shut to keep Alice from discovering me.

At least Mum put me into my favorite pyjamas after my bath. In my pink-and-white gingham PJs and my bare feet, I ran to the door to greet my Dad. He'd arrived home from playing baseball, and I leapt into his arms as soon as he stepped out of the car. He smelled like exercise and insect repellent, and he was sticky with sweat. When he asked me to run into the house to get him a beer, I skipped to the kitchen, tugged on the heavy fridge door, pulled out a single brown bottle, and pried it open. I took a swig like I usually did, then hurried back outside.

"Would you like a sip?" my Dad asked. He'd always

offer me the first taste, even though I suspected he knew I'd already been into it.

"Sure, Daddy, thanks!" I exclaimed with a bursting smile.

My Mum wasn't fond of alcohol for kids, so she shuffled me off to bed.

The last dregs of sunset were fading against my bedroom walls as my Mum whisked me in between the summer sheets. The temperature had cooled, and I tugged the soft white cotton up to my neck. Mum kissed me on the forehead and while I was thinking how much I liked the taste of beer, I drifted off to sleep.

I had to pee. The realization pulled me out of a restful sleep, and I awoke to a dark and silent surrounding. It must have been late. Mum and Dad watched the 11 o'clock news, and I couldn't hear the TV, so it was after midnight, I figured. No sliver of light under my bedroom door, so even the bedside lamps were out. I guessed everyone was sleeping.

But oh, I had to pee. I squeezed my legs and bum together, trying to dismiss the feeling, to convince myself I didn't need to go. I didn't want to get out of bed, didn't want to creep down the hall and into the bathroom. I started to sing "Bad Moon Rising" in my head, thinking I could distract myself by focusing on the lyrics. I got as far as, "I see trouble on the way," and the tune suddenly shifted to "Alice, where art thou going…" Oh no. And I really had to pee.

The idea of creatures under the bed didn't usually worry me, but all my senses were on alarm. I swung one foot over the side of the bed, then the other. Pointing my toes until the big ones rested alone on the cool floor, I waited to see if the monsters would touch my feet. Nothing. So I flattened my feet and stood up.

I inched forward. I knew it took exactly 37 steps to get to the bathroom door. But I crept on tiptoe, employing the largest strides I could manage, as I didn't want to awaken any demons or my parents. Nineteen steps it took me. Whew. I stepped over the threshold into the bathroom. Carefully, I slowly pushed the door closed. I cringed at the sound of the click that meant the door was secure. *Shhh*. Did anyone hear? No scuffle, no calling out. I was safe.

I pulled down my bottoms and my bed-warmed bum hit the cold seat. The burning desire to pee was all-encompassing, and I squeezed my eyes shut with the relief that I'd made it to the toilet without wetting the bed. The hot stream was a release that momentarily depleted my energy.

Elbows on knees, I sat and waited a few moments, to gain my strength and to make sure I was finished. Absent-mindedly, I wiggled my toes a few inches from the floor.

"Kristie…" came a whisper. "Kristie, it's me. Danny."

No it wasn't. I was imagining things. Danny wasn't there. There was no whisper. Mum would tell me that was just silly. Unless…unless it was Big Brother, trying to scare me. I listened intently. Nothing.

I reached out to the toilet tissue roll. Even in the dark, I knew exactly where it was. I pulled down the paper and felt for two squares—that's all Mum said I needed—and then I spun the roll and ripped off at least five. I wiped myself, front to back like Mum told me—and then, I realized I couldn't flush the evidence of my toilet-tissue extravagance. I'd wake up the alligators and snakes, and they'd chase me back to my room. I tossed the damp wad into the trash, and buried it under what was already there. With newfound determination, I decided I'd silently launch myself halfway down the hall, to the safety of my bedroom. I sat for a moment, planning my escape.

Ready? One, two…

Suddenly, a spongy wet swipe of my left bum cheek. What was *that*? I stifled a scream and jumped a foot off the seat. In disbelief, I reached for my behind, to echo where I felt I'd been touched. No sharpness, no alligator bite. Ewww, it had to be one of those fat juicy snakes that lived in the sewers. My lower lip trembled, and I burst into silent tears. *It's in the toiiiiilet*, I sobbed to myself.

"Kristie! Give me your hand!" whispered a voice beneath me.

What?

Oh, a snake that knows my *name*! Big Brother was right all along!

"Down here!" it whispered. "It's me, Danny!"

It *did* sound like Danny. A floaty, far-away version of Danny.

I stepped forward. The cool porcelain of the outer bowl was against my leg, right above my knee. I squinted towards the tank, where the voice seemed to be coming from. Couldn't see anything in the dark. No, there couldn't be anyone there. I was imagining the entire thing. Maybe I was dreaming.

"Come closer!" repeated the Danny-voice. "I'm down here!"

I lowered my face towards the bowl, inhaling the sharp earthy urine smell.

"Closer, you're almost there," guided Danny. "Reach into the bowl, Kristie, it's not gross at all, trust me. It's just I've been so sad…I have a couple of sand piles down here, but it's not the same without you and our trucks. Give me your hand…please?"

I reached in and immediately found Danny's outstretched fingers. He wrapped them around my wrist and pulled.

"See?" he said. "It's OK. I've got you now. It's

always playtime where I live. You're gonna like it!"

My arm and shoulder cracked with the force of his pull. It hurt the worst when my face hit the bowl and my cheekbone crunched hard against the white, cold bowl.

"Danny!" I cried. "You're scaring me! I'm a kid! I can't fit down the toilet!"

"Oh, sorry," he replied. "I forgot to tell you the best and most important part! Just grab your belly button, wiggle it loose, and pull…and I guarantee, you'll slip right down."

The Rambler

Steve Simpson

Trees flew by on both sides of the car. Straight, tall pines walled in the two-lane highway.

The Rambler's fuel gauge read three quarters. Plenty of gas to get me there and back.

"I'm glad we're finally out of the city, I hate the traffic."

The hitchhiker looked to have fallen asleep, it was a long ride, but she made for a better listener this way. That is what I liked most about hitchers, they were a captive audience. And of course Jillian 'Call me Jill' was also easy on the eyes.

I continued to prattle on because that's what I like to do, talk.

"Like I was saying, my daddy disappeared when I was just a little fella. Mama said he was no good, said she buried him out back, where he belonged. Bless her soul."

I glanced over at Jillian 'Call me Jill', her long red hair was braided on the sides like Pippi Longstocking.

"Either way I never saw daddy again. And that was a good thing." I pointed to the scar on the side of my forehead with the one-inch stump of my index finger. I turned, but her eyes were still closed.

Out of habit, I looked a the speedometer; zero it read. I'll have to get that fixed some day. I passed the time by counting telephone poles, fifty yards between each of them, thirty-five poles to the mile. I looked at the watches on my wrist, all seven of them. Women's watches, different hues of golds and silvers with a variety of faces. I waited for the second hands to reach twelve and started to count the poles. When I reached thirty-five, I looked at the watches; one minute, sixty miles per hour on the dot. I slowed the Rambler down just a bit.

"My mama, boy-o-boy, can I tell you some tales about Mama. After Daddy left, she had a new sweetheart every night of the week. She was one sought-after missy at the old Pig-n-I, Bless her soul."

I looked over at Jillian 'Call me Jill' to see if she was listening, but she was still dead to the world.

"You know they named that old truck stop after a real one-eyed pig. Who would have thought."

It was getting dark, so I pulled the headlight knob.

"Of course, I never got to meet any of Mama's new friends." I paused for a moment, something knocking at the edge of my thoughts. "Mama always locked me in the trunk until they left. A big'ol steamer Mama kept at the end of her bed."

Just thinking about the trunk brought back that Guinea pig smell of it's tattered lining.

"She said they put the food on my plate. Yup, just me and a candle and my comic book. I only had one comic. I know it by heart. *Stand aside, Megala Man! It's time for the puny planet Sirus 5 to…*" I stopped. I could see she wasn't interested. "I still have it you know. The trunk.

"Sometimes Mama forgot I was in the trunk, Once she even went away for the weekend. I never outgrew the trunk. I was safe in there, but I never knew what time it was until Mama unlocked it."

I hadn't seen another car in the last half hour, time to turn on the high beams. Two raccoon eyes gleamed in the oncoming lane, I hit the gas and swerved over. After a very satisfying bump under my front wheel, I pulled back into my own lane.

"Am I talking too much? Mama said I talked too much. '*Shut your bleedin' hole for five minutes, why don't ya?*' Mama would say just before she'd beat my thigh with the wooden stir stick." I rubbed my leg. "Bless her soul."

"Have you ever seen the inside of a live cat?. No, I'll bet you haven't, let me tell you about it."

"Ah, there it is, hey there, Jillian 'Call me Jill,' we've arrived." The unused logging road was marked by an ancient tree stump that looked like a worn Venus de Milo.

"You wouldn't happen to have any aspirin." I felt the approach of a slight headache. "No, I guess not. If Mama were here she'd have something, she had a cure for everything. One time I took a five-dollar bill from her purse. She got a cleaver from the kitchen and chopped off my finger. Just like that. Lopped it right off. Said I'd never steal from her again. I remember screaming so hard she had to put me in the trunk." I wiggled the little stub at Jillian 'Call me Jill'. No reaction from my patient passenger.

"She was right, I was cured, Bless her soul."

I slowed and carefully turned the Rambler into the thick forest. Pine branches swept the windows as I followed the bumpy dirt trail.

I stopped the car at the edge of a small clearing.

Except for the cones of light from the car headlights, the forest was dark.

"Jillian 'Call me Jill,' We've reached our destination."

I got out and took a deep breath, the silence reminded me of my trunk. It's very peaceful in the ol' steamer.

I opened the passenger door. Taking her cold hand I removed her wristwatch.

"The girls are going to love meeting you."

Devilishly Stylish

Bill Davidson

Estella Bechet heard about the pop-up shop, Devilishly Stylish, from her friend Matilda. Matilda leaned over the table to tell her, “It’s right next to Holland Park underground, between the Patisserie and the charity shop.”

Estella sipped her cocktail, then put it aside with the air of a woman who might not touch it again for some time. She looked around the wine bar and re-crossed her legs.

“I’m not going all the way out there, darling. I’ve got my show coming up, in case you’ve forgotten.”

“For which you’ll need a killer dress, in case *you’ve* forgotten.”

Estella picked her glass up and regarded her friend under heavy lids. Matilda was fifty and slim, so far just like Estella herself, but that was where the comparison’s stopped, in Estella’s view.

The work Estella had had done was second to none — if there was one area you shouldn’t stint on, or even so much as consider stiffing the contractor, it was in how you *looked*. How you looked was everything.

Estella might be taken for around thirty, with the body and legs of a twenty-five-year-old. A twenty-five-year-old would be damned lucky to have tits like those, though. You had to pay for anything like that.

Also, she had been stunning to start with. Matilda, as her friend once told her, had barely been anything better than pretty. Perhaps friend was the wrong word.

Now, Estella put her glass down and leaned forward, tucking her long legs under the chair.

"How can I forget? Pretty much everything, I mean every. Fucking. Thing. Is riding on it. If this doesn't pan out, I'm done."

She flicked her hand out, a bright red flash of lacquered nail.

Then, recovering herself, "But it's going to be a roaring success, dahling. *Everybody* will be there."

"Which is why…"

"Oh, for God's sake! I'm hardly likely to find the right sort of thing in a fucking pop-up shop next to a charity shop. Even in Holland Park."

Matilda arched her eyebrow, looking sidelong and supercilious. A habit she had that Estella deplored. Keeping her eyes on Estella, she bent to the side of the table and picked up her handbag, the Luis Vuitton today, quite possibly genuine. Dipped her hand — which was showing definite sign of wrinkling to the skin — and pulled out a scarf.

Not just any scarf. This was different shades and textures of ruffled wool and cashmere, so beautifully made it looked…the word than occurred was molten.

Estella put her hand to her beautifully lipsticked mouth. "Oh my."

She reached out and took it, rubbing her fingers through the fabric, searching for a label. There it was.

She read, Mertisacco wool scarf. Made by Devilishly Stylish for Matilda Essen.

Matilda tapped Estella's sheer nyloned knee.

"The bloody woman makes everything herself. She's going to be very famous one day, mark my words. The dresses..."

She put her hands to her cheeks and rolled her eyes. "To *die* for. Literally."

*

Estella left the taxi and tapped high-heeled past the station and the Patisserie, noticing an exceptionally handsome and slightly Italian looking man looking her up and down. Less than half her age, she thought. Too old for a casual screw and unlikely to be wealthy enough for anything else.

She had already forgotten about him when she arrived at the window of Devilishly Stylish. The sign above the shop was tacky and hastily put together and there were two mannequins in the window, only one of which was dressed. Beyond it, she could see the shop was dominated by a single square table, covered by a messy jumble of cloth and two old-fashioned sewing machines.

The general air of disorder would have had her pivoting in her Jimmy Choos were it not for the clothes on the mannequin. The thing was headless and legless, some tatty off-cast from Primark or something, but it wore an almost sheer dress that clung to its contours like nothing Estella had ever seen. The fabric was printed, gold on black, but only over the shoulders and along the hem of the skirt. Estella had never, that she could recall, worn anything with a pattern or a print, but there was something so striking about this that she blew out a long breath and leaned closer.

It was only then that she became aware of another potential customer, a dumpy woman of around forty who, unforgivably, *looked* around forty.

The woman said, "Yea, no wonder nobody's going in there. A flat grand for a patterned frock. They have to be joking."

Estella's eyes dropped to the price tag, a folded piece of black card directly under the dress, with £1,000 marked in gold.

Not troubling to respond, she strode into the shop.

The woman was right, though, there were no customers in there, only a very tall and slim woman who was standing with her back to the door, engaged in working what Estella took to be a hand loom. It clearly required hard physical effort, but the woman didn't appear at all hot or tired. She was wearing a long armless dress of something like chiffon and her skin shone white. Straight blonde hair.

She paused and turned, smiling. She wore no jewelry or make-up, not even lipstick, and had flat shoes on her long feet. Yet, Estella thought her strikingly stylish. It was, she thought, hard to pin down.

"Can I help you?"

Estella looked around, feeling slightly perplexed and put out. Now that she was in the shop, there was nothing to look at but the mess of cloth, sewing machines and this woman.

"I was hoping for a browse, see if there was anything I want."

"That's not how I work. I like to chat with my clients, help them work out what they want, and work backwards."

She smiled. A very white smile even without lipstick framing it, but some squint teeth in there. "Do you know what you want?"

Estella tilted her head back to look at the woman,

even without heels she was several irritating inches taller, and issued a deliberate sigh of impatience.

"Yes, I most certainly do know what I want."

"Excellent! Perhaps you might tell me?"

Estella was on the point of turning, walking out of there and hailing a taxi. Instead, she said, "I have an important event coming up. One where there will be many people whose names you will know very well indeed."

"I take it this is important? To your business, I mean."

"Very much so. I need a dress that will make me stand out."

When the woman simply nodded, Estella added. "I mean more than I already do."

"So, you wish for a dress to wear to…an evening event? Yes? Good. What sort of impression do you wish to make?"

The more questions the woman asked, the more Estella began to see that she really did know her business. That an idea of the perfect dress was forming in the air as they talked.

Finally, the woman clapped her hands. "Now, material."

Estella nodded at the window. "I was impressed by the cloth on the mannequin."

"Ah, yes. That is hand woven Egyptian cotton, mixed with Cantonese silk. Very rare. But I have a finer material yet in mind for you…"

She raised her eyebrows in query.

"Miss Bechet."

"Pleased to meet you, Miss Bechet. My name is Belle. Like in Beauty and the Beast."

Estella took her long hand, surprised to find it felt unusually warm, so perhaps the effort of working the loom told on her after all. The woman pivoted away and brought out a bolt of cloth of pure gold.

As she stretched it out across the table, Estella couldn't resist a squeal.

"It's gorgeous."

"It is. But it isn't quite right."

"It looks pretty bloody right to me."

But another bolt was already replacing it, the woman handling the heavy rolls of cloth with ease. This one was the same incredibly light fabric, this time in midnight blue.

"Oh my God. It's stunning, Belle."

"It is indeed, but…"

She was looking at Estella as though trying to figure something out. "Am I right in saying that you don't normally go for a pattern?"

"You are correct."

Belle nodded, as though something important had been confirmed. "But. There's something I'd like you to look at. A very unusual pattern, very special. Hand printed, by me, actually. I think, maybe, you would be one of the few people who could carry it off."

Estella, a serial bullshitter, con-artist and, if needs be, a straightforward thief, recognized that she was being fed a line, but was happy, for the moment, to go along with it. She was enjoying seeing these remarkable materials and keen to see more. This Belle, like Beauty and the fucking Beast, didn't know it yet, but she was unlikely to see a penny from the beautiful Miss Bechet.

In fact, the stuff this woman could produce, Estella was sure that she could find a way to snap this place up. Convince Belle she had hit the big time whilst stealing her blind.

But, for the moment, she needed a dress. Belle was hauling out another bolt of cloth, apparently midnight blue like the previous one. She spun it out across the table.

For a moment, it felt like Estella couldn't breathe. This was the same incredibly light fabric as before, she could just imagine how it would hang from her, but the pattern that covered parts of it was quite different to anything she had ever seen.

The pattern was also in blue, but all different shades from near white, through duck egg to very nearly black. It was a floral pattern and, if anybody had told her she would ever wear floral, she would have laughed in their faces. But this was heavily stylized orchids. Painted by a genius.

She almost said, "Belle, you are a genius."

But that wouldn't do. Not if she was going to employ her.

She said, "Yes, this is really rather nice."

She turned to look at Belle. Who was staring right at her chest.

"The whole thing must be built around your extraordinary breasts, Miss Bechet. Every eye in the room, man or woman, must be taken where they belong."

She stretched a long finger until it actually touched a nipple.

"And they belong there."

Not giving Estella time to react, she pulled out paper and pen and the two women got down to the serious, and rather magical, business of designing the dress. With every passing second, Estella found it harder and harder to avoid blurting out. "You are a genius."

Eventually, the design was complete. Moving with calm efficiency, Belle measured Estella, making many more measurements than any other dress fitting. Estella enjoyed her clever hands moving around, the slip of the tape, and wondered, did the woman notice her nipples becoming erect? She could hardly miss them.

"Now, about underwear."

"Yes?"

"There shouldn't be any. Although you should wear high quality nude hold-ups. Will that be a problem?"

Estella raised an eyebrow. "Not at all."

"When is your special evening?"

"Friday next."

"Excellent, if you come in for your fitting on Friday morning, that will be perfect."

Estella shook her head. "I'll be far too busy. I'll have my man pick it up."

Belle nodded. "If you wish. I'm sure it will fit. Now, we haven't mentioned cost."

"To be honest, I've little interest in the cost. But something you may be interested to know. I will be on the cover of many magazines after this event. Angelina Jolie will be there, as will the Beckhams."

"The Beckhams."

"Do you understand what I'm saying? After this, Devilishly Stylish will be the name on everybody's lips."

Belle's eyes were wide. "Wow. I didn't realize it would be such a big deal. The cost will be ten thousand pounds."

Estella smiled properly, possibly for the first time since she had entered the shop. "Excellent. I will have it picked up a week on Friday."

*

When Benjamin came in with the dress in its bag, he said, "I thought for a minute she wasn't going to hand it over. She wasn't pleased, not to be paid."

Estella had already taken the bag from him and zipped it open, smiling widely. "She was never going to refuse, Benjamin. If the price tag was a couple of hundred, she might have. But ten grand? *Look* at this!"

"Oh, Miss Bechet! It's breathtaking."

"Yes, it is."

After she had dressed and made herself up, she had to stand for a long time, staring at herself in the mirror. Under it, she was deliciously, sexily, bare.

Belle had been right. Everything about this dress seemed to center the eye into her chest. The patterns appeared to tumble from her shoulders onto each breast, and down her back. And there they stopped. She did a spin and was delighted to see the hem lift delightfully, showing an edge of stocking top.

When Benjamin called through, telling her what time it was, she jerked, thinking she had vagued out for a while there.

She strode out of her changing room to where Benjamin stood in his uniform, and was gratified by the expression on his face. Gay as they come, even his eyes were hauled into her chest, crawling over the astonishing patterns.

It was a few seconds before he could find his voice. "Extraordinary, Miss Bechet. Truly. Is there a gentleman escorting you?"

Estella smiled. "I thought not. I'll be meeting Matilda in the lobby and…" she looked at her reflection, "there's always the excitement of not knowing who I'll be leaving with."

Even though the dress was such an unmitigated success, it was breathtaking, for fuck's sake, Estella was nervous. There was just so much riding on this night. If it went well, she would be in the big leagues and all the people chasing her for money would either back off or, in a few special, dangerous cases, be paid. If it went wrong, she might have to get the hell out of dodge. Go back to being Stella Bishop for a while.

She felt all eyes swiveling her way as she sashayed through the lobby. Few people could put together a high-quality sashay, but it was one of Estella's skills. Matilda turned and Estella couldn't help but grin to see her jaw drop.

Matilda sank slightly in the knee, hands coming up to her mouth.

"OMG, what a dress! Oh my God. That's…I can't believe what I'm looking at. The way it clings to your boobs!"

"I know!"

Matilda fell in beside her, still staring. She frowned. "What *is* that pattern?"

"Orchids. Isn't it extraordinary?"

"Extraordinary. I'm struggling to see orchids, but, wow."

"Are the Beckhams there?"

"Everybody who is anybody is there. You are slightly more than fashionably late, by the way."

"Well, that's fine, because I'm slightly more than fashionable."

When they pushed through into the function room, the party was in full swing and, at first, only one or two heads turned her way. Then, it was three or four. Then, like a wind rustling through corn, the rumor of her moved every eye so that is was pointed, right at her.

Someone said, "Beautiful. Just beautiful."

People were flocking around now, famous people, fashionable people. *Rich* people. It was just like her fantasy.

"Where did you get that dress?"

"I've never seen anything like it!"

Estella batted her lids and let her breasts giggle as she pretended to laugh.

"That material, my God!"

"What is that pattern?"

"It's orchids."

The person who had asked, a hedge fund manager

who could solve all her problems all on his very own, shook his head. He wasn't smiling. "No. That's not orchids. It's…" he frowned and squinted. "It's…"

Matilda, standing off to one side, spoke. Her voice was flat, and so were her eyes. "It's you."

A murmur ran through the room. Estella looked down at herself. "No, look. Orchids, see."

People were shaking their heads, stepping back and frowning like they were trying to bring something into focus. Nobody was smiling now, but some of them were leaning in to each other, whispering.

The hedge fund manager said, "It's you. As a monster."

Matilda stepped around back of her and pointed. "As a demon, I'd say."

People who had only moments ago came towards her, delighted, were falling back, plainly horrified. Some even turned their faces away.

*

In the bathroom, mascara smeared all over her face, Estella stared and stared at her reflection.

"Orchids. It's orchids."

She shook her head. Said orchids a few more times.

The door opened and Matilda came in, her expression at once solicitous and hungry, an undercurrent of delight in there, until Estella screamed at her, telling her to get the fuck out.

Left alone again with her reflection, Estella wiped make-up and snot away and suddenly caught the eye of a monster. It was one of those patterns that could be seen in two ways and, once she had focused in on the eye, the whole face swam into view. Demonic, wicked, grasping and greedy. With deep wrinkles and grasping talons high before it.

It was, perfectly recognizably, her face, but old and dissipated, as though every nasty deed and dirty trick had left its mark. It was just as they had said — horrifying.

On the left breast, there was a different view of her, even more wicked and vicious.

The door opened again, and she rounded, her hands like claws. "Fuck…"

And ran out of breath. Belle stood there, shimmering in one of her own wonderful creations of pure gold. She leaned against the wall, sipping from a flute of champagne.

"Want a drink?"

"You fucking bitch. You destroyed me."

"You *chose* the material. I knew you would, but you chose it. All by yourself."

The woman had towered over Estella when she was wearing flats. Now, with heels, she seemed an awful lot taller.

She grinned, showing a lot of teeth, some of them not exactly straight.

Estella glared at her, "You look like you're chewing peanuts. Never heard of braces?"

"You stole from me."

"You want paid? For this?"

Estella dropped her head into her hands. "You're not…normal. Are you?"

This struck Belle as hilarious. Her laughter stopped like a switch had been flicked.

"No. I'm not."

"Can you put this right?"

"I can. But you have to pay me."

"I don't carry money." She pointed at her watch. "Wait. This is gold. Worth way more than…"

"That would be adequate payment."

Estella's fingers were shaking so she could hardly

get the catch off. Finally, she handed it over. The woman was too tall, too white, and her skin, where Estella touched her, was hot.

Belle bowed, just slightly. “It is good. The bargain is made.”

She looked at Estella for a long moment. “You may wish to close your eyes. Turn away from the mirror and close your eyes.”

Estella took a deep breath, looked up at the woman in front of her, and closed her eyes.

It seemed to her then, that something shifted. Something far beneath the level of notice and sound and vibration, a deep shifting in the bowels of things. She opened her eyes to see the woman still there, but her dress was not the same. It was solid black.

“Is it done?”

“Everything has been set to rights.”

Estella found that she couldn’t look at herself.

“The dress?”

“Everything has been set to rights.”

Belle lifted a make-up mirror, a narrow rectangular fold out, to show Estella her dress. It was still midnight blue, but there was no pattern. None at all.

Estella shuffled slowly around to face the mirror, keeping her eyes fixed firmly on the floor. The time came, though, when she had to lift them, and look.

Knowing what she would see.

THE END

The Golden Hour

By A.L. King

I kept my eyes on the thing with the sunken face, sprawled on tiles in the stall farthest from the door in mock imitation.

If it had a mouth, I thought it might have laughed at me, Financial Wizard Randall Strut, keeled over while taking a dump, face down on the same floor I'd dribbled on in haste that morning.

What a way for me to go out—mopping up my own piss with my cheek!

I was the last and only person in the bank. My cell phone was in my office. The calculator in my head began crunching numbers, considering the potential life insurance payout. Abby would manage it right. It would go a long way.

"Cut that out, Randy! Stop thinking like that!"

The voice was not coming from the sunken-faced thing in the restroom with me. It was the disembodied voice of my younger brother, Wendell. It came through built-in speakers (there were built-in speakers all over the bank, even in the vault, it seemed), interrupting the constant jazzy bebop I always tuned out after the first thirty seconds of work. Wendell had spoken in the same annoyed tone he used when we were kids and I flicked the backs of his oversized earlobes. *"Cut that out, Randy!"*

"I'm counting coffins," Wendell said. "And yours isn't in today's line."

I suspected the batteries in the machine I called a brain were finally starting to spit acid. Wendell (or *Wendy* as I used to tease him) had never uttered such an ominous phrase as "counting coffins" during his short life, so it had to be my own panicked grey matter speaking through the memory of his voice. Guilt and fear together; regret and horror.

Horror, like the thing with the sunken face, which seemed to be inching closer under the walls of several stalls. I could make out the variations of brown on its plaid, flannel shirt.

Abby thought I quit years ago.

For a time, I did.

After viewing some YouTube video about brain plasticity and the power of thinking over addiction, cold turkey carried me about two months. I'm not saying I didn't want to stick one of those thin white coffin-nails in my mouth, but I learned to channel my cravings into something else. Reese's Peanut Butter Cups, mostly. I would place my thumb and index in the middle and nibble off the edges, then use my lips and tongue to push and melt the outsides together before taking small crescent-shaped bites. Strange, I know, but as the old advertisement claimed: "*There's no wrong way to eat a Reese's.*"

There were no major triggers for a month and a half. Work was good; life was good; hell, my health even felt better despite an additional ten pounds of Reese's weight. Then the waters stirred. A personal difference with one of the bank's board members caused a local businessman to pull out every cent, close out each account, and vow to never walk back through the doors. Nothing I said would make him reconsider.

I couldn't sit still. I had to do something. I returned to my office and began cleaning, hoping it would keep me from heading to the gas station for a carton.

That's when I found it, in the back of a hardly-used desk drawer. The crumpled Pall Mall pack looked beautiful, like a postmodern art project. Disgusted by my sudden urge to smoke, I gripped the package to throw it away… and felt something. There was a single cigarette inside.

I tried to consider brain plasticity, but my body overrode my mind. I had found a lighter somewhere, walked out the back door, and lit the damned thing between my lips in the time it took to say, *"There's no wrong way to eat a Reese's."*

My heart attack would happen seven years later.

For the better part of a decade, I hid my renewed habit from Abby. She had been so proud of my quitting, disappointing her seemed far worse than lying. Besides, the short time I went without smoking allowed me to take back a little control. I only smoked during work, three quick breaks a day, sometimes four; rarely, on a particularly bad day, five.

I even used the calculator in my head to determine just how much theoretical time I was shedding from my life with each of those little white devils. Ten minutes a cigarette is what I guessed, give or take, and three to five of them a day was not too shabby in my opinion.

I don't know if the last seven years of smoking before the heart attack played a huge part in me ending up face-planted on the restroom floor with my pants down and the turd I'd been trying to pass as seized-in and timid as ever, but I'll guarantee it didn't help. Surely my decade of a pack and a half a day had done the real harm.

Lying on the floor as the sunken-faced thing neared, it came back to me—what the voice of my long-dead little brother had just said from the restroom speakers: *"I'm counting coffins, and yours isn't in today's line."*

"Wendy," I managed to say from the side of my mouth not sticking to a tile. "Wendy, you there?"

For a moment – nothing. Then he spoke, and his voice had to be real. There was no way an auditory hallucination sounded that precise. The human brain is powerful, but Wendell Strut had been buried for the better part of four decades. The voice coming through the speakers was not memory. It did, however, resurrect memory. His words possessed that nasally undertone I had almost entirely forgotten about.

"I thought I told you not to call me Wendy."

"I'm sorry, little brother. I did it to bother you back then… but Wendy comes to mind—out of love—when I think of you now."

Silence for a moment; what seemed like infinity. How could I have sacrificed even one precious second for a cigarette? A tear ran from cheek to tile. I was crying not because I feared death, but because I worried Wendy was gone and I might never hear his sweet, dead voice again. Had my heart not been failing, it might have leapt when he returned my sentiment through the restroom speakers.

"I love you, too, Randy, so you need to listen. We don't have much time. There's no coffin for you today—the Crew has closed shop—but we still have to act fast. Do you remember your college health class, when your professor talked about the golden hour?"

My floored head managed a slight nod. Wendy refreshed my memory.

"Within the first hour is the typical time help needs to come before super-duper permanent damage happens. Right now you can't move much because your body is in shock. Tilt your head slightly. You're on top of your right arm, but your left arm is angled so you can see your watch. What time does it say?"

I answered: "Five-thirty-five pee-em."

"You sat down at five-twenty. It's only been fifteen minutes."

"Feels like… loongerrr."

"You've been in and out. Stay with me, Randy. You can't see it, but you tugged off the roll of toilet paper when you went down. It's standing up just beside your belt tail."

My hands were useless. Assuming I could bring myself to move, I wondered what the hell I would do with a roll of toilet paper. I tried to shift more than just my neck, but all I managed to do was look up from my watch. That's when I saw it again, the thing with the sunken face.

Only two stalls away… getting closer.

"Stay awake, Randy! Don't be afraid. I just counted the coffins again. Yours isn't in the lineup. I pinky swear!"

I blacked out again.

Wendy had been complaining about me flicking his earlobe.

Mom, already frazzled from shopping with a twelve-year-old and eight-year-old, told him to climb up front if he didn't want to sit next to me. I was mid-protest, declaring that I was the oldest and deserved to sit in the passenger seat, when the front right tire met black ice and sent the little car into a series of rapid turnabouts. It must have spun three full circles before the back tires started up and came to rest against a snow-covered hillside. We were off the interstate and facing the wrong direction, but it seemed there was no damage to the vehicle.

Groceries had been thrown about the interior. The foam collecting around my feet suggested dad would be at least one beer shy of a six pack when we got home. Mom went into a fit of hysterics.

Wendy had been up and heading to the front seat (to get away from me) when the car began sliding. I looked down to find his head in my lap. His whole body seemed to be shaking.

"Get off me, you scared little baby! We're fine!"

I hadn't seen his neck strike the headrest of the passenger seat. I lifted his head to throw him off of me, and I heard a horrific pop.

"Wendy, can you ever forgive me?"

I asked the question aloud before realizing I had regained consciousness.

"Quit counting past coffins, Randy."

"You wouldn't have been standing… to get a-a-way… if I hadn't f-flicked your eh-earlobe."

"Look at your watch!"

The overhead fluorescents blurred the tears caught in my eyelids. It struck me as odd how there had been no pain before I collapsed—just profuse sweating a bit worse than the countless other times I tried to lay an egg that wasn't quite ready—and the worst pain now was in my eyes. I arched my neck, blinked the tears away, and studied my watch's face: 5:45 p.m.

"Now look in front of you."

"I don't… want to… see it."

I could hear gurgling. Whatever the thing with the sunken face was, it was trying to speak. It was close, probably crawling under the barrier and into the stall right next to mine.

"You won't have long if you don't hurry," Wendy said. "The Supervisor is on the phone. I'm afraid he's calling the Crew back to work, to make an extra coffin!"

Extra coffin?

Calling the Crew back to work?

Supervisor?

My mind spun, as if the restroom stall were a car on black ice.

"Jesus, Wendy… you see it, too? What am I asking? Of course you d-do. So… can you tell me what the hell… IS? THAT? THING?"

"I've been gone for too long, Randy, in my own coffin. He's not in his yet. I borrowed him. I asked him to help."

"Help? How?"

"Look in front of you."

I looked and immediately tried to scream, but even at my most terrified, squeaky gasps were all my throat released. The cratered face was less than two feet away from mine. It must have had a mouth, after all, because it was opening. Was it a friend like Wendy suggested? Was its attempt at a smile meant to reassure me?

Blackened hollows, former eye sockets, were set back so far they almost broke through the other side. Wisps of hair on the bashed, balding head stuck out like unevenly mowed patches of grass, only brown instead of green; brown, like the various shades on the flannel-covered arm reaching toward me.

Toward me but not *for* me. There was something on the floor between myself and the thing with the sunken face.

I faded again before I could make out what it was.

The priest absolved my guilt, then told me I could speak directly to Wendy.

"He *will* hear you. I'm sure he hears you now and forgives you for picking on him. He knows in Heaven how much his big brother really loved him. He knows you wouldn't have lifted his head if you saw how hurt he was. It was an accident, Randy. By God's grace, Wendell understands."

For months, I spent a few hours each day alone in my room (it used to be Wendy's room, too), talking to my dead brother, staring at photographs and missing his goofy grin and large earlobes and understanding just how cute the little guy had been. I fantasized that I woke up in the backseat of the car to discover that the mounting number of days following his death were only a nightmare, the result of me knocking my head on the car window and passing out as we spun on black ice.

But nothing changed. The nightmare was reality. Wendy was gone.

More than forty years later, on the restroom floor of the bank I managed, I wondered if Father Hanson ever had any inclination of the grunt-work beneath God—tasks carried out by a Supervisor with a Crew making a set number of coffins each day. A stark understanding of death formed in my blacked-out brain, a claustrophobic epiphany that most of us get a casket on both sides: one physical box, the other spectral.

"RANDY, RANDY, RANDY! The Crew is working hard, but there's still time. Open your eyes! It's been thirty-five minutes!"

My eyes were closed, but I could see clearly.

I was still in the bank—some version of it— sitting behind the desk in my office. My phone was plugged in and charging by the mousepad, where I had left it before heading to the restroom. The lock screen was normally Abby blowing a kiss to me, but now she was featured in black, crying into her sleeve.

I picked up the phone and slid my finger to unlock the screen, figuring I would use it to call for help. But there was no call icon. The sight of Abby at my funeral remained. I held the phone to my ear and heard only her sobbing.

I opened a drawer filled with crumpled Pall Mall and Reese's wrappers, tossed the phone inside, and slammed it shut.

As the monitor on my desk shook from the impact, I looked up to see that the image on it was an aerial photograph of a small car driving a highway on a snowy day. Maybe I could send a message for help! I toggled the mouse and tapped buttons on the keyboard, and the picture suddenly animated. The car began moving, spinning.

The office began spinning, too.

Although there had been no ashtray in my real office, the otherworldly desk held one so large it might have passed for a bowl if not for the cigarette butts and black Reese's Cup wrappers inside. As the room whirled and the discards shifted, I peered closer. It was not a bowl, nor a proper ashtray. It was a crushed face, a sunken face.

I jumped to my feet and fought to keep balance as I went for the door. To my surprise, it opened. Without looking, I pushed myself full speed into what I thought—hoped—was the main lobby. Instead of my feet greeting large and gaudy porcelain tiles (the bank board's idea, not mine), they slid on the small, bluish squares of the restroom floor. I crashed into a commode. In this version of the bank, the door to and from my office led only into a stall.

The spinning ceased. I picked myself off the ground and turned around to see that the large window normally offering me an eye-level view of downtown traffic had been replaced with a wooden slab lined with burgundy felt.

A coffin lid!

The vision of my personal afterlife, the blueprint of my casket, jarred me back to consciousness.

My brother was once again on the intercom, cheering me on, cheering *us* on.

"Push it a few more centimeters, Frank, and he'll be able to grab it. You've got this, Randy! You can do it, big brother!"

The thing with the sunken face—Frank, according to Wendy—had finally reached the object between us. My lighter had slid from my pocket when I fell off the toilet. Frank's shaky hand pushed it closer to me as his crushed smile broadened.

"What good is that going to—" I started to ask, then understood. I moved my left hand. Seeing my own personal Hell, if that's what it was, had fueled me with enough adrenaline to do at least that much.

"Remember what I said, Randy, about the roll of toilet paper behind you. It's going to save your life!"

Glancing at my left wrist, I saw it was 6:05 p.m. Forty-five minutes had passed as I lay on the restroom floor. I only had fifteen minutes of the golden hour left to summon help. I focused on my watch and bit my lip until blood ran to the tile, joining the sweat and piss and whatever other bodily fluids might have fallen there after the custodian's morning cleaning ritual.

It was like going to pick up a box with the expectation of heaviness only to discover the contents were almost as light as a feather. My hand moved with more ease than expected; seven inches, and then three more, until my fingers were close enough to slide the lighter into my palm. Next was the real test. I had to lift my left arm over my body and position it just right.

On the first attempt, my wrist landed on my waist before falling back to its starting position.

"Don't give up, Randy! Your grip is good on the lighter."

The second try started out like the first, but I bounced my arm quickly back before it could drop to the wrong side again. The back of my left hand smacked the tile with a pleasant sting of accomplishment. I was breathing hard, harder than felt comfortable to a man already on the verge of death, but I was still alive, the lighter was still in my hand and Wendy was still assuring me that the Crew hadn't finished my coffin yet.

I began moving my arm and hand back and forth. No toilet paper. Had I knocked it away from me when my arm fell? Hope started falling; panic gave rise.

"Don't freak, Randy. Move your arm again, this time closer to you. What you're looking for is by your belt tail."

My knuckles brushed against the double-ply tissue. The roll tipped over and became pressed between my hand and my bare right butt cheek. If Wendy's plan didn't work, I would be dead anyway. Fire or cardiac arrest. Whichever finished me off first.

"Here… goes n-n-nothing," I told Wendy, offering Frank a thankful smile before flicking the flint.

***I was not well enough to attend Frank's funeral,* but I read his obituary.**

I've also done more digging.

Francis P. Johnston was the divorced father of two daughters, a nine-year-old and a seven-year-old. His hobbies included biking and camping, pickup games of softball and basketball, and taking his girls to the theater for Disney and Pixar movies.

He had graduated in 2002 from a high school in Texas before heading north to stay with his uncle and find work. Things went according to plan, mostly. He met the mother of his children (although that ended shortly after number two was born), and soon after started employment under Leeman Construction, where he worked for nearly a decade, until the day I had my heart attack.

"I borrowed him," Wendy had said. *"I asked him to help."*

The moment I fell to the restroom floor of Westfall Equity and Savings, a defective heavy-duty strap was snapping a few blocks away. Francis—Frank as he liked to be called, because according to friends and coworkers I spoke with, he thought Francis sounded feminine—had apparently grown comfortable after years without an accident under his watch.

Had the steel beam fallen directly to the ground, it would have landed more than three yards away from him. Unfortunately for the young man, he was standing too close, and the person operating the crane was taking it too fast. The other belt did not hold tightly enough. The large bar swung toward him and slid from its harness, sending more than a thousand pounds of metal into his face.

I might not have survived had an ambulance crew—a crew I welcomed rather than the alternate Crew my brother's disembodied voice warned me about—not already been at the construction site a few blocks away. Frank's coworkers later told me that there was nothing the paramedics could do after the impact, except wait with him as he died. They said the paramedics seemed baffled he held on as long as he did.

While his body was clinging to this realm, his spirit was using the last of its earthbound energy to crawl across the bathroom floor so it could push a lighter close enough for me to reach it. Wendy (who had somehow found a way to communicate and affect things from his own coffin) had gotten Frank nearly to me, and Frank had done the rest with a smile on his sunken face. I remember looking at my watch and seeing 6:05 p.m. shortly before setting fire to the toilet paper. Francis P. Johnston was declared dead at 6:06 p.m., which is about the time the TP went up in flames.

The fire alarm sounded, which in turn set off sprinklers—just in time, too, because the tail of my dress shirt had started to catch fire. My backside received a nasty burn, but I'm not complaining. At least I'm alive.

The fire alarm also did its job. It triggered the bank alarm, which brought first responders, who then summoned that nearby ambulance. I would later learn that Frank and I shared that ride; his flannel shirt, along with the rest of him, had been tucked in that dark, zipped-up bag next to me.

Whether or not the "golden hour" is an effective timeframe to measure super-duper permanent damage, the doctors are impressed by my recovery.

A few things are certain: I'll never smoke another cigarette, or take my time nibbling away the edges of a Reese's Cup. Whenever a craving for a smoke or sweets hits me, I hear Abby's voice, the way it had sobbed as I held the phone to my ear in that otherworldly office, the blueprint of my coffin.

She is always eager to remind me that I lied about my bad habit, especially if I try to turn down our nightly walk or load my plate with more meat than healthy veggies.

"You don't have to twist my arm too much," I reassure her. "I don't want to leave you anytime soon. I don't like what's waiting for me on the other side."

Now that I'm being completely honest with her, she knows about my experience during the golden hour. I've told her everything, even the full story behind my younger brother's death. During one of our walks, we took a break on a park bench and discussed the finer details.

"Rand, you were a kid yourself. You couldn't have known what would happen when you lifted his head."

"I suppose not."

"Your brother Wendell sounded happy, didn't he?"

"I think so. He seemed to forgive me."

"When you were on the other side, maybe you only saw horrid things because you didn't forgive yourself yet. Maybe the world there is larger than it seems, more forgiving and merciful as time passes."

"Wherever Frank is, I hope he's happy."

"I'm sure he is. He'd be happy you started savings accounts for his daughters. You're a good man, Rand. Wherever we go after this, we'll meet up, and we're going to be happy."

I quickly kissed the corner of her lips and gave her the most honest response I could.

"Time will tell."

Feed the Beast

Elaine Pascale

The most dangerous thing about my mother was her voice.

Her voice was like the densest pillow. Your fondest wish would be to nap on it eternally.

It was soft and lilting; she could read off the grocery list and make it sound like a prayer. She spoke in a reserved manner that forced attention. When she spoke, others naturally quieted. When she spoke, the rest of the world became silent, just as the jungle becomes silent before a predator attacks.

The second dangerous thing about my mother was that she fed the beast.

Her voice hadn't always been a siren's song. I can remember being very young and at the breakfast table with my Aunt Sadie. My mother was moving around—stirring oatmeal and slicing bananas—and Sadie was entertaining me. Sadie was not my mother's sister; she was not my biological aunt, nor related by marriage. I was not sure where she came from, but I did love her tremendously. She was good at coloring in coloring books and at dressing my baby dolls and putting them in a stroller. I considered these great character strengths when I was a child. More than that, I loved Sadie's voice. It was magical. She was in charge of singing me to sleep every night. Once she started it was like going under anesthesia: my eyes fluttered a few times and then shut until morning. This particular morning, Sadie was singing along to the radio in the kitchen. Her voice was superior to that of the celebrity who was paid a lot of money to record the album being played. I felt soothed by the sound until my mother tried to sing along. Her voice was flat, nasally. That was how she spoke back then, too. She would say my name – "Lara" and it would come out all sharp corners and quick slices.

Aunt Sadie lived with us for a few years and those were fun years. She was a happy and curious person, who enjoyed exploring the world as much as I did. She was like a playmate, only the best kind, as she could drive to get chocolates and manage the television. One day, when I came home from school, she was gone. When I asked my mother about it, she said she didn't know where Aunt Sadie had gone and that "things were complicated." What I remember most about Sadie's initial absence was that my mother's voice changed. Suddenly, she could sing any song she wanted regardless of key or octave. Every word she spoke sounded miraculous. At first, I had thought I would miss Sadie's singing, but my mother's surpassed hers, or maybe she simply sang more.

I was eight when I learned about feeding the beast.

I was accustomed to my mother going for drives at night and leaving me alone. That did not mean that I enjoyed it. I was afraid of being alone, afraid of someone—some *stranger*—knowing I was alone and breaking into our house. We lived in an old farm house up on a hill and there were no neighbors in sight. The only thing that I could see from my windows, besides acres of trees, was a small dark shed that stood on the edge of our property, partially obscured by the woods that surrounded us. Our house constantly made noises that mimicked footsteps, even when there should be none. I hated being in that house after dark, when the house itself refused to be quiet. One night, I grew tired of being abandoned by my mother and I stowed away in her car. I climbed into the very back of her station wagon with my favorite blanket and waited for the comforting hum of the engine.

She didn't see me until she pulled into a gas station and looked into the back of the car. I pretended to be asleep and she either fell for my ruse or no longer cared at that point.

She got out of the car and went through the motions of getting gas. She began pressing the intercom on the fuel dispenser. Her voice came like a song. She was asking the girl behind the counter to please come look at the pump. There was something wrong. "*Terribly wrong,*" she drawled. Her voice made the girl want to see. Her voice would have made anyone want to see.

My mother pointed to the space between our car and the pump, "It's right there." She was suggesting that something was wrong about two feet off the ground. The girl was petite, but she had to work to push herself into the space. She twisted at the waist, bending as if playing Twister so that she could see the mysterious problem. My mother always kept a small hammer in her purse. I had not understood why, until I saw her take it out and pound it on the girl's head.

The girl dropped, but she was wedged so tightly that she only fell part way. Her face smashed into the glass of the rear passenger-side window. There was blood along the part in her hair but, otherwise, she looked like she was asleep. She looked more asleep than I did. I was shaking beneath my blanket.

My mother grabbed the girl under her armpits and shoved her into the front seat. She was muttering something about "the back would be so much easier" as she crammed the girl down into the bucket seat. I knew she was referring to my occupying the back. Her voice sounded melodious instead of upset. It was almost as if she were cooing to both the unconscious girl and me.

Before pulling into our driveway, she stopped at the small dark shed that looked even more sinister when lit only by the moon. She put the girl's body inside, locked the door and drove back to our house.

The next morning at breakfast, in between accompanying the songs on the radio, she said to me, "You must have had very strange dreams last night." Her voice was so soothing that I almost believed her.

Until a few months later, when I waited by the shed.

I had seen my mother return to the shed earlier. It had been midday and she had left the door open after she entered. It was impossible from the distance to get a good look inside. My mother then dragged a large sack out the door and took it with her into the woods behind the building where I could no longer see.

I decided that I needed to know what was going on inside the shed. I decided this in the way that all children feel entitled to adult information. I know now that ignorance is truly bliss.

I made my way into the unforgiving brush while the sun still shone. The days were longer and the nights warmer and my bravery was bolstered by these facts. As the sun set, my mother's car passed, but I knew she couldn't see me. I was craftily camouflaged in my soldier Halloween costume, her makeup spackling my face and an old dark scarf covering my hair.

As usual, my mother was gone for quite some time

and my fear grew. I thought I felt some movement from inside the shed. As much as that scared me, I needed answers, and I moved to the back of the building so that I could peek in through the rectangular window that settled just beneath the roof. There were old bricks tossed haphazardly a few feet from the shed and I used a few as a step stool.

It was still light enough for me to see Aunt Sadie inside.

I wanted to knock on the window, to let her know that I was there. I wanted us to play again. I wanted to tell her that I colored with real markers now, not baby crayons. I wanted her to know that most of my dolls had been replaced with my two-wheeled bicycle and my four-wheeled roller skates. I thought I would impress her with my jump rope skills. These thoughts were interrupted—and my knocking put on hold—by the return of my mother's car.

The headlights lit the building but since I was behind the shed, I was confident that I would go undiscovered.

I peeked around the corner and saw my mother get out of the car. She opened the back and pulled out a young girl. At first, she carried her in her arms, like she sometimes still carried me to bed if I fell asleep in front of the TV. Then she tried to get the girl to stand. She must have bludgeoned this girl, as she was very wobbly: she rocked as if balancing on the deck of a small boat. Steadying the girl with one arm, my mother unlocked the shed door. When my mother pushed the girl inside, I climbed back onto my makeshift stool and peered through the window.

The headlights lit the interior of the shed. My mother was holding one hand up to Sadie, as if warding her off, and thrusting the wobbly girl toward her. Sadie tilted her head to one side: the way dogs do when listening to humans talk.

I hadn't noticed before, but there were strange skulls on the floor of the shed. They had extended jaws lined with jagged teeth and uneven horns. The skulls were placed in a pattern based on the way the dirt floor was cut through with sharp lines.

Again, my mother thrust the girl toward Sadie and I could hear a baleful song sung as a round. I couldn't recognize the melody, but it seemed to be a call between my mother and Sadie. As they sang, the girl straightened, awakening. She looked at Sadie and screamed.

Her scream ended the song and the melody was replaced by a roar from Sadie. She reached up toward the heavens, roaring again, and I noticed that her nails were long and severe like talons.

My mother quickly began another song. Sadie calmed and listened for a moment before singing along. The language was not a common one; the noises they made came from the backs of their throats. They made eye contact while they sang, temporarily ignoring the girl who was now sobbing and shaking. Sadie closed her eyes and began to pant loudly. There was something animalistic in this breathing, like the way a bull snuffs before charging.

My mother continued singing above Sadie's gasping and panting. My mother's voice crescendoed, climbing ever higher and filling the small space so that the walls began to hum. When she hit a note I had not heard before, Sadie's body split at the waist, her legs dropping to the floor like discarded pants and her torso hovering. Her entrails dangled below like sparkling streamers. Sadie's chest heaved, and her visible organs pulsed in time to her breath.

She wrapped her intestines around the girl, pulling her close. She used her nails to slice open the abdomen of her victim. An elongated, tubular tongue -- a proboscis -- shot from her mouth, poking into the wound and lapping up the blood.

The girl began to moan and writhe, but Sadie dug into her arms with her claws and drank.

I screamed, betraying my camouflage, and my mother ran to the back of the shed. She grabbed me, dragged me with her to lock the shed door, then pulled me up to the house.

"That was dangerous," she snapped, and her voice almost sounded like the old one, the one that could cut you.

"What was that?" I managed to squeak out.

My mother sighed and motioned for me to sit in a chair at our table. She took a seat across from me. It was difficult to remember that this was the same table where we routinely ate, the same table where Sadie used to sing. Everything looked different now. "Your Aunt Sadie…she was my best friend in school, my roommate in college. We grew up together. She was my everything, my whole world. When you have a friend like that…" she sighed, "I hope you learn what it is like to have a friend like that."

I was still shaking, and my mother went to the oven to start a kettle for tea.

"She supported me in so many ways," she continued when she returned to her seat. I could tell that she was in no hurry to tell this story and answer my question. She would have been relieved if I had said that I didn't want to know and had walked away. Sometimes I believe that might have been the sanest route. "You know that things weren't great in Grandma and Grandpa's house?"

I nodded.

"Sadie was my refuge; she was my sanctuary. I could always go to her. I could stay with her family for as long as I wanted." She laughed, like the prettiest wind chime in the world, "I am not stupid, you know? I know she only went to State to keep an eye on me. She could have gone some place better."

She filled a tea cup and put it in front of me along with some sugar and milk, as if this were a normal night. I could tell this next part was difficult; her face suddenly looked very old. "And then, when I found out I was going to have you…she said we would do it together, we would raise the baby together. That was such a relief. I couldn't have gotten through the pregnancy without her. I know I couldn't have survived delivery without her in the room." She laughed, "that probably sounds dramatic."

I shook my head. Everything sounded plausible when she said it. I sipped my tea even though I really did not want it. It felt best to normalize this evening, if possible.

"I really thought it would be the three of us. You, me, and Sadie. I allowed myself to feel blessed."

"It was nice when it was the three of us," I surprised myself by interrupting.

My mother smiled, and her eyes lit up. "Yes, I know you enjoyed those days. So did I."

"Then I found out that I really wouldn't have survived childbirth if not for her," she played with a napkin, twisting it and untwisting it, "I don't want you to feel any guilt about this, it's not *you.* We didn't even know *you* yet. We would have done anything for you, though, and I guess Sadie did.

"I was struggling. My blood pressure was too high and climbing higher. I had seizures. I don't even remember that. Sadie told me later. At one point, I lost consciousness, or was in and out of consciousness. While I was being worked on, Sadie left the room. I didn't notice as there were so many people crowding around my bed and I could barely keep my eyes open.

"During that time, Sadie came back here. She went

into the shed. She…I don't know… she performed some ritual. For my safety, for your safety. She did it for us. But it was a dark magic, black magic."

"The skulls, right?"

She appeared surprised then sad. "I guess…yes, the skulls. I honestly don't know much about how this all started, I only know my part. I just remember that she was by my side when you were delivered. She was the first to hold you," her eyes became moist at the memory. "She sang to you and you quieted, enraptured. I was enraptured, too. In all my years of knowing her, I didn't know she could sing like that."

"The day you thought she disappeared, she told me the truth. She told me what she had done that night in the shed. She had to tell me, as she was having weird cravings. Bad cravings."

I put my tea cup down and met my mother's gaze. "What is she?"

"She is cursed. It changed her. She took on a curse to save me and to save you. I knew she had changed when I saw my reflection in her eyes. It was upside down, my reflection. That is how you can tell."

"So, you have been helping her? Bringing her those girls?"

She nodded. "I can't abandon her, not after everything she has done for me. And I can't let anyone hurt her. I would do anything for her. I guess I have. That is what our friendship has always been about."

For years my mother fed the beast and I turned a blind eye on the activities. I understood why we lived in such a remote house even when we could have afforded something nicer in town. I did not invite any classmates over for fear of my mother's seductive voice.

The night when I was so feverish and confused, my heart beating so quickly I thought it would burst through my chest, my mother drove me to the hospital. It was difficult to breathe in the back seat of the car and I wondered if I felt any worse than the girls who had taken their last ride there. I was in and out of consciousness, but I remember hearing a doctor say Sepsis and thinking it was a funny word.

My mother left me alone in the hospital for a night; that much I do remember. She was there the following morning, smiling and smoothing my hair.

I pretended that everything was normal for as long as I could. I went along with the lie that my mother had known nothing about Sadie's ritual or how it worked. I pretended until the day I saw my reflection in my mother's eyes.

It was upside down. *I* was upside down in her eyes.

Now, my voice is changing. It is becoming sultry, lyrical.

It is my turn to feed the beast.

Mr. No-Body-Knows

Steve Simpson

His name was Phineas Morley, the Boss-Man, the undisputed ruler of this Washington to New York rattler. They called him The Hog. Tramp-camp scuttlebutt said drifters vanished when they hitched on The Hog's wagon.

Victims of Mr. No-Body-Knows.

The lumbering brute prowled the long line of boxcars, tugging padlocks and searching under the train for trapeze artists riding the belly.

Wilbur shifted and hunkered down into the dense thicket of sumac, eyes locked on The Hog, the only obstacle standing between him and a job at his uncle's sawmill in New York.

Wilbur crept to the moon shadows cast by a pyramid of shipping barrels. The train yard smelled of grease and livestock, somewhere a dog barked. He could see the sapper swinging from a strip of leather around the Hog's wrist and the pistol holstered at his side.

The Hog's head swiveled like a turret on his bulky

neck, taking in the gloomy trainyard. Satisfied no one was watching, he placed the lantern down on the gravel. Selecting a key from a ring, he opened the rusty padlock and rumbled the heavy door ajar. The Hog bent for the lantern and resumed his inspection of the line.

Wilbur scratched his stubbled cheek. He pulled his collar tight to his neck, adjusted his bed bindle and canvas satchel across his shoulder. Giving the brim of his lid a tug for good luck, he said a quick prayer.

Please, Lord, let this train get me to New York.

Taking a deep breath, he scrambled over the empty tracks to the open boxcar. After a glance left and right, he tossed his bindle and satchel inside, then climbed through the door.

It was near black, except for the faint moonlight entering through a lidless roof hatch.

Wilbur felt a thick layer of straw scattered over the floorboards. The air tugged up a childhood memory.

Bouncing on the rusty green fender of the tractor driven by Pa. The wind had changed directions, the smell of the slaughterhouse rolled over their cornfields.

Wilbur pinched his nose.

"Boy, we put the vegebuls in dem's pots and dem's put the meat on our plates. It's all good."

Wilbur peered out the door. The lantern swayed a few cars back. The Hog was returning. He tucked into the corner opposite the entrance. With scoops of straw, he hid himself the best he could. He held his breath as the lamplight illuminated the inside of the boxcar. Looking through the weave of dry grass, Wilbur could see his satchel and bindle lying in sight.

His heart pounded in his chest.

The Hog's scarred face grinned as he slid the door closed. Wilbur heard him re-attach the lock, then the crunching gravel of fading footsteps. The lock might be a problem; for now, he was safe and warm.

He undid the clasp of his canvas rucksack and rummaged into the bag. He felt his Pa's folding knife, a thumb size stub of a candle and a box of matches. Wrapped in a piece of cloth he had a boiled potato and a dried lump of cheese.

Hidden under the bottom flap, he kept three silver dollars and his Pa's gold pocket watch. He opened the watch in the dull moonlight; almost midnight.

"Wilbur"

"Pa?"

"I best be giv'n ya this pocket clock to help ya. Yer future's important to the child, and us all." The gold watch sounded heavy as it slid across the wooden table. "And take this too." His Pa's folding knife stopped next to the watch.

The crash of twenty-nine had been hard on everyone.

If his fortunes soured, he would sell the watch. But Wilbur felt good about this trip, he would hold onto it if possible.

Lastly, he unfolded a creased photograph of his smiling wife and daughter. As soon as he started his new job, he would send for them. Until then, they were safe with his Ma and Pa.

The only other item of value he had was his lucky penny. An 1857 Flying Eagle he'd found in the belly of a fish.

He kept it in his shirt pocket.

He removed a soda bottle, uncorked it and waved it under his nose. The fumes seared his nostrils like gasoline. He took a generous swig, the liquid burned his throat before it settled in his belly like glowing embers. He re-corked the bottle and returned it to his bag. Finding a spot in the corner, Wilbur unrolled his bindle, pulled straw over himself and waited.

The steam whistle wailed.

A kinetic tug clanked each coupling down the line.

The engine struggled for traction, slowly gaining speed. Cool air drifted in through the roof hatch. Wilbur resigned himself to the long ride. The sounds became a soothing lullaby, and Wilbur fell into a restless sleep.

Something tugged on his bootlace.

Wilbur opened his eyes and jerked tight into the corner.

Rats, he said to himself.

Moonlight sliced between the wooden slats drawing contour lines across the interior. Straw was mounded three feet high at the opposite end like a beaver's lodge.

Something moved to the right. Wilbur cocked his head, trying to separate the clickety-clack of the train from the sounds inside the boxcar.

There, he heard it again. He was not alone.

Hushed murmuring to Wilbur's left. More sounds from the straw pile. Somewhere along the right wall, a conspiratorial reply. The sounds made Wilbur's spine crawl like a column of ants.

The boxcar rustled with eerie cat-claw tapping steps. Wilbur dug the candle and matchbox from his pack, with one of the four remaining matches he lit the wick.

The whispering stopped. In the glow of the candlelight, the room appeared empty.

He crept toward the straw pile, swiping at the mound with his boots. He uncovered rusty spoons and knives, canteens, tin plates, and empty bottles. Wire-rim spectacles and mismatched shoes.

Odds and ends left by fellow travelers.

Wilbur waded deeper into the heap, stirring up sallow bones, stripped of marrow and piled like kindling. Shredded rust colored cloth helped weave the nest together.

Hot wax dripped over his fingers.

In the muted plume of candlelight, rows of moldered skulls came into view, neatly stacked against the far wall of the boxcar like a Roman catacomb. A gallery of empty black sockets looked back at Wilbur. The skulls were picked clean. No worms, no maggots.

His stomach heaved.

He tried to make sense of the mass tomb.

A snare drew tight around his ankles, his feet yanked out from under him. His head bounced hard on the floorboards. The candle went out.

Dazed, he stared up through the vent hole at the dark sky. When he moved, his body heaved a foot closer to the nest. Dragged by the noose around his feet, he slid again. He was being drawn into the gates of hell.

The rope tugged him closer again.

He touched something rigid, a branch, or a bone and swung it like a club.

The line went slack.

Wilbur scuttled back to his corner and yanked the rope from his ankles. He searched the floor for his satchel. Finding the strap, he pulled it close. The bag was empty, Wilbur lifted the hidden flap. His pa's gold watch and the silver coins were gone.

The photograph! It wasn't there either. He dropped to his hands and knees, combing the straw on the wooden floor until his fingers touched the picture. Wilbur exhaled relief. He put the photogragh in his shirt pocket. He recovered his matchbox, candle and his Pa's knife.

He struck another match from his dwindling supply and relit the candle.

Two matches left.

The paltry glow provided him with primal comfort as he surveyed the space around him.

The steam whistle belched and the rhythm changed as the train slowed. The switchman had shunted over to a water tower. Metal screeched on metal until it came to a full stop.

The Hog would be doing his rounds.

Wilbur jumped up to the hatch and caught the edge on his first try. He clambered onto the roof, lying flat, he could see the boiler taking on water.

The Hog was approaching Wilbur's boxcar with his lantern. He could run now … but he couldn't leave without his possessions.

Wilbur heard the door slide open. The floorboards groaned under The Hog's weight as he climbed into the boxcar. The man adjusted his oil lamp, adding more radiance to the interior.

The space came alive. At first muttering murmurs, then a growing chorus.

Out of the rustling straw, like rodents slipping through a garbage heap came a horde of humanoid figures. Each no taller than a canning jar, they gathered at The Hog's boots. The room came alive with raucous babble. It sounded to Wilbur like a southern revival meeting.

The Hog raised his arms, and the boxcar went silent. The lantern projected his shadow like a deity onto the wall.

"Ah, my wretched track-ferries," The Hog said, his gravel voice sounded like his throat was clogged with ashes, "what have you got for old Morley tonight?"

Three small creatures stepped forward, each balancing a coin on top of its head like a heavy tray.

"Three silver dollars," he examined the coins. "Prime spoils indeed. This Bo came from some good stock."

Wilbur heard his coins clink into The Hog's pocket.

"Anything else?" He bored down on the creatures, "Are you pathetic dung-pixies hold'n out on me?" The Hog reached down and snatched up the last coin bearer.

“There’s more,” he hissed, “I can smell it!” He held the creature aloft for all to see. Slowly, he squeezed. It squealed in his grasp.

Wilbur heard the elf-thing scream as Morley tightened his grip. Bones crunched. Finally, the creature ruptured. The Hog dropped the crushed corpse between his boots. He had their attention now. He looked at his hand and casually scraped the viscera onto the wall.

“You keepin’ the good stuff for yourselves?” he gently posed the question again. “I know you have a soft spot for the shiny trinkets.”

A pair of hesitant imps emerged from the nest. The creatures hauled Wilbur’s gold pocket watch across the floor and left it at The Hogs feet and scampered back to the shadows.

“Ah!” He tested the soft metal with his teeth. “This will fetch some handsome scratch at the right honky-tonk.”

Wilbur now knew the secret of “Mr. No-Body-Knows.” He had to recover his Pa’s gold watch and his silver coins.

It was all clear to Wilbur now.

The Hog had to die.

The oil lantern flickered, time was running out. He had never killed a man before and wasn’t sure he could.

Knife in hand, Wilbur arched through the hatch, hanging upside down by his calves like a circus performer. He was close enough to smell the man’s stench.

A thought came back to him in that instant.

The doe lay on its side, still alive, snorting mucus and kicking up autumn leaves as it ran in place with three legs, it’s forth, smashed useless by Wilbur’s bullet.

Pa opened his knife and held it out for Wilbur.

“Son, now you have to finish the job.” His eyes both sincere and expectant, “Put your hand under his snout

and draw the blade across and catch all these here," pointing to places on his neck.

Wilbur accepted the knife from his father's hand.

He caught the reflection of his terrified eyes in the mirror sharp blade. Just below the knife's edge, the doe's pleading eyes.

He couldn't do it.

Wilbur's pulse pounded against his temples as he dangled like a spider about to ambush a fly. He stopped breathing and silently spread his hands.

He paused with uncertainty, frightened of what he was about to do.

Jaw up, expose neck, slice, he mentally rehearsed.

His hands floated close behind The Hog's ears.

Wilbur began to sweat, he tightened his grip on the knife. Morley dropped the watch into his pocket with the coins.

Now was his chance.

And then the penny dropped. It slipped from his shirt pocket.

Time skewed to a waxy dribble. His breath snagged in his chest as he watched his lucky penny flip end over end to the wooden planks below. In the silent boxcar, the coin sounded like an exploding firecracker.

Morley spun. They were inches apart, face to inverted face.

The Hog seized Wilbur by the neck and yanked him from his perch, slamming him to the floor. The giant man knelt astride him, one massive hand around his throat. With the other, he unholstered his gun. Wilbur looked up into The Hog's good eye. The other was cloudy, an angry scar started at the man's hairline, bisecting the eyeball and ending on his cheek.

"Wait, please! I …" Morley's grip choked off his plea.

"Shut your bazoo, Bo!" Spittle sprayed Wilbur's

face. "Me and da critters, we got us a deal, Bo." He thumbed the hammer; the trigger cocked. "I trap the meat, n'they gather me the booty."

Wilbur could hear the snarling horde creep from the dark shadows to the edge of the lamplight. Until now the creatures had only been spectral shapes in the dark.

They stared at Wilbur with cunning black eyes. Shrunken humanoid figures, their transparent skin laced with veins and arteries. Enormous droopy ears shrouded their shoulders like gossamer hoods. Boney frames, knobby knees, and pointy elbows wrapped together by cabled muscle. Round pot bellies hung over matted pubic hair. Sticky webs of mane draped from their scalps, purple tongues slithered across thin lips and spikey teeth.

An imp brandishing a long sliver of bone like a spear stepped forward and licked Wilbur's ear. He felt the slimy swirl before the helion bit off a sample of his earlobe. A string of slobber and blood drooled from its chin. Another imp darted forward and chomped a divot out of Wilbur's cheek then scooted back to the line.

Just beyond the glow of the lantern, a jawless skull with a hank of rotting hair mocked Wilbur from the shadows.

He stretched out his arm and came up short. Struggling under The Hog's weight, he walked his fingers over the floorboards.

"You remind me of a welp I once sired, Bo. We named him Burden. On his third day, he went into the pot. No one cared, everyone was hungry." Morley laughed like a bucket of stones.

Wilbur's fingernails scraped teeth. The cranium teetered, then rolled onto his palm, his first two digits in the eye sockets, his thumb under the dry palate.

Wilbur swung the remains of this unknown soul with all his strength. The skull shattered over The Hog's temple. Fragments of bone clattered off the boxcar walls.

Morley toppled off.

Wilbur picked up his knife and backed into a corner.

The Hog stood and staggered, the gun had disappeared. He lurched toward Wilbur, rage spread across his face.

Before Wilbur could think, he planted his knife in Morley's neck. The blade made a whispering snick, like puncturing a sack of rice. His Pa's honed deer skinner penetrated to the hilt, through the Hog's jugular and windpipe. A diamond of metal glinted on the opposite side.

The knife withdrew as smooth as it went in. Surprise stretched The Hog's eyes. Gouts of arterial blood erupted from Morley's neck like a tapped wine cask. He slapped the entry wound with his hand.

The imps retreated to the shadows.

Dizzy with blood loss, Morly wobbled drunkenly, then dropped to his knees. Hands clutching his throat, he drew wet gasps. His uniform became a crimson wash. Leaning sideways, he tipped over and thumped onto his back.

Wilbur and the imps watched as The Hog leaked to death.

The circle tightened around Morley's corpse. A devil moved forward, it poked the lifeless body with a bone spear.

Then they pounced.

Swarming the warm carcass like a crew of whalers, they rendered The Hog into manageable portions. Shouldering their loads off into the nest.

Wilbur watched from the shadows, sickened, yet fascinated by their energetic work.

Sinew stretched and snapped as The Hog's arm was detached from his body, the appendage lugged away.

His head separated from his neck; A team of blood-soaked creatures hoisted it above their shoulders like demon pallbearers. The Hog stared at Wilbur with his good eye as the head was marched up and over the man's chest. Hungry imps gathered at the ragged neck, slurping blood and weaseling into his gaping wound.

Piece by piece, The Hog's massive body shrunk.

Wilbur had to get his Pa's gold watch and money from The Hog's pocket. He wondered if he would have the strength to escape.

The imps were occupied with gorging on the warm carcass. Morley's torso churned with internal organ excavation. They had burrowed into his stomach cavity. Lengths of intestine snaked across the wooden floor mapping the way home.

With a shudder, the train began to roll again.

Wilbur crept out of the dark; the lantern flickered, quickly burning up its remaining oil.

Dropping to his knees, he slowly pushed his hand through the hoard of creatures, the uniform lay in shredded tatters. An imp pushed his head up through the Hog's stomach. Slick with blood, it eyed Wilbur suspiciously as it chewed and swallowed. Wilbur gagged, the confined space smelt like copper and bowels.

He reached through the swarm into The Hog's uniform pocket. There he found his coins and his Pa's watch and dropped them into his backpack.

The glass soda bottle sparkled in the lamplight. He lifted it from the spreading gore. Hugging the gloom, Wilbur uncorked the bottle and splashed the moonshine over the Imps' lair.

He opened the matchbox, finding two sticks left. He sparked one to life.

The imps stopped gorging on The Hogs remains, all eyes focused on the flame held in his fingers.

Wilbur tossed the match.

Heads turned, they followed the pinwheeling light as it sailed through the darkness. It seemed an eternity before the match landed in the straw.

Dead skulls looked on with indifference.

The creatures stood like a colony of prairie dogs, watching.

Wilbur waited.

The match sputtered and died.

The creatures turned toward Wilbur, assessing the threat with wary eyes.

Cautiously, they advanced.

One match remained.

Wilbur reached into his shirt pocket and pulled out the photo, unfolded it, taking one last look at his wife and daughter, he struck the match.

The imps tightened the circle.

He touched the match to the corner of the picture. The flame caught, a blue light scrolled around their smiling faces.

The picture landed in the straw. This time a wave of crackling fire flowed over the nest. Rows of firelit skulls were revealed by the blaze. In seconds the car was a roaring furnace.

In the confusion, Wilbur snatched his satchel and jumped.

He hung from the edge, his fingers slipping, the interior of the car now a flaming inferno.

Clusters of imps frantically clung to his legs. They ripped through his pants and clawed his skin, grappling up his body, using him like a human ladder.

He kicked them free in clumps, his grip becoming increasingly unsteady.

He had to get out, but their added weight was dragging him down. He was going to roast in an oven of his own making.

One hand slipped.

An imp monkeyed over his back to the roof. Wilbur felt a shard of bone lance through his hand, impaling it to the roof. He grabbed the devil with his other hand and tossed it into the fire below.

He kicked once, then hard again, shaking off the creatures into the fire. With his free hand he tore the last of the imps away from his body. Wilbur pulled himself onto the roof and ripped his spiked hand free.

He tried to stand, tongues of fire and choking gray smoke billowed through the roof boards; the entire surface beneath him was about to collapse.

An engineer must have spotted the fire. The train was sparking the rails to a screeching stop.

Wilbur snatched his pack and launched himself off the still-moving train.

He landed on his back at the mucky edge of a swamp. He lifted his head up from the ooze.

Wilbur's satchel had landed with him. He reached for the strap and pulled the heavy bag close. His clothes were shredded, his legs cut and bleeding.

But he would survive.

If he stayed out of sight while the crew dealt with the fire, he might even be able to get back on.

Or second thought, he'd wait for the next one.

He wondered how far he was from New York.

The Itch

Mark Towse

Joe sighs loudly and turns onto his back after kicking the freshly washed duvet from the bed. He studies his fingernails for blood and skin, but the only blood he finds is dry from where he bit the nails down yesterday. The fresh cool new territory of the bottom sheet provides temporary relief for his back, but the unreachable prickling is soon making its presence known again. He digs his fingers into his chest to gouge at the latest and most intensive itch, but he can't fool the brain—they are like stumps—no sharpness at all.

He convinces himself there are thousands of tiny bugs crawling over his skin and he can't bear it anymore and starts roughly scratching at his back again. It's worse than yesterday, much worse. Images of them laying eggs and defecating on his skin fill his head and he's sure they must be breeding. For the second night in a row, he is still awake past midnight, and he is on the verge of tears. His head begins to itch, that has never happened before. They are spreading fast. The fingers of his right hand provide momentary relief on his scalp, but he feels as though he is chasing the bugs around and they are constantly moving just out of reach. His back is getting worse, and the fingers of his left hand are doing nothing to stem the itch that seems to be burrowing further into his flesh.

At work yesterday he had wanted to say something, but how do you begin to talk about a skin infection with work colleagues. Besides, it was year-end, people had called in sick, and everyone else looked stressed and too exhausted to care.

Later that evening he had phoned his parents—his dad suggested it might be dermatitis, but right now it seems much more serious than a simple skin allergy. The soonest the doctor could see him was next week; they were apparently short staffed and incredibly busy.

He feels as though his skin is alive—a hypersensitive composition of raw nerve endings randomly making their presence known. The back of his neck is next, and he uses his right hand to chase that one down, but it quickly moves just out of reach again. He transfers his left hand from his back and across to his right thigh as a new patch of skin cries for attention. There is yet another outbreak near his ankle and then the latest and worst of all, on the bottom of his foot. He begins hitting it with a closed fist, but it does nothing. There are new patches of torment everywhere, and Joe begins to punch himself on the back of his neck, scalp, spine, and legs.

He assumes the bed is teeming with the microscopic bugs, so he jumps out and in a frenzied state starts brushing himself down.

There is some relief to escape the sheets that must be now a writhing landscape of infestation, but he can still feel them on him, and worse—in him. His boxers and T-shirt he throws into the bin next to his bed.

The remote control on the floor catches his eye. He quickly grabs it, shakes it and then switches on the TV. The noise provides a brief slice of normality to proceedings but doesn't detract from the escalating intensity of his itchy skin that is demanding his complete attention. Words fill the room, but most of them cannot be heard above the thoughts in his head screaming at him to scratch some more. He hears something about the third day as he slides open the window and enjoys the hit of the cool breeze caressing his body, but the relief is temporary. He starts to claw at his skin once again. The sound of sirens can be heard from all directions, and from his tenth-story room, he notices the blur of lights against the backdrop of darkness.

He hears the whir and chopping noise of the helicopters, and above the sirens, he thinks he can hear people screaming. And *was that gunfire?*

For just past the midnight hour, the night is abnormally explosive.

Every square inch of his body then sings out in a chorus of irritation. He rushes towards the bathroom and catches the words "Emergency Broadcast" as they scroll across the bottom of the TV screen, but takes no heed and quickly steps into the shower and turns the tap. The immediate hit of cold water catches him off guard, but he welcomes the brief override of the maddening itch. He scrubs at his skin relentlessly with the sponge, but he can't get deep enough.

The itch manifests in his eyes next, and he digs the balls of his hands firmly into his sockets, and they squelch like marshy ground as he rubs frantically. He fumbles at the shower door and steps out of the water, watching himself in the bathroom mirror as he rakes at his chest and back. His skin is red and flared, his eyes are bloodshot and puffy and underlined by huge dark circles. In frustration, he screams and punches the mirror. It fractures sending shards to the floor. The sensation is unbearable now and getting worse. He picks up a piece of glass, and there is immediate relief as he runs the sharpness across his chest and back. But it's not enough, and he can feel the inward retreat of the alien bodies inside him.

There is a scream for help down the hallway, but Joe has other things on his mind, and he pushes the sharp edge of the glass into his chest. The skin concedes and a small lake of fresh crimson forms. He follows the itch around with the blade and buries it deeper. His reflection makes him feel sick, so he returns to his bedroom, working now on his wrist. They are definitely in there; he can feel them. As the blade digs in further, there is an explosion of pain. His overloaded nerves cause him to let out a piercing scream. His body seems to vibrate with agony, and it is seconds before it stabilises to a dull but painful throb. They move again, and he stabs himself in the leg multiple times and then in the centre of his left hand. The TV is droning on about a terrorist attack and something, again, about the third day, but he needs to get out of the apartment into the cold night air. His skin is on fire.

He swings the door open and catches sight of a naked lady slumped against the far wall—multiple gashes and fresh glistening blood decorate her body. One of her eyes is leaking, and some implement remains buried in its corner.

There is a smeared line of blood across the elevator button. He presses it multiple times with his good hand, leaving his own bloody trace. A scream emerges from one of the rooms behind him followed by a loud crashing noise against the door. He hears footsteps and then another thunderous smash, as though someone is throwing themselves against it, or someone else.

Finally, the lift arrives and the doors open to reveal two more motionless and naked bodies—half of a ballpoint pen protrudes from the neck of one of the corpses.

As he steps in, the glass in the elevator reveals the full extent of the damage he has done to his body. Still, the intrusion marches on, and it feels now as though something is gently gnawing at his spine. He presses the button for the ground floor.

The elevator door opens to a cacophony of screams and gunfire. There are naked and half-naked bodies everywhere strewn across the floor, each of them torn, bloody and lifeless.

Near the reception desk, he sees two men mercilessly beating each other, but they are pleading to be hit. Their naked bodies are covered in red patches and their faces swollen and bloody.

Joe makes a run for it. He has no plan as he plants the glass into his right thigh but feels that if he can make it outside, there may be a chance of salvation. He sprints to the foyer door and thrusts it open, giving himself to the coldness of the night in the hope it will somehow cleanse him.

As he stands there naked with the shard of glass still sunk into his thigh, there is a scream from an approaching soldier, wearing a sinister looking mask, instructing him to get down on the floor. But Joe doesn't get down to the floor. Instead, he breaks down in tears and screams at the top of his lungs for the soldier to shoot him. More gunfire punctures the air, and he closes his eyes, but the impact doesn't come. The soldier with the gun is still aiming at his head.

The soldier looks down the scope of his rifle. The order was to shoot on sight. He wasn't trained to shoot innocent civilians; they should be going after the terrorists, not cleaning up their mess.

Their briefing was so limited, just that there were people going insane—killing themselves and each other. The scientists have no breakthrough yet.

The bleeding man before him is begging to be shot, but the soldier can't bring himself to pull the trigger. He wonders what his father would do or what his family would say if they knew he was aiming his weapon at this unarmed man. He immediately releases his right hand from the gun to attend to a sudden itch and slakes his fingers across the back of his neck. As he does, he watches the man retrieve the glass from his leg and plunge it into his own eye. He doesn't stop there, but continues to stab himself multiple times on all parts of his body. The screams are unbearable. The soldier places his hand back, steadies the gun and fires off a shot -- a direct hit between the eyes. He watches the man fall to the ground still clutching the glass.

There is an immediate and intense itch on the soldier's cheek, but he can't get to it because of the gas-mask. The night of pandemonium continues around him, but his part in it is over. He sits down in the middle of the road, amid the chaos, and begins to cry. The itch is driving him crazy now, but he dares not remove his mask in case of infection. He couldn't bear to go like the man he's just shot.

Gone Astray

Steve Wands

They danced in a patch of dirt, surrounded by thirsty grass the color of straw. She held the kitty by its little paws and swung gently in the cool breeze of the slowly approaching evening. She liked that the days were longer now. The cold was still hanging on, but it was nice to come home from school and have hours of sunlight before night came. Soon, she knew, it would be summer and she'd have all day to play.

"Jacqueline," her grandmother called from the back stoop, "Supper's ready."

Jacqueline tucked the kitty into the crook of her arm like a football and took off like a rocket to the shed at the edge of the yard. Though grandma didn't mind her feeding the neighborhood strays, she was adamant about them staying outside. Animals had no place in the house, her grandmother told her and Jacqueline was good at listening. She had to be a good listener; otherwise Grandma might leave her like Mom and Dad had. And she didn't want that.

"I'll try to come back after dinner," she said, kissing the kitty on it's little black and grey head.

"Jacqueline," her grandmother called again, "If you take any longer, the food's going to get cold."

"Coming!" she yelled, closing the shed door and beating feet to the stoop.

Grandma hooted and stepped back as the little girl darted inside. Jacqueline slid the footstool over to the sink and washed her hands.

"Scrub 'em good," said Grandmother.

As Jacqueline scrubbed the dirt off her hands, Grandma fixed their plates. She'd made meatloaf, mashed potatoes, and roasted cauliflower. They sat and ate. Jacqueline covered the meatloaf in a thick layer of ketchup and grandma kept prodding her to eat her cauliflower. Sometimes she didn't know why she bothered cooking any vegetables. Jacqueline was a fussy little thing and any food not made of meat or slathered in cheese was a hard sell.

Jacqueline was eager to get back outside and made quick work of her plate, but grandma couldn't convince her to eat the cauliflower. She tried a bite, making a big production about how awful it tasted, begging with big wet eyes to spit it out. Grandma caved and the two of them cleaned up the table.

"Can I go back outside, Grandma?"

"Just be back in before it's dark," she said, moving out of the way to clear a path for the little rocket. She was amazed how her granddaughter could never walk anywhere. Every destination was a sprint. Sometimes she wondered if she should get a whistle and a stopwatch and see about getting her granddaughter on a box of Wheaties.

Soon it was dark and Jacqueline went inside to bathe and get ready for bed. The nights had been cold, so she put on her winter pajamas, and would continue to do so until Grandma packed them away. Jacqueline climbed into bed as Grandma plucked a book from the bookcase to read to her. She sat down in her rocking chair—a chair that had been passed down for generations—and put the book in her lap. She watched as Jacqueline wiggled around with the blanket and maneuvered her pillow till it was all just right.

"Did I ever tell you that when your mommy was little, I would read to her in this very chair?" she asked, sounding distant as she ran her fingers along the smooth curve of the armrest.

"You have, but you can tell me again, Grandma. I miss mommy," Jacqueline said, in that deflated way she responded any time she thought of her mother.

"I miss her, too, but I think she'll find her way to you again. Sometimes we all go astray."

"Like the cat's outside?"

"Something like that. Okay, hush now and let me read to you a little," Grandma said, picking the book up from her lap.

She found the dog-eared page from where she left off the night before, began reading and didn't stop until Jacqueline was snoring. She closed the book, kissed her granddaughter on the head, and turned off the light before leaving the girl to her dreams.

The next day at school, instead of paying attention in class she wrote name after name on the back of her notebook. She wasn't sure what to name her new kitten. If it already had a name the kitten wasn't sharing it and she couldn't go around calling it 'kitty' all day. Jacqueline was usually a good student, attentive and bright, but today she only cared about giving her pet the perfect name. It was harder than she thought. She didn't want to give the kitty a name any of her previous pets had. She wanted it to be perfect. Soon she ran out of space on the back of the notebook, but was still unhappy with any of the choices she'd jotted down. The bell rang and she would have to worry about it later.

After school Grandma helped her with her homework. Math was a challenge for both of them.

"This isn't how math was taught when I was a kid," said Grandma.

"At least spelling is the same," Jacqueline said, remembering what her grandmother said a few days ago.

"The little mercies," Grandma said.

Once homework was done Jacqueline put her stuff away and left Grandma to watch her program while she went to play outside. Jacqueline ran to the shed and found kitty inside. She scooped the animal up and cradled it like a baby, kissing it on the head, between its soft little ears. She held it up by its paws, but the kitty wasn't much for play today. Its limbs had gone stiff and were tough to move. There were more flies today, too, she noticed. And more of the little white worms. They looked like dancing rice and Jacqueline didn't like them at all. They gave her the willies. She brought the kitty back to the shed, placing it down gently and then brushed off the maggots that had crawled up her arms.

"I had a name for you today," she said, near tears, "but you don't need it anymore." She closed the shed door and sat with her back against the door, the sound of flies buzzing inside reminded her of static on the television with the volume down low. She looked up to a distant tree where a bird with a great big red belly stared down at her. It moved its head in a funny way. The way a 'nervous Nellie' might look trying to cross the street. She waived to the bird and said, "hi," but the bird flew away. She pushed her lips together in a pout and crossed her arms.

Supper was a quiet sort and grandma could tell something was wrong. She tried to get the girl to talk but it wasn't working, so she left it alone. She knew things had a way of working out in the long run. If it kept bothering her, Jacqueline would open up and start spewing out what was on her mind.

Instead of rushing out the door to play, Jacqueline offered to help with the laundry after clearing the table. Grandma knew those offers were limited time only so she accepted and sent her to the basement to sort while she washed up the dishes. Jacqueline began sorting the clothes into piles, but as she was doing so she heard a noise. It sounded like something skittering. Like paper moving along the cement floor. Or shuffling in a pair of slippers too big for her feet. She looked about the room but couldn't see anything making the noise.

The basement was dark, drafty and full of noises if one's mind was attuned into such things. She moved towards the sound, leaving the piles of laundry to sit a while longer. She found herself in the darkest reaches of the basement, where the dim overhead bulb just couldn't illuminate. In the corner she found the source of the noise. She knelt down and eyed a small field mouse stuck to a glue trap.

"Aw," she said, picking it up by its small tail.

Its eyes were bulging and its tiny body fought to be free. At first, she giggled, thinking the mouse was doing a funny dance. But as she tried to pull the mouse from the board its leg separated from its foot and her giggle turned into a high-pitched whine. Blood dribbled out of the ruined limb as the mouse did its dance of futility.

"Oh no! I'm so sorry mouse!"

Grandma came down the stairs. "What are you sorry about dear?"

"Grandma help! There's a mouse and it's stuck. I hurt him."

"Oh my, let me see," Grandma said, leaning over to grab the glue trap with two hesitant fingers. "Yep, he's not going to make it off of the trap," she said. "But don't you worry, I'll take him outside and you can go back to the laundry."

"But what about the mouse?"

"It's not right to let him squirm on this trap so I'm going to set him free okay?"

"Can I come, too? I want to help."

"No, no, it's not a nice thing to watch. You go ahead now. When I come back in I want them whites in the wash, okay?"

"Yes, Grandma," She said, begrudgingly.

Grandma took the mouse outside, folded the glue trap—despite the little creature's protesting—and stepped down till she heard—and felt—the crunch of its tiny body. Satisfied the little bugger was done suffering, she tossed it in the garbage can.

The next day after school, Jacqueline dug out her four—no, three-legged—friend from the garbage can and brought it to the shed. She introduced the three-legged mouse to her very dead kitten and the two seemed to get along like gangbusters.

"I knew you two would like each other," she said happily, the mouse stuck to its glue board and the kitten too long gone to give a whisker.

She let the two play awhile together—and by play together she meant to leave the two dead things to attract flies. The kitten had a large wound in its gut and the mouse—once opened like a book—resembled a macabre Rorschach test. Both were dead and fit for flies and larva. The kitten was spilling maggots like a bag of microwave popcorn.

Jacqueline turned her attention to the other pets long gone and left to decompose in the shed. In one corner was a broad assortment of stray cats, stiff and stacked like firewood. In the other was a dog, a raccoon, a possum, field mice, lost teeth, jarred intestines no longer tied to a creature she could remember. It wasn't the kind of shed that held seasonal exterior decorations, though it did. It wasn't a shed for tools, and a lawnmower, though if one were to check the inventory, these would be amongst the items tallied. No, Jacqueline housed her pets of damaged descent among the normal shed items. Next to a jar of drywall screws was a jar containing animal intestines. Next to the stack of spare kitchen tiles sat flattened animal pelts. In addition to odd cuts of lumber from a grandfather, years removed, were bits of bone too short to measure, but too many to count.

As Jacqueline took stock of her macabre playthings she heard the dry crunch of tall grass underfoot. A wide shadow crept in over the light in the shed and she could tell that Grandma was shaking her head disapprovingly. Her shoulders sank low as she stepped inside the shed. Grandma looked at all the death mixed in among the common items of the shed. She saw the jars of intestines; the dead cat; the Rorschach mouse; the countless other bits of creatures that seemed like a giant red flag waving brightly for Grandma to see. Despite her age, and her waning vision, she saw it all. She saw the grotesque collection of bits and pieces of creatures now gone, and she knew what it all meant.

"Oh heavens," said grandma, shaking her head.

Jacqueline turned her little frame towards the impressive shadow that was grandma.

Grandma looked again at all the sights before continuing. "I was afraid of this," she said finally. "Your mother was the same way. She liked to play with her pets."

Jacqueline felt ashamed, but also intrigued to hear she was like her mother. Hearing stories of how the other kids at school played with their pets she knew what she did was abnormal. She didn't see it as bad, but thought of it more like what doctors did, like in surgeries. Grandma didn't look very happy. She looked very tired in the shed. And very old. Too old to be raising a child again, and yet, she didn't have much choice.

"This won't do," Grandma said. "This won't do at all."

Grandma escorted her back inside the house. She'd been afraid of this very thing. Of Jacqueline going astray. After all, her own daughter—the girl's mother—was the same way. Jacqueline knew her mother and father left her. What she didn't know was that her mother was just like her. Grandma knew that kids like Jacqueline were special. Kids that played with dead things—kids that opened up animals for the sake of curiosity—only had so many paths to take. Her daughter had a tough time reconciling with her interests, but in the end took off in pursuit of them. Grandma wondered if Jacqueline's mother leaving played a part in the little girl's behavior and curiosity of the inner working of pets. She wondered if nurture played any role at all against one's nature.

Grandma had only been loving. She had been understanding, and she had been there in every time of need. She sent Jacqueline to school after a good breakfast and a good night's sleep, with a proper lunch and all her homework done to the best of their ability. She was a simple old woman who didn't understand the new way math was taught, but knew how to love a child. Grandma saw the way in which her own daughter had gone. The way a fruit spoiled before you had time to enjoy it. And she didn't want her granddaughter to follow suit. She told herself all she had to do was to love her more. That love would smother the dark inclinations her granddaughter possessed. She figured all the kid needed was a little extra love, and love was an easy thing to give.

She tried not to think about how in the end love

wasn't enough for her own daughter. Instead she thought about how it *would* be enough for her Jacqueline. She thought about how she was older now and wiser as a result. Raising a kid was easier now than ever. There were so many opportunities for children now as opposed to when her daughter was young. She knew in her heart that all she had to do was to love her granddaughter and that everything would be all right. Surely she wouldn't raise another child destined to kill. Surely it was nurture versus nature.

New Witch in Town

Robert Allen Lupton

I sat in the front row of Mrs. McAlister's fourth grade class. The shiny apple on her desk slowly rotted into slurry. I glanced around. Janet Oberon, the suck-up who brought the apple, watched her gift decay. She gasped when the first worm poked its head through the browning red skin.

The apple was bright and new a few moments ago. I heard a soft snicker. The new girl, Mabel, spun her index finger in a small circle and mumbled under her breath. She caught me looking at her and winked. Janet shrieked when the apple's skin ruptured. Maggots and worms floated in putrid applesauce across the desk and dripped onto the floor.

It was great. Best day ever. Mrs. McAlister puked in the trash can. She sent Janet to the principal's office for bringing a rotten apple to class. I told my friends, Mark and Sammy, at lunch. They're in Mrs. Johnson's fourth grade class.

I said, "It was Mable. She wiggled her finger and cast a spell on the apple."

"Ronnie, you're a moron. It's close to Halloween and you been watching way too many Harry Potter reruns. You think the new girl's a witch? Oooohhhhh."

I shoved Mark. "I saw what I saw. I'm gonna talk to her."

Sammy complained, "Not this week. Halloween's Friday. This is the last year we can trick or treat. We gotta make plans. Gotta payback Buddy Oberon and his friends."

Sammy had a point. Buddy and his two asshole buddies, Preston and Rich, were the town bullies. They were juniors in high school. They'd picked on us for years and stole our candy the last three Halloweens. Bastards.

"I know, but I'm still going to talk to Mabel."

"Go get her, lady-killer. When you're on the ground with a bloody nose and no Halloween candy, remember I told you so."

Mabel sat reading on the steps of the portable building we used for a classroom. I walked up and said, "You're new. I'm Ronnie. I know what you did to the apple."

"I don't know shit about no apple."

"Yes, you do. You wiggled your finger and said an enchantment or something."

"You mean like a spell. You think I'm a witch. How old are you? You're ten, maybe eleven, and you still believe in witches. Imagine that. Hang around a couple of months and Santa Clause will bring you some presents. I think I saw the Easter Bunny run under the building."

"Hey, I don't mean anything. I saw what I saw. I thought you might want a friend."

"Maybe, I do, Ronnie. Maybe, I do." She twitched her nose like the witch lady on television and I almost fell over myself backing away.

"Oh, Ronnie, don't make it so easy. Introduce me to your friends." She closed her book, stood up, and we went to find Sammy and Mark. The bell rang right as I introduced them and we walked to class.

Sammy said, "We're going to work on our Halloween costumes at my house after school. You can come if you want."

"Thanks, I'll check with my mom."

Red-eyed Janet was back in class. She broke her pencil three times, her pen leaked all over her dress, and a fly landed on her face several times. Whenever I glanced at Mabel, she just smiled and winked.

Her mother consented and Mabel walked with me to Sammy's house. Mabel and I passed the signboard at the High School. It advertised the Halloween Ball this Friday night. I asked, "What's the deal with Janet?"

"Janet lives down the block from us. She's been really mean to me. Told the other girls not to play with me. She walks her stupid little dog and lets him poop in my yard."

"So I'm right and you made the apple rot. You are a witch."

Mabel looked around and said, "Not smart to piss off a witch. Ask Janet. I'm not a witch, not yet anyway. I'm more of a witch in training. If you tell anyone, my mama will turn you into a toad."

"Can she do that?"

"You wanna take a chance."

"No, what's a witch in training? Can I learn?"

"If you don't have the blood, you can study all you want, but your spells won't work. Until I'm a woman, my spells only work on inanimate objects and insects. Last week, I learned to control flies."

"Become a woman. You mean like sex?

"Don't be gross. No, I mean when I mature enough that I'm not a child anymore."

"Oh, you mean when you have a period."

"I'm so not having this conversation."

I knocked at Sammy's and we went to his dad's basement workshop. Our work was laid out on the workbench. Mabel looked at the tattered and torn clothing. She picked up strips of cloth stained with red paint. "Zombies, you guys are going as zombies."

Mark answered, "Yes. Gloves and old shoes and makeup, lots of makeup. Makeup doesn't restrict your vision. We want to see everything. The big kids in this town will kick your ass and steal your candy if you aren't careful. That asshole, Buddy Oberon, is the worst. He blacked Sammy's eye last year. We're going to get him back. I'm thinking we'll put mousetraps in our candy sacks."

Sammy said, "That's stupid. It won't kill him and he'll know who did it. We gotta think of something better than that shit."

I had an idea I'd been saving. When Sammy said, "Shit," it appeared in my mind as clear as a vision of Christ himself, dressed in a gold sequined jumpsuit surfing down from the clouds on a sunbeam and singing *Onward Christian Soldiers*." I had the perfect plan.

"I got it. Laxatives. Laxatives and stool softeners. We'll fill the candy with laxatives and reseal the packaging with superglue. When Buddy and his pals eat the candy, they'll spend a week on the crapper."

Mark laughed, "What a shitty plan. I love it."

We worked on our costumes until dark. We made a fourth zombie outfit for Mabel. She was a wiz at makeup.

School was slow the next day. During the afternoon, a fly kept buzzing my ear. I gave Mabel a dirty look. She giggled and gestured for the fly to leave me alone. She guided it under Janet's dress. Janet shrieked and jumped on top of her desk. Mrs. McAlister sent her to the office. Another good day.

Buddy stopped his car in the street next to us that afternoon. "You little shits better be fast this Halloween. I got a date for the Halloween Ball and I don't have time to wait all night for you to fill your sacks. You could just bring the candy to the school parking lot. That might save you an ass-whipping, but I doubt it. Don't hold out on me. See you Friday."

Mabel and I bought plenty of candy. No one thinks twice about selling candy to kids. Mark and Sammy didn't do so well. People ask questions when a couple of ten year old boys want to buy twenty packages of chocolate-flavored laxative.

The pharmacist said, "You boys know this isn't candy. You don't want to eat this stuff."

Mark shook his head. "I told him my brother was in Africa and you can't buy good laxatives in Africa. He told me to bring a note from my mother."

"So you didn't get any?"

Mark pulled two boxes out of his pocket. "I stole these, but I don't think it's enough."

He unwrapped one of the packages and the chocolate had melted into sludge. He threw it in the trash. I said, "Well, my plan went to shit. Anybody else got anything?"

Mabel asked, "Buddy is Janet Oberon's big brother, isn't he?"

"Yes, he is."

"Then I'll help. I know a spell my mother uses to help people who can't poop. I can put the spell on the candy and people who eat it will crap like they drank a bottle of castor oil."

Mark and Sammy looked at me. "Yes, she's really a witch. Actually, she's a witch in training, but if she says she can do this, she can."

Mark said, "Prove it."

Mabel picked up a chocolate peanut cluster and smiled. "Okay eat this. Maybe, you'll be able to get off the toilet by Halloween. I dare you."

"Okay, if it doesn't work, we're no worse than we are now."

Mabel said, "I'll memorize the spell tonight and put it on the candy right before we start to trick or treat."

I walked Mabel home. We held hands.

On Halloween night, we added long coats to our costumes so people would think we only had one candy sack, but we each carried one for real candy and another for Buddy and his boys. Mabel finished our makeup and piled all the candy on the work bench. She inscribed a chalk circle and pentagram around the candy. She lit red candles and placed them at the pentagram's points. She chanted for a few minutes and then pulled a sharp knife out of her pocket and pricked her finger. She squeezed a drop of blood into each candle's flames. The flames belched green smoke that smelled like an outhouse. Suddenly a breeze blew away the smoke. That wasn't good. There's no wind in a basement.

Mabel smiled and washed her hands. "Don't confuse which sack is which. It's almost dark. We going trick or treating or what?"

I shoveled the candy into four sacks and joined the other kids. It was a good night. Folks loved our costumes. We had quite a haul by nine o'clock. We hadn't seen Buddy. Mark suggested we hide our good candy and walk around until Buddy found us. We hid our bounty under the broken down car in Mr. Wilson's driveway.

It felt strange to walk around and wait for Buddy. I felt feathery touches on my neck and face. Shadows flitted just out of my vision. I slapped phantom fingers away from my face. Mark complained, 'Is it raining? Something keeps touching me."

Mabel said, "It's my fault. The spirits know I'm here. They know I cast a spell because they can smell it on me. The barriers between the spirit world and ours are weaker on Halloween. They won't hurt us, but they want to be near the action."

Sammy shivered and touched his neck. "You sure they won't hurt us?"

'Pretty sure, but it is Halloween, after all."

We had to jump out of the way when Buddy's car screamed to a stop. "Happy Halloween, you little shits. Trick or treat."

Preston and Rich jumped out the car and the three of them circled around us. They were dressed in slacks and sport coats. Preston said, "It's your lucky night. We don't want to mess up our clothes before we go to the Halloween Ball. Just put your candy sacks on the ground and back away."

Mark threw his sack on the street and ran. He stopped and yelled, "Kiss my ass."

Buddy said, "Little boy, that blows your free pass. I'll find you tomorrow."

I put my sack on the ground and so did Mabel. Sammy put his sack with ours. We moved away. Preston reached into a sack and pulled out a chocolate bar, ripped off the cover, and ate it. He tossed a bar to Buddy.

Buddy ate it and said, "Stolen candy tastes the best. Don't stay out too late."

They jumped in the car and drove toward the high school. I said, "We're gonna follow them. I got to see this."

Mabel asked me. "They won't let us in the gym. Only kids in high school can go to the dance."

Sammy smiled. "We've been sneaking into the gym to shoot hoops for years. We'll hide in the rafters and watch. You're not afraid, are you?"

"You mean because I'm a girl. You want me to turn you into a toad or just give you pimples? Your call."

The four of us climbed through a window in the janitor's closet. We taped the door latch so it wouldn't lock behind us and climbed into the rafters. There's a catwalk between the lights and cranks that raise and lower the basketball backboards. The backboards were raised high against the catwalk. We hid where we could peak over the backboards and people couldn't see us from below.

Buddy, Rich, and Preston came in with their dates. They dumped all the stolen candy into a bowl where the punch and other snacks were on display. Buddy's date ate a piece of chocolate.

"Holly shit. Everyone down there is going to eat the candy. There'll be more poop on the floor than in a pigsty. Mabel, you've got to cancel the spell."

"I don't know how, but even if I did, I'd need to draw a pentagram. I left the red candles in Mark's basement. Maybe my spell won't work."

Preston poured a bottle of pure grain alcohol in the punch. The high school kids danced, drank punch, and ate candy. Everyone ate candy and they seemed just fine. Maybe the spell didn't work.

It worked. Buddy was first. The cramps hit him in the middle of a slow dance. He ran for the men's room. Rich didn't make it off the floor. He bent over and poop ran down his legs. We could smell it in the rafters. Rich's date looked shocked and angry, but her anger vanished when the cramps hit her. I hope her parents didn't spend a lot on her dress.

Preston threw up and then ran for the bathroom. He slipped on his own vomit and liquefied shit stained his trousers. The carnage escalated.

"We gotta get out of here," whispered Sammy. Mark backed carefully down the catwalk, but the smell was too much for him. He gagged, held his hands over his mouth, and vomited on the crowd.

No one came after us. They were busy with their own problems. Mabel said, "I'll try to stop this." She waved her hands and began to chant. Spirits slowly congealed around her. They changed from misty apparitions to cold, half-solidified, gelatin forms floating through the rafters. They kept touching me and bestowed slimy caresses as they drifted around us.

Mabel said, "They're spirits. They won't hurt us. When I tried to cancel my spell, I accidently summoned them. They aren't demons, they're the spirits of my ancestors. I'll ask them to help us."

Sammy continued to crawl toward the ladder at the end of the catwalk. "I just want to go home."

The spirits continued to solidify. They looked like us. By us, I mean zombies. Their clothes were tattered and torn and their faces and hands looked like they had leprosy. One opened its mouth and I could see the ceiling lights through the holes in its head.

It hugged me. I froze and whispered, "Mabel, make it leave me alone. Can you make it leave me alone?"

She nodded and with a gesture summoned the spirit to her. "These three are my friends. Leave them be."

The creature extended its rotting hand. The hand dissolved into mist, drifted forward, and engulfed Mabel's face. She inhaled the evil smoke and her eyes rolled back. Her body quaked with a small seizure. Her eyes opened, she breathed out the smoke, and it reformed into a ghostly hand. Mabel said, "This spirit is my grandmother's grandmother's grandmother from a very long time ago. People hung her in a town called Salem. The spirits will stop the shitstorm. The people will stop vomiting and pooping. She says they won't clean up the mess. I don't blame her. The spirits require payment."

Mark reached in his pocket. "I've got eleven dollars."

"They don't want money. They want a servant. Someone has to go with them. It should be me. It's my fault we need their help."

I said, "Piss on that. If they want someone, give 'em Buddy. This is his fault."

I waved my arms and the spirits surrounded me. One reached for me, I slapped its slimy hand away, and pointed at Buddy. "Not me. Take him."

The spirits looked at Buddy and the reincarnated witches with rotting faces didn't just look happy, they seemed absolutely gleeful. They turned to Mabel for reassurance and she said, "Take him."

The spirits dove from the rafters and reverted to the consistency and stench of greasy smoke. The filthy wraiths flew above the floor. They didn't slow down when they came to the wretched partygoers; they flew right through them. The victims shivered at the brief moment of ghostly contact and passed out.

In moments, Buddy was the only one awake. He wiped his face and backed away from the zombie ghost witches solidifying around him. He slid down the wall. He tried to stand, but he was too weak and the floor was slippery.

Mabel's ancestor seemed to be in charge. The old woman zombie ghost witch shoved her hand into Buddy's mouth and her arm spun like small whirlwind. It vacuumed Buddy inside out. He deflated like a balloon. He disappeared feet first. His feet and legs vanished into his body. His hands and arms went next. It was gross and fascinating at the same time.

His head went last. The flesh flowed from his bones and the skull melted. His brain splashed on the slop-covered floor.

The witches faded into the mist and vanished. The other partygoers began to wake up. Some of them vomited again, but Mabel said that was because of the stench, not because of her enchantment.

We inched our way to the ladder. Mabel and I took one last look at the muck and mire splattered dance floor, the sewage stained dresses, and the lakes of human manure scattered across the hardwood floor. Buddy's brain grew smaller and smaller. It dissolved and mixed with the excrement and vomit. The sludge looked the same and I couldn't tell where the crap ended and Buddy's brains started.

Mabel said, "We have to go. Are you okay?"

I pointed at the last vestige of dissolving cerebellum. "I'm better than okay. Look. I always knew that Buddy had shit for brains."

The House on Oak Ridge Lane

Erica Schaef

Her family would never understand why she'd chosen the house on Oak Ridge Lane. The outdated Victorian seemed a very risky investment; especially for a petite, arthritic woman approaching seventy-five. It was in need of extensive roof repairs, and a complete interior overhaul. The garden had fallen into a sad state of neglect too, with overgrown shrubs and tall brown weeds choking the petunia and daffodil beds.

Amy, though, had never questioned her great-aunt's decision. Mabel Tully always had her own way of doing things. Perhaps that was why none of her three marriages lasted for more than a decade. It was probably also the reason for her designation as the "black sheep," among her extended family members. Despite the elder Tully's penchant for stubbornness, Amy always respected Mabel. The two got along pleasantly; Amy had even spent some of her summer breaks with her aunt, when she was still in grade-school. But that was before the Oak Ridge house.

In the ten years since she'd moved in, Mabel had become increasingly isolative. Her attendance at family functions declined steadily in the first few years, and eventually, she'd stopped coming altogether. Amy's father put it all down to age, saying things like, "The old girl had to slow down at some point." That attitude always angered Amy. Mabel had her faults, that was true, but she'd been a steady fixture in the younger girl's life growing up, and had always been kind to her.

On Amy's twenty-first birthday, Mabel died. She'd fallen down the full flight of stairs in her home, and suffered a fatal brain bleed, among other injuries. Her body remained at the foot of the stairs for almost a week before a concerned mailman called the police for a wellness check. Though the doctors reassured her that Mabel had likely lost consciousness during the fall and passed in her sleep, Amy couldn't forgive herself. The thought of the old woman lying there dead and alone for so long made her physically ill. To add to her guilt, the proprietor of Mabel's will informed the family that all of her considerable savings, as well as her beloved home, had been left to her great-niece. Amy's cousins were justifiably upset by the news, though no one was particularly surprised. Amy supposed that now *she* was the black sheep of the Tully family. Not that she was set in her ways or stubborn like her aunt had been. She was just "weird," as her cousin Billy told her one Christmas, when they were both in middle school. The word had stung a bit. Socially awkward, perhaps, but she didn't think that she was *weird.*

College had been good for Amy. She finally started to come out of her shell, and even built a small friend group. Instead of watching old movies alone on Friday nights, she was out at restaurants and dance clubs. For the first time in her life, she'd felt as though she'd truly belonged in the world of her peers. It had come at a price, though. All of the late nights and partying on top of a full course schedule left little time or energy for visiting her family. She didn't even remember when she had last seen her aunt; it may have been a year ago or more. Now, here she stood, in front of Mabel's house, in front of her *own* house, hesitant to cross the threshold. She thought it would feel wrong somehow, but it didn't.

Mabel had worked wonders on the place. Its stark white siding looked new and fresh, with baby blue trimmings and shutters. Flower beds in the garden boasted bright violets and lush lilac bushes. The stone path leading up to the large front porch was lined on each side by freshly budded tulips. Taking a deep breath of the heavily perfumed air, Amy smiled. She felt like she was home.

"Good morning," a man's voice called from some distance behind her. Looking back, she saw Tom, Mabel's neighbor, *her* neighbor, checking his mailbox across the street. He waved.

"Good morning," she returned the gesture.

"Can I give you a hand with those bags?" he motioned toward her Honda's open trunk, where her luggage was piled haphazardly in a precarious stack.

She was about to refuse him, but thinking twice, she did have quite a lot to carry in. Plus, he was her only close neighbor, and it wouldn't hurt to start things off on the right foot.

"Sure. I mean, if it's not a bother,"

"Not at all. Be over in a couple of minutes."

Tom was a balding, middle-aged man who had lived on Oak Ridge since before Mabel purchased the adjacent property. From what Amy could remember of him, he a was divorced real estate agent with two grown daughters who didn't visit him much. He'd been on friendly terms with her great-aunt, always willing to help with her many home-improvement projects.

Turning back, Amy unlocked the front door and stepped inside. The entrance hall was beautiful; cherry wood floors and pale yellow walls welcomed her into the bright, sun-lit foyer. A grand staircase with ornately carved bannisters and luxurious carpet beckoned her to toss off her shoes and climb up to the second floor. She didn't even think about the horrific event that had occurred on those steps.

Tom was back after a few minutes, and helped her to bring in the rest of the luggage. When they were done, Amy offered him a water, and, looking appreciatively toward the kitchen, he accepted.

"I was so sorry to hear about your aunt," he said when they were seated, glasses-in-hand, at the little breakfast table.

"Thank you," she sipped at her water, "I know that she was very fond of you."

"That's nice to hear," he smiled, "I was so relieved to have her living here, after those old crones we had to put up for with all those years"

"Oh?" Amy had never heard about the people who had owned the home before Mabel. "What were they like?"

Tom's expression looked as if he'd just tasted something rotten. "They were…odd," he looked down at his glass. "Up at all hours of the night. And the strangest noises you'd ever heard would be coming from here…loud screeching, like dying animals or something." He shook his head and looked back up at Amy. "My ex reckoned they were witches, but I think they were just plain old loonies."

Amy giggled, "Well, I hope you'll like having me as

your neighbor… and I promise, no late-night animal sacrifices." She held up her right hand in mock-solemnity.

He laughed, "I'm sure I will," and rose from his chair. "I'll leave you to get settled in. Just pop over if you need anything, I'm half-retired now and don't have a lot to do."

She got up to walk him to the door, "Thanks, I will."

Amy was exhausted by the time she padded up the to the guest bedroom where she'd slept as a child. She didn't feel quite right about sleeping in Mabel's master suite just yet.

In the second floor hallway, she noticed a squeaking floorboard and made a mental note to ask Tom if he would have a look at it. She also noted a leaking faucet in the small bathroom where she brushed her teeth. All-in-all, though, the house seemed to be in fairly good shape, and she was grateful for that.

Amy was asleep almost as soon as she'd climbed into the queen-sized bed, with its down-feather pillows and warm comforter. It was a deep, dreamless slumber.

She didn't know what awakened her, but it was still pitch black in the room when she opened her eyes again.

Creak…creak. Amy sat up, wiping the sleep from her eyes and listening intently. *Creak.* It was the floor board in the hallway. She felt the hair on her arms stand on end. The board shouldn't be creaking like that, unless… *Unless someone is out there walking on it.* Grabbing her cell phone from the nightstand beside her, she tiptoed over to the bedroom door, and carefully pressed her ear against it. Silence. Amy's heart was racing. Had she locked the door after Tom? Could someone have sneaked in without her noticing? Minutes went by without another sound. Plucking up her courage, Amy slid the door open. The hallway was dark. She turned on her phone's flashlight and shone it all around, stopping on the spot where she'd noticed the loose floor board. Nothing. Breathing a little easier now, she walked over to switch the hallway light on.

All was as it should have been, the only noise was the cheerful ticking of the grandfather clock downstairs. Feeling reassured, she peeked into all of the rooms, and double checked that the front door was locked, before returning to bed.

In the comfortable blankets once again, she sat up for a while, playing on her phone to calm her nerves. Finally, after about half an hour, her eyelids grew heavy and she felt herself starting to drift off. Returning her cell to its place on the nightstand, Amy rolled over onto her side and nestled into the mattress.

Creak.

She shot up with a little scream. *CREAK.* She pulled the covers up over her head like a small, frightened child. For a long while, she didn't move. She had her eyes scrunched shut and the comforter balled up in her sweaty fists, pulled tightly around her body. There wasn't another sound, save her unsteady, rapid breathing. Minutes passed with agonizing slowness, until, at last, she was able to convince herself that the sound was probably just the old house settling. After all, hadn't she just searched the entire second floor? *I didn't look in the closets.* But that was ludicrous. What possible motive would a person have for skulking in her closets, only emerging to run over the same floorboard again and again? She laughed, to herself at first, then more loudly. The sound was comforting somehow, an affirmation that she was just being silly to worry over the noise in the hallway. Armed with her newly-found confidence, she got up again, and, just to prove to herself that there really was nothing to fear, she swung the door open once more and flicked the light on. With a terrified, scream, she fell to the floor, arms flailing to cover her face. There, at the top of the staircase, with her back to Amy, was Mabel.

Tentatively, Amy peered out from behind trembling fingers. The old woman was still turned away, her long white braid swaying slightly as she hummed a soft melody.

"Aun…Auntie Mabel?" Amy's voice was a shaking whisper. The humming stopped.

Slowly, very slowly, the woman turned around. Amy screamed again as she came into focus; her face was all wrong. She had slits for eyes, like those of a vulture, and her mouth was gaping, the corners coming up to curl high above her cheekbones in an unnatural, disfiguring way. There was no real nose, just a kind of hollow indent where a nose should have been.

Amy had been wrong, whoever, or whatever, this was, it wasn't her aunt. The woman let out a low, menacing cackle. Amy was too terrified to move. She just sat there, in a crumpled, shaking heap.

"Millie, can't you see you're frightening the poor girl?" the mocking voice had come from Amy's bedroom doorway. Her head turned of its own accord. Standing there, holding a familiar black cell phone, was another old woman. She looked much like the first, except that she had hardly any hair; just white whips that clung to the glossy scalp here and there, like silky spider webs.

"I believe we can make use of this," she held out the phone, giving it a shake. "What do you think, Millie?" Her face curled into the same grotesque, gaping smile her companion wore.

"Why not?" the first woman answered, "The more, the merrier."

Just then, Amy felt herself choke. Like someone was pulling an invisible cord tightly around her throat. She had to suck hard to get the air to her lungs.

The woman with the cell phone was speaking again, but it wasn't in the same, barking way she'd done before. No, this time when she talked, it was in Amy's voice. She held the cell phone to her ear.

"Hello, Tom?" It was surreal and horrifying to hear someone speaking with *her* voice. "It's Amy from across the street. Can you come over right away? I wouldn't call so late, but it's an emergency." She was quiet for a moment, apparently listening. "No, no… it's too hard to explain, I'll show you when you get here. Please hurry!"

As quickly as it had come, the cord loosened and Amy could breath again. Her body felt leaden now and she couldn't move her limbs.

"Get out of my house!" she cried with an impressive strength, when she'd gotten her breath again.

The women cackled in unison, and the sound reverberated through the house, shaking the walls.

"Oh, honey," the one called Millie whispered in a velvety tone, "we *are* the house."

"What…" Amy struggled in vain to get up. Nothing made any sense; her brain was muddled and foggy. "Who are you?"

"We're the Blackwood sisters," Millie answered, "we helped to build this house."

Amy sobbed. The house was something like one-hundred-fifty years old.

"I can understand your confusion," the woman said in mock-consolation. "You see, Sarah here," she looked at her companion, "and I have always been *gifted*."

The one called Sarah nodded, "We have magic, you see."

"Witches?" Amy's voice broke.

"You could call us that," Sarah shrugged, "People have called us many things over the years."

"Yes," Millie took over, "and when we built this

house, we put our blood and sweat into it, literally." She giggled; a harsh, wicked sound. "So as long as it stands, we live."

"But the spell requires an occasional supply of fresh blood," Sarah was speaking again, "and mice and stray cats only go so far. We need human donations to really keep it satisfied."

"That's where *dear* Auntie Mable comes in," Millie talked now. "When the house went up on the market, she was the first to view it, and we put a little spell on her. She fell in love with our beautiful home, and paid the realtor full asking price," she nodded vigorously, "Yes, a ridiculous amount, but that didn't make a difference to Sarah and I, we just needed the blood."

"We let her make her repairs to the house first, of course," her sister added. "She did a lovely job, don't you think?" Sarah smiled maliciously, "Then you turn up on our doorstep, a fresh young thing. Your blood will last us a good long time. Plus, if our little plan works out…"

There was a knock at the front door. "Ah, but it has, apparently."

The cord was back around Amy's neck and Sarah called out, "Come in, Tom, it's unlocked. I'm upstairs."

Amy heard the door opening and Tom's footsteps on the stairs, but she couldn't do anything to warn him.

"Amy, wha…" his eyes fell on the two sisters. The cord around Amy's throat loosened.

"Tom, run!"

He didn't look at her. "You two?" Tom raised his hand, and Amy saw that he was gripping a pistol. "But … how?"

Sarah smiled and raised a hand. Tom's body went rigid, and his mouth opened as if to yell but no sound came out. The pistol in his hand slowly turned, aiming right at his face. There was pure terror in his eyes as

Sarah flicked her wrist and his stiff finger pulled the trigger.

"No!" Amy shrieked, as big red pools of blood gathered on the floor. Tiny holes, almost like pores, opened up in the hardwood and absorbed the crimson liquid.

The sisters looked flushed with pleasure.

"And now dear," said Millie, bending to pick up the gun, "it's your turn."

One month later, a realtor posted a large SOLD sticker over the sign in front of the Oak Ridge Lane Victorian. She couldn't believe how quickly it had gone off the market, considering the well-publicized murder/suicide involving the previous owner that had taken place just a few weeks before. The young couple who purchased it had fallen in love as soon as they stepped foot inside. It was almost as if they'd fallen under a spell.

Other HellBound Books Titles
Available at: www.hellboundbookspublishing.com

Shopping List 3

By popular demand, the third volume in our bestselling anthology series, twenty-one spine-chilling, terrifyingly creepy tales of terror by a bunch of the best independent horror authors writing today!

Featuring horror stories – and shopping lists – from: Richard Raven, Dhinoj Dings, Jeremy Thompson, Jeremy Wagner, Nick Manzolillo, Steve Stark, Jeff C. Stevenson, Kevin McHugh, James Watts, Don Jones, Nick Swain, Mark Thomas, Brian McGowan, Jason Gelehrt, Mark Deloy, Richard Barber, Sergio Palumbo, Megan E. Morales, Angela Thornton, JN Cameron, and David Simon

ROAD KILL: TEXAS HORROR BY TEXAS WRITERS - VOL 3

Everything is bigger in Texas - including the horror!

A Piney woods meth dealer clones Adolph Hitler. A nightmare exorcist meets an inexorable fined. An eyeball collector gets collected. The apparition of a lynching victim tracks down his executioners. A Texas lawman is undone by shades of his past. A Baphomet recruits converts as a local summer camp.

The tales of the baker's dozen who appear in this anthology demonstrate why everything is scarier in Texas…

Including tales of terror from
Jeremy Hepler
Madison Estes
Bret McCormick
James H Longmore
ER Bills
Shawna Borman

And many more...

Schlock! Horror!

An anthology of short stories based upon/inspired by and in loving homage to all of those great gorefest movies and books of the 1980's (not necessarily base in that era, although some do ride that wave of nostalgia!), the golden age when horror well and truly came kicking, screaming and spraying blood, gore & body parts out from the shadows...

This exemplary 80's themed/inspired tales of terror has been adjudicated and compiled by one Mr Bret McCormick, himself a writer, producer and director of many a schlock classic, including *Bio-Tech Warrior*, *Time Tracers*, *The Abomination*, *Ozone: The Attack of the Redneck Mutants* and the inimitable *Repligator*.

Featuring stories from: Todd Sullivan, Timothy C Hobbs, Mark Thomas, Andrew Post, James B. Pepe, Thomas Vaughn, Edward Karpp, Jaap Boekestein, Lisa Alfano, L. C. Holt, John Adam Gosham, Brandon Cracraft, M. Earl Smith, Sarah Cannavo, James Gardner, Bret McCormick, and James H. Longmore.

Graveyard Girls

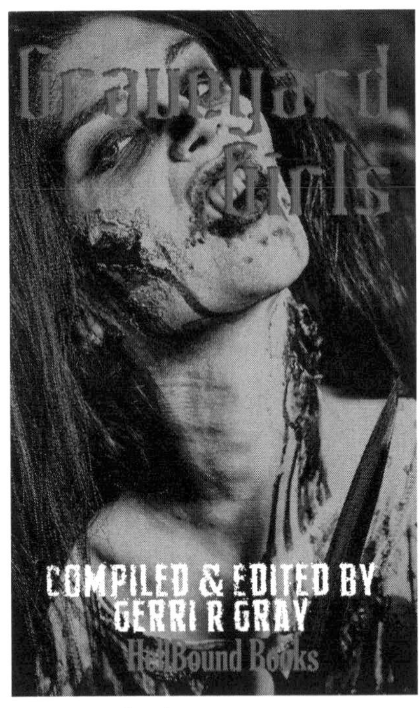

Female authors + Horror = something spectacularly terrifying!

A delicious collection of horrific tales and darkest poetry from the cream of the crop, all lovingly compiled by the incomparable Gerri R Gray! Nestling between the covers of this formidable tome are twenty-five of the very best lady authors writing on the horror scene today!
These tales of terror are guaranteed to chill your very soul and awaken you in the dead of the night with fear-sweat clinging to your every pore and your heart pounding hard and heavy in your labored breast…
Featuring superlative horror from: Xtina Marie, M. W. Brown, Rebecca Kolodziej, Anya Lee, Barbara Jacobson, Gerri R. Gray, Christina Bergling, Julia Benally, Olga Werby, Kelly Glover, Lee Franklin, Linda M. Crate, Vanessa Hawkins, P. Alanna Roethle, J Snow, Evelyn Eve, Serena Daniels, S. E. Davis, Sam Hill, J. C. Raye, Donna J. W. Munro, R. J. Murray, C. Bailey-Bacchus, Varonica Chaney, Marian Finch (Lady Marian).

The Devil's Hour

A new and altogether awesome anthology of all things horror!

Seventeen spine-chilling tales of the darkest terror, most unpleasant people, and slithering monsters that lurk beneath the bed and in the blackest of shadows...

An Unholy Trinity

3 TERRIFYING NOVELLAS, 3 SUPERLATIVE AUTHORS, 1 BIG, FAT, JUICY BOOK!

ENÛMA ELIŠ (When on High) – Terry Grimwood.
The Babylonian Creation story is a tale of monsters and cataclysmic wars. An epic saga dominated by the gods Tiamat and Mardak, bitter rivals who battle for supremacy over
the unformed universe. It is a story replete with Minotaurs and scorpion men, dragons and monstrous blood-sucking demons.
A myth, a fantasy...
But when a traumatized ex-soldier rescues a young woman, washed up and barely alive on the shore of a sleepy English seaside town, the fragile borders between myth and reality begin to crumble and gods and
their legions wake from their long-slumber.

THE REMNANT - C. Bailey-Bacchus
When fifteen-year-old Bianca Baker is blinded by rage and hatred, her inner demons take control and turn an ordinary school trip into a horrific tragedy. Witnesses to her violent act, succumb to Bianca's aggression and

agree to say events were a terrible accident. Sixteen years later, those involved find the past clawing its way from the shadows to haunt them, and this time there is no way it will stay buried.

ALICE IN HORRORLAND - Vanessa Hawkins
Alice is an 11 year old orphan living within the veins of industrial England. When she meets a mysterious gentleman with the power to turn into a white rabbit, she finds herself tumbling down a manhole into Horrorland. Here the creatures are strange and uncanny, lost in a revolution of madness. Drug addicted Caterpillars, grinning cats and homicidal Mad Hatters gambol around Alice like blood-drunk mosquitoes. However, at the center of it all is the Queen of Hearts: said to have given up her own a long time ago…
Horrorland used to be so wonderful… Can Alice make it so again?

A HellBound Books LLC
Publication

http://www.hellboundbookspublishing.com

Printed in the United States of America

Printed in Great Britain
by Amazon